John Harris w.   _z_ best-selling _The Sea Shall Not Have Them_ and wrote under the pen names of Mark Hebden and Max Hennessy. He was a sailor, airman, journalist, travel courier, cartoonist and history teacher. During the Second World War he served with two air forces and two navies. After turning to full-time writing, Harris wrote adventure stories and created a sequence of crime novels around the quirky fictional character Chief Inspector Pel. A master of war and crime fiction, his enduring fictions are versatile and entertaining.

JOHN HARRIS

THE LONELY VOYAGE

HOUSE OF
STRATUS

This edition published in 2001 by House of Stratus, an imprint of
Stratus Holdings plc, 24c Old Burlington Street, London, W1X 1RL, UK.

www.houseofstratus.com

Typeset, printed and bound by House of Stratus.

A catalogue record for this book is available from the British Library.

ISBN 0-7551-0218-5

BOOK ONE

one

It was a cold place, that police-court, with the cold of an old man's bones. There was a musty chill over the whole building, the chill of time, of tremendous age.

Shafts of dusty sunlight streamed through the brine-splashed windows and fell in square patches on the cold green paint opposite. A couple of banners and a ship's crest nearby caught the splash of gold. High on the wall, over the magistrates' bench, one of Nelson's captains, whose name I can't remember, stared bleakly over his nose from his gilt frame.

Down in the well of the court there was a gloom where the sun never reached. The stone floor was covered with strips of rush matting to deaden the sound of heels, and the oak of the furnishings was smeared where hundreds of fingers had gripped it during hundreds of petty sessions. In the public gallery, which was the dignified name given to the three or four raised benches at the back of the court, there was an uninterested group of spectators – a snuffle-nosed old man who'd come in for a rest as a change from the reading-room of the public library, I suspect; a hawk-nosed battleaxe in uniform who represented some women's organisation, and a Salvation Army official complete with bus conductor's cap and red sea-jersey.

There was a lot of whispering between the sergeant and the policeman on the door before we were shepherded inside. The chill of the place struck you as soon as you left the

3

passage where the defendants and witnesses were waiting in whispering groups, apprehensive and afraid because they didn't know what was coming. Only the old hands who'd been there before showed no nervousness and lounged outside in the fresh air, smoking and even chatting with the bobby on the steps.

At the other side of the heavy oak door, where we'd heard muffled voices for an hour past, the solicitors were collecting sheaves of papers or leaning across their table to whisper with their clerks. The police superintendent just below the magistrates' high throne ran a podgy finger round the collar of his tunic, and made himself comfortable. Just above him, to his left, the Mayor and the other magistrates sat, bored and uninterested. It had been an unentertaining morning, full of paternity orders, dockside drunks and backyard squabbles. I'd been outside talking to them for an hour, so I knew.

The Mayor fiddled with his case-sheet as the door closed behind us, leaned his cheek on a fat hand and sighed out loud as he eased his behind.

"Call the next case," the magistrates' clerk said. He was a little chap, with a ferret-face and a neck as stringy as an old tomcat's. His voice was like drawing a file across the corner of an anvil. The superintendent waited for a signal from him, then tugged down his well-filled tunic and stood up, rattling a sheet of paper.

"Your worships," he said, and he seemed to be speaking to somebody in the next street, "one of the defendants in this case is a boy of fifteen. Normally, of course, he'd come before the juvenile court, but in the circumstances that exist it's been decided to bring him before the bench today with the other two defendants."

The magistrates concurred, nodding to the superintendent with about as much interest as if he'd been talking to himself, and he turned towards the well of the court again.

"Patrick Fee, Jess Ferigo, Horatio James Boxer," he declaimed, reading from his charge-sheet.

The old man from the library stirred as we were pushed forward and manoeuvred by bored policemen into the dock, two youngsters and a great raw lurcher of a man in a shabby suit.

Old Boxer stood leaning on the rails, resting his weight on his hands. His hat was stuffed all-ways into his pocket, and he eyed the court with an air of defiance. He'd been handsome once, but the years and the rum that even there in the police-court betrayed its presence in his breath had left their mark on him. His grizzled hair still clustered in small curls above his ears, but his heavy figure was flabby and his face had a ravaged look about it. He seemed to me like some heroic ruin, some crumbling monument. There was the same sense of decaying grandeur about his craggy features.

He wore an air of false good humour that admitted a fair cop and didn't give a damn about it, a suggestion of indifference that the look in his flickering eyes made into nonsense. He was trying to give himself Dutch courage by an act of contempt for everything that was taking place around him.

Pat Fee's attitude had the same suggestion of carelessness, but his aged eyes showed none of Old Boxer's uneasiness. He was a sharp customer of eighteen then, was Pat, who'd already got the shady tricks of half a dozen trades at his finger-tips, and there was a cocksure boldness in the tilt of his head that indicated self-confidence far more than Old Boxer's studied calm.

I must have seemed a child by contrast with him.

While I waited for the fun to begin, I studied the pale face of the Mayor, whom I'd seen somewhere before wearing a red cloak and a fur Sunday-go-to-meeting hat. The magistrates' clerk just below him was reading the charge against us and the plump red-faced police superintendent, who'd whispered outside to me that there was nothing to be afraid of, was waiting for him to finish, fidgeting with his papers as he leaned against the bench. Farther down the court was an array of bobbies, curiously human without their helmets, and, near them, my father, Dig Ferigo. He looked slight alongside the policemen, and shy and stooping, screwing at his hat with worried fingers. He was an accounts clerk at Wiggins' boat-yard down by the river, where he worried into their proper places all the red and black figures that made everybody else but him go cross-eyed.

'Is the boy's father in court?" the magistrates' clerk demanded suddenly, lifting his ferret-face from his papers, and as Dig half rose, embarrassed and unhappy, a solicitor jumped to his feet, energetic and efficient, as confident as Dig was self-conscious and unsure. Dig was paying him the best part of his savings for it, so he wasn't doing it for fun.

"He is, your worships!"

"And what's the plea?"

"May it please your worships, my client pleads not guilty."

I gathered from this they were trying to make out I hadn't been poaching when I was caught with Old Boxer and Pat. But that was nonsense, of course. I'd not only been poaching but I'd been the one who banged the life out of the furry body they found in Old Boxer's pocket.

The superintendent broke into my thoughts as he began to read a summary of the evidence against us, and suddenly, so unexpectedly it made me jump, Old Boxer began to speak. His manner was aggressive as usual.

"Yes, I am Horatio Boxer," he said. His tone indicated he wasn't in the habit of answering questions about himself.

Ferret-face scowled at him. "Don't be insolent," he snapped venomously. "Do you plead guilty or not guilty?"

Old Boxer stared at him as though he were something unpleasant. "That's for you to decide. You brought me here."

Ferret-face went puce. He knew Old Boxer was taking the mike out of him. "Be quiet! Do you plead guilty or not guilty, Boxer," he snapped, his voice sharp with anger. "You must know."

But Old Boxer obviously intended to keep him waiting as long as possible. "I only know," he said, "that all this is a lot of damn' nonsense." He spoke as though he were more used to giving orders than receiving them.

"If you don't behave we'll have you taken below," the magistrates' clerk almost shouted, looking as though he'd like to throw the inkwell at him. "Now, do you plead guilty or not guilty?"

"Pah, it was no bigger than a backyard rat!"

"You plead guilty," Ferret-face snapped sourly and with an air of finality, and he signed hurriedly to the superintendent to carry on before there were any more interruptions.

I felt an elbow dig into my ribs and turned to see Pat Fee winking. There was nothing in Pat of his Ma, a prematurely old woman who kept a sailors' lodging-house near the docks. But from his father, who was Irish, a greaser on a coasting freighter, he'd inherited a glib sauciness that made him indifferent to his position in the dock. He was a sly bit of goods, was Pat, sharper even than his father, and he'd no fears of the police-court. I envied him. He reckoned on more than holding his own.

"The old lady's brought Katie's new shoes with 'er," he whispered, indicating his mother in the public gallery. "Bang they go to Levy's pop-shop if there's a fine." He grinned and I felt vaguely ashamed at being concerned in any lark that might jeopardise anything that belonged to Katie Fee. She was a nice kid, serious and dark, and always friendly in a grave way that never let you pull her leg. She'd been waiting outside the police-court for her mother as I arrived, silent and preoccupied, apparently prepared to kill time to the last trump if necessary...

The case dragged wearily along, through all sorts of by-ways that didn't seem to have anything to do with it at all. Questions kept popping out at me from nowhere and old Ferret-face kept getting mad at us. Old Boxer deliberately baited him, and was warned a couple of times for it by the Mayor.

"One more interruption from you, Boxer," he was told sourly, "and we'll put you away to cool your heels for a while. Perhaps you'd listen then to some of the things we're trying to say to you."

"God forbid," Old Boxer murmured.

I don't know whether the Mayor heard or not. I think he did, although he pretended not to and signed to Ferret-face to carry on. But Ferret-face was having a worse time of it than *he* was, and I reckon he'd just as soon have left it to the Mayor. Old Boxer was more than a match for him – even though he kept a wary eye on the Mayor and didn't get into trouble again. But I could see he was fed up with the whole affair and was getting ready to throw his hand in.

He seemed to lose all interest in the arguing, and began to glower boldly at the old battleaxe from the women's organisation in such an aggressive way that she blushed. Pat was counting the knobs of plaster that ran round the room high up near the ceiling. I did the same for a while, bored with the wordy wrestling, then I began to stare at the clouds that hurried past outside the windows, obscuring the sunny blue of the sky from time to time. The police-court was stuffy and smelt strongly of carbolic soap that seemed to stick, sharp and acid, in my throat. I was itching, and had been for half an hour, to be outside where the wind blew the spray over the blunt bows of the ferry on the river to St Clewes and across the shipping crowding the estuary.

I could see sparrows fighting and twittering in the eaves of the building opposite, and a few cold-eyed, yellow-beaked gulls goose-stepping along the lichen-covered roofs. Before you could say Jack Robinson I was out of the drab court-room and miles away where the sun glinted on the oil-slicked water of the river. I was never behind the door when they handed out the ability to daydream. I could see ships on pond-calm seas that shimmered in a brassy glare, and waving palm fronds and foreign ports with names that made your head ring – Pernambuco, Port o' Spain, Singapore…

"Boy! Wake up, boy!"

An acid voice whirled in space, focused suddenly and stretched in a vast shout in front of me. I started and straightened up in a noisy shuffle.

"What's the matter? Asleep or something?" Ferret-face was scowling at me as though he'd have liked to box my ears.

"No." I was hardly able to make the word come from my stiff lips.

"Say 'sir'," the superintendent prompted.

"Sir," I repeated dutifully.

"Then pay attention!" Ferret-face was wagging a pencil at me. "This is no place to go moonstruck, is it?"

"No."

"Sir!"

"Sir."

"Now! Were you with Horatio Boxer and Patrick Fee on the day in question?"

As Ferret-face leaned forward suddenly and peered at me, I tried to make my clumsy thoughts function. I hadn't heard half of what had gone before and I could see Pat grinning alongside me.

"Come now! Answer me quickly! Were you with the other defendants on the day in question?"

"I – I dunno," I said. "What day was that?"

"Ach!" The magistrates' clerk slammed a hand down on his ledger with a gesture of annoyance. "You haven't been listening to a word that's been said! Now, have you?"

"No, sir." My guilt seemed enormous.

Up popped the solicitor from his bench, brisk as a jack-in-a-box. "May it please your worships, the boy's probably frightened a little by his surroundings. After all, this isn't a juvenile court." He coughed deprecatingly and the Mayor nodded sympathetically.

The magistrates' clerk took the hint, left me gratefully alone and rounded on Pat:

"Take that grin off your face! This is a court of law and a serious business!"

Pat's face became an austere mask.

I tried hard to concentrate. I'd long ago admitted all my guilt in the affair to Dig, and all this performance seemed to have broken away from reality. I began to study the superintendent, deciding I'd be safe if I kept my eye on him. I was determined Ferret-face shouldn't catch me again.

Then I noticed the superintendent didn't seem to know what to do with his hands. First he poked out an ear and pulled at his long nose. Then he fiddled with his papers, shoved his hands in his pockets and sat quietly for a while. Eventually, however, I noticed in fascination, his hands reappeared and he used them to stroke his hair, smooth the creases out of his tunic and ease his collar. I watched, spellbound, until finally he appeared to stare at his hands in distaste, as though wondering what to do next with them, and shoved them under his broad behind and sat on them to keep them still.

I fought hard against boredom. The superintendent helped a lot, but I gradually lost interest once more. All this arguing seemed unnecessary. I'd been through it all before with Dig.

The minutes slid by in unhurried monotony, with my mind anywhere but on the avalanche of words, then suddenly I realised the Mayor was speaking and started to attention.

"We shall bind the two younger defendants over for six months in five pounds," he was saying. "We'll deal with the defendant Boxer in a moment."

I saw a stir in the public benches and caught a glimpse of Pat Fee's mother half-rising to her feet, then a sharp "Pay attention" made me realise Ferret-face hadn't missed anything. He still desired me inside the orbit of his ministrations.

He stood up on his raised dais and pointed a pencil at us, wagging it with every word he spoke.

"You are bound over in the sum of five pounds," he said in a nasal monotonous voice, "to be of good behaviour for six months, and that you appear at this court for conviction and sentence if-called-upon-at-any-time-within-that-six-months."

He seemed to lose interest towards the end and babbled the last few words in a meaningless jumble. A policeman with a fair moustache took my arm and piloted me gently from the dock. Then, as I moved towards Dig, I heard the superintendent reading out Old Boxer's record, a lengthy recital of wrongdoing that seemed to feature drunkenness rather than criminality.

Old Boxer listened intently, almost as though he were anxious that none of his misdeeds should be omitted. He was deliberately making a farce of the proceedings with an attitude of studied carelessness that didn't seem quite genuine.

At last the superintendent came to a stop with a shrug.

"There's another sheet like that one, your worships." he concluded.

"I've lived a long time," Old Boxer pointed out sardonically.

The Mayor sighed for silence, and Ferret-face hushed Old Boxer to quietness. Then the Mayor began to address him in that cold, high voice he read the lesson with at the chapel every weekend.

"Horatio Boxer, we've decided that you alone are responsible for leading these two youngsters into wrongdoing. A man of your age and undoubted education ought to be ashamed of himself." He paused to let this sink in before continuing, "But for you, we're convinced these two youths wouldn't have been before the court today."

Old Boxer snorted angrily. But for the persuasion of the two youths he'd have been sleeping off his lunch-time drinks in the ramshackle sail loft where he lived, instead of scuffling round the woods with a couple of policemen after him.

The Mayor was leaning forward now over the edge of the bench, pointing at him with a pencil, almost enjoying himself. Old Boxer treated him to a scowl in return.

"A man of your intelligence ought to know better," the Mayor was saying. "Yet you prefer drinking and breaking the law to making an honest living. You've a boat-yard that could make money," he went on. "A business that could thrive – "

"It's nothing but a set of musty mortgages and bad debts," Old Boxer snapped back. "It's the dustbin for all the rubbish in the river."

"An energetic man could make it work at a profit!"

"All right. You have a go," Old Boxer countered as rudely as he could. "I'll sell it to you. Cheap!"

The Mayor went red. "You're incorrigible!" he snapped.

"And you're a sanctimonious old ass!" Old Boxer snorted, losing his temper. "Tell me what I've got and let's get on with it."

While I was still gaping at the way he was flouting authority, I heard Dig mutter something under his breath and felt him tug at my arm. But I hung back, determined to hear the end of the drama.

The Mayor had sat back stiffly in his chair, clutching its arms, taken by surprise at the insult. Then he slapped a hand on to the bench in front of him and glared down.

"You will go to prison – " he said, and old Boxer's eye-brows shot up.

"Prison?" he yelped. "For a rabbit not worth three-halfpence."

" – for fourteen days," concluded the Mayor, and began to scribble something on his charge-sheet.

"Fourteen days?" Old Boxer said in a loud incredulous voice, and the police who'd been watching him ever since he crossed the threshold closed up behind him. "Fourteen days! Why, you smug, self-righteous old sea lawyer!" The police grabbed him by the arms and the Mayor went pink with indignation.

I was enjoying the scene, taking in Dig's startled face, Pat Fee's stare and his mother's working mouth as she watched from the back of the court.

"You pale parasite," Old Boxer said with vibrant con-tempt. "You sit there with your silly little chain round your stupid neck and criticise me for leading two youngsters astray. And no one ever overworked his articled clerks more than you do."

The Mayor seemed to swell with fury, and I found myself praying Old Boxer would put a lashing on his tongue before he brought fresh disasters on himself.

The trouble was done, though, and the Mayor was itching to get his own back.

"Release him," he said to the policemen, and Old Boxer was allowed to stand in the dock, his thick fingers gripping the rail, his breast heaving at his anger.

"Listen to me, Horatio Boxer," the Mayor snapped, secure on his raised bench. "You're a disgrace to the town, a defiant, lying rogue and a persistent drunkard." He sat back and announced almost as an afterthought, "Ten more days for contempt of court."

"Contempt!" Old Boxer almost shouted the word. He'd drawn himself upright into a figure of impressive dignity that was incredible considering the state of his clothes. "Contempt it is! Contempt for your psalm-singing, sanctimonious pi-jaw!"

The police had his arms again immediately and were trying to drag him from the dock. But he was strong and had a good grip on the dock rail. He was obviously determined to get in his share of insults before they got him out of the court.

"You, who've been moored by your fat behind," he said coldly, "to an office chair as long as you've lived, and voyaged as far as the chapel and there stopped..." The policemen heaved but he clung on tighter. "...you have the impudence to sit in judgement on *me!*"

Half the court was on its feet now, staring at the commotion. Pat Fee's eyes were wild and excited.

"Go it, Dad," he whispered.

"Come along, Jess!" Dig dragged at my hand, but I hung back, eager to see the finish of the contest.

"God, man, you don't know what living is!"

A policeman brought his fist down on Old Boxer's fingers, and he was dragged reeling from the dock. The Mayor stared with studied indifference at his charge-sheet, pretending not to notice.

The superintendent suddenly saw me gaping from the back of the court, and he waved a hand wildly to the policeman on the door. "Get the boy outside, you fool!" he snapped.

But he was too late, and I managed to be slow enough to see the scene played out.

The policemen were reinforced now, and Old Boxer was giving ground. But his voice hadn't decreased in strength, though it was broken and panting as he jerked and heaved at the blue-clad figures around him.

"...I've seen finer men than you or me offer their lives to protect just such a pious old fool as you."

All of this wasn't strictly true, I suspect, but Old Boxer seemed to be enjoying the thundering broadsides of words and the grandeur of his anger. They had him now at the entrance to the cells, but he gripped the door just long enough to get out his last explosion of contempt for the Mayor.

He hung on long enough to glare at the sergeant who was twisting his fingers one by one from the door and said in a resounding voice across the court. "You, you've had no time to see half of what goes on around you."

Then he was out of sight, but not quite gone. From the back of the court we heard his last withering comment, "Pah, the child of a man..." before a door slammed and the cries became muffled.

The magistrates' clerk looked up from his book – he'd been studying it all through the commotion as though it hadn't anything to do with him – and stared at the super-intendent.

The Mayor looked down at him and nodded, just as they shoved me outside.

"Next case," he said, then the door slammed behind me.

two

Dig was silent on the way back to No 46 Atlantic Street, where we lived, and it was hard to make out exactly what he was thinking.

He stalked gloomily along the vast miles of pavement that fronted the terraced houses of the dock area, a drooping figure with the long face of a horse.

Normally, his thoughts were occupied entirely by the dusty ledgers that lined his office at Wiggins' boat-yard, and by the articles he sprawled across the cheap foolscap sheets each week for the local paper, his one link with a literary existence he'd always hankered after and never known.

I wasn't very old, I remember, before I realised that even this one thing he enjoyed sometimes lost its savour for him in a bitter awareness that he couldn't do it well. His writing reflected that same pathetic inefficiency that was a part of everything he did. Even his ledger-keeping didn't bring him any satisfaction, for his lack of self-confidence prevented Wiggins' from promoting him.

As for the articles he wrote in the threadbare kitchen in Atlantic Street, they were out-of-touch and a bit crackpot, set down in a flowing language no one could be bothered to read. I'd known for a long time, and probably so had he, that they were used for the *Gazette* only as column-fillers.

As he trudged between the screaming children who played hopscotch and football on the littered pavements it was obvious that only half his attention was on the process of

getting home. The other half seemed to be groping in the
dusty recesses of his mind. He was seeking a decision on my
future, I knew – almost as if he'd worn a label round his
neck.

He covered the long walk from the town centre without a
word, his pale face moist with the heat of the day. I followed,
watching him carefully, not speaking. We'd never understood
each other very well, Dig and I. He'd never done much more
than lecture me in an apologetic fashion, even when I was
caught with Old Boxer by a Trinity House vessel tied up to
one of their buoys way out in the Channel. His anger always
seemed to be directed at a spot just beyond me, as though he
couldn't quite come to grips with me – as though he were
missing his aim all the time. It was a good job I never took
advantage of him; I could have caused him a lot of trouble...

The sun had reached its zenith now and the clouds were
skating along the blue highways of the sky at speed before
the warm breeze. As I watched them, away I went again after
them, as I had in court, soaring over the salty roof-tops so
that I barely noticed the moving people who thronged the
dirty streets and the noise of the dockyard hooters.

Long before we reached Atlantic Street I was far beyond
the dingy district where we lived. It wasn't a district you
could get much kick out of at the best of times. All the pop-
shops in the town seemed to be gathered there, all the street-
corner beer-offs, and the grey dives where Lascars and
Maltese and Negroes and Chinee stokers kipped while
ashore. Ship chandlers' stores rubbed shoulders with
shebeens; and boozers with the Missions to Seamen.
Children screamed in hordes about the pavement, and
slatternly women gossiped in the passage ends. At night it
was noisy with courting cats or rattling dust-bins.

The streets and everything in them that lived and died
there were shadowed by blank walls beyond which reared
the funnels and masts of ships. They were solid-looking and

high, far above the houses that quivered to the rumble of lorries and the clatter of sardine-tin trams on the main road as they jolted their passengers over the points and set their heads wobbling in unison until they looked like a lot of roosters with their necks wrung.

But I never noticed them. I rarely did. And that morning I was in a daze. It must have been the chilly court-house that had done it. And besides, past the bare walls and between the iron sheds I could see the river shining in the sun. Through open gateways and down the narrow alleys I kept catching bright tantalising glimpses of its hurrying traffic of small boats and the yachts and launches lying at anchor out towards St Clewes, on the wooded bank of the stream – the fashionable bank.

My mind travelled effortlessly down-river and over a calm sea that was stirred with long quivering feathers of light across its surface as the breeze touched it; far and away past the headland at the river mouth, past the horizon even, beyond sight itself. I'd long since tasted the sea both east and west beyond familiar landmarks, but the feel of it was only an urge to wander farther. Always I wanted more than the narrow pathways of water that surrounded the town. To me, they were only the merest fringes of the greater plains of ocean over the horizon.

The episodes with Pat Fee and Old Boxer that were a constant course of irritation to Dig, and which had reached their culmination in that morning's proceedings, were merely a makeshift. I was after more than the dockside or even the busy boat-yard where Dig worked. I always had been. As long as I could remember.

The train of thought carried me on suddenly to Old Boxer, who was more to blame than anyone for the love I had for the sea. In those days I'd never met anyone like him. I thought he was God's gift to small boys. Make no mistake, when he was sober there was something tremendously impressive about him, despite his sagging frame and greying hair. Some odd charm there was that held me tight in spite of his sour tempers and the chilly speechlessness that came on him at times, something that showed through his moodiness and sardonic bitterness in a bright, flashing, unexpected smile or a gesture of tenderness.

It was just such a gesture that had landed him in gaol. Mostly, he'd take no notice of me, staring through me, or even being rude. But occasionally, and that was one of the occasions, he'd treat me as though he couldn't do enough for me. I'd fished out young lobsters with him, tender as they come, from the rocks round by St Andrew Head. I'd gone egging with him, or trailed a mackerel line from the stern of the old boat he ran. I'd even been with a gun after mallard in the creeks inland. He seemed to like me to go with him, when his temper was good. I was the one who'd persuaded him to go poaching. Pat had just happened to be there at the time.

When he was sober and feeling on top of the world he was as good a companion as anyone my own age, and interested in what I was learning at school. And even on the days when the bitter black temper was on him I always came back for more. While Dig could offer nothing more exciting than a grey life in a drab street or a disinterested account of the business of the boat-yard, Old Boxer could talk in a sailor's picturesque speech that was flavoured with salty sarcasm of adventures that featured names like San Francisco and New Jersey, names that never failed to make my head whirl, names that spun in my brain as I lay in the park overlooking the bay on a summer evening, staring into the glow of the sky…

I was brought sharply back to reality as we pushed open the door of No 46, with its peeling paint, and Dig spoke to me, "Want to see you, young man," he said heavily as I hurried inside the house. "Don't go away yet."

As I hung my hat in the shabby hall where the skirting-board had warped away from the plaster and left great gaps, I heard a heavy voice calling me from the living-room.

"Come in here," it said. "Let's see you while the guilt's still in your cheeks."

Ma was downstairs, pottering about the house in her aimless, disinterested fashion.

For years she'd made only spasmodic appearances outside the bedroom, where she spent the better part of her life. She lived upstairs almost entirely, nourishing some private grievance I'd never been able to fathom but which had long since wrecked her marriage and Dig's happiness. By dramatising some early mistake I'd never discovered, she'd made a vast tragedy of her life, a Wagnerian charade played in the twilight of her own angry mind, with herself as the central unhappy figure.

There was little love lost between Ma and me, and I faced her reluctantly. She'd become gross, and gloomy in the way that old actors – ham actors – grow gloomy. She stared at me out of lustreless yellow eyes from underneath a fringe of blousy hair. Over the years I'd come to realise that the rare occasions when she ventured out of her room invariably meant frustration for me and ridicule for Dig, and I'd acquired the habit of stubborn unfriendliness.

She was pointing to a spot about three feet from her toes, and she fixed me with a dull eye that was ringed with an unhealthy violet.

"Stand there," she said. "Let your Ma see you in the flush of your crime."

I stood on the spot she indicated and, aware of the baleful look she was directing at me, I kept my eyes fixed on a point beyond her chair. On the faded wallpaper there, as though in mockery of her, was a photograph of her on her wedding day, young and lovely and radiant, a slender figure in white – though even then seeming to seek the drama of the occasion.

"Don't look much like a criminal," she observed. "What happened?"

"They had a fight in court."

"Did anybody get hurt?" The dull voice seemed to show a spark of interest.

"Not much, Ma."

"I expect Dig scuttled for safety."

"No, Ma," I said, "he helped the bobbies."

I told the lie without blinking, my face innocent and honest as the new-born day. I'd been telling lies of this sort about Dig as long as I could remember. The embarrassing comments on his gentleness seemed like a challenge.

I couldn't remember when Ma had said a kind word either to or about him – nothing only bitterness and contempt for his mildness.

"He's quite brave really," I blustered on. "P'r'aps you've never seen it."

"And never will," Ma said, and she heaved herself out of her chair. She was a big woman who'd once been attractive and strong, but through the years since her marriage to Dig she'd allowed herself to grow fat and slothful. Her tall frame had broadened to hugeness so that her clothes hung awkwardly on her.

I watched her as she moved towards the door, hoping she was going back upstairs. Both Dig and I felt the edginess when she left her room. She'd been sulking there with her imaginary illness for fifteen years and we'd got used to the house down-stairs without her. As she reached the door, though, she halted with her hand on the knob and looked back. I stared out of the window, pretending I hadn't noticed she'd stopped. She swept a lock of untidy hair from her eyes as she spoke.

"Stewin' in that grubby office among his books till his britches' behind shines," she said bitterly. "And home at night over the kitchen table. Words. Words. Words. They only use the rubbish he writes to keep him quiet."

I stared harder as Ma's voice grew louder and more incoherent with a passionate outburst of petty temper.

"Clerk. Pah! My father was a master mariner. Captain of a sailing ship he was, with an extra master's certificate. He brought us things home from abroad. A parrot. A walking-stick made out of a shark's spine, and sharkskin slippers. And what did *I* marry?" She snorted. "My God," she said, "me, who could have picked a sailor like my father! Stuck in that office. Afraid to put his feet on the deck of a boat. Afraid a breath of sea air might blow him away."

She sniffed, and in her eyes were tears of temper. Then, angry because I didn't reply, she flung open the door and, as she stalked out, almost bumped into Dig.

"Ha," she said, and the contempt in her voice drove away the self-pity, "here comes the head of the family. Doing nothing as usual."

Dig watched her sweep out of the door, ridiculous in a foolish masquerade of dignity, his eyes unhappy and hurt.

He'd been looking after Ma ever since she'd begun to imagine she was ailing; doing the housework, cooking the meals and trying in addition to earn his living and scrape a bit of pleasure from words written on cheap lined notepaper.

"What brings your Ma downstairs?" he queried, shaking his head like a boxer fighting off the shock of a blow.

"Awkwardness," I wanted to say. But he never blamed Ma – never once all the time I knew him – so I kept the words in my throat and said nothing.

"P'r'aps there's something she wants," he suggested.

"No, I don't think so," I said, and there was a strained silence.

Dig stared at me for a moment, then, almost instinctively, he picked up a book from the sideboard, a leatherette-backed volume given away with nine companions in a newspaper publicity campaign. He fingered it gently, lovingly, speaking to me over the top of it, as though most of his mental concentration was on the book.

Only half of his apologetic mumble reached me.

"...time you started work," I heard, and my eyebrows shot up.

"Work?" I said, startled.

Dig had moved towards the window so that the sunshine that edged over the tall, blank wall of a warehouse opposite fell across his thin, sensitive face.

"Yes, Jess," he said, and his eyes were still on the book, as though he were unable to look me in the face.

"I hoped," he was saying, "you'd continue your studies a bit longer, but it seems you don't like school and you're always with that Boxer chap."

"I needn't be," I pointed out.

"I know you needn't," Dig said, turning over the pages of the book. "But you are. He encourages you."

I stubbed my toe in the carpet, playing with the frayed edges round a worn patch. "Seems to like me to go with him," I admitted. "Says I'm the best deck-hand he's ever had."

"Because you're the cheapest, I expect," Dig commented.

He glanced shyly at me over the top of the book as though half afraid of defiance, then he slapped it to with a bang that stirred the dust in its leaves, and tossed it on to the table.

"Jess," he said with an unusual briskness, "I'm not much of a one for telling a story, but it's time you knew a bit about Old Boxer. You'll have heard it all before, I expect – or at least *his* version." Already his eyes were on the bookshelf again, and his fingers were touching another volume. "Boxer's a good-for-nothing," he said.

He paused, as though wondering if the word were too strong. "Such a shame," he commented thoughtfully. "He's a lot of good in him if he'd only give people a chance to find it."

It was just like Dig to say that. He was generous as they come, and full-hearted, for he'd always disliked and been a little afraid of Old Boxer. The old man, huge, shabby, imperious for all his meagre station in life, had always been rude to him. Adventurous as a backyard fowl, he'd called him more than once to his face.

Dig frowned at the threadbare carpet that showed the paper underneath in parts and took the book he was fingering from the shelf. He fiddled with the fly-leaf for a while before continuing.

"I suppose," he said, "you couldn't hardly call *me* a success. Mind, I've not gone backwards like he has. I was born around here and I was brought up here. And there are worse places in the town to live in than this. After all, it is a house. It isn't an old barn like he's got, with the rain coming through the roof and rats making love of a night underneath the floor-boards. Old Boxer's been used to better than that, you know, Jess. You can tell that. He wasn't brought up in a two-by-four a stone's throw from the docks."

It was true enough what Dig said, and it was generous of him to say it the way he did. Anybody else but Dig would have accused Old Boxer of putting on airs and graces. In fact, everybody I'd ever heard talk about him did. But they were wrong and Dig was right. The airs and graces Old Boxer wore were bred in him. He'd been used to them all his life, and it was because they were so natural to him that they made everybody detest him – even people like the Mayor, whom he'd treated with a cold contempt that seemed to suggest he was only a piffling little solicitor.

"He's not made much of his life," Dig went on, interrupting my thoughts, "going down the nick the way he has. Boozing and that. Wasting his money. Letting that boat-yard go to rack and ruin. Mind you," he added, half embarrassed, "give him his due: give him the occasion and he'd come up to it, I'll bet."

I waited in silence as he paused. The leaves of the book whispered as they were turned over idly, then Dig put the volume aside with a gesture of futility.

"But why can't he always come up to it?" he asked.

He looked again at me. His lecture was not having much effect and he must have realised he was drifting away from his original subject.

"You're fifteen now." He seemed as he spoke to be bustling himself back to earth. "It's time you left school and made something of yourself. It's hard lines, Jess," he observed, and I had a feeling he was sorrier about it than I was. Perhaps he'd had hopes for my future that wouldn't ever reach fruition. "You'll have to start work on Monday. I've got you a job on the newspaper."

"On the newspaper?" I was aware of a feeling of bitter disappointment.

The worst I'd expected was a summons to the boat-yard, and the sunshine and the smell of the river and new wood. Where I could watch the tugs plying between the ship-yards and the river mouth, and bear the boom of their sirens as they butted and tugged the great vessels upstream to the repair yards, grey and rusty and weatherbeaten, steam trailing away in feathers from their hulls down the wind.

"Yes, Jess," Dig said, and his face was in shadow as the sun sank beneath the great grey wall opposite that brought evening to Atlantic Street before its time. "It's better to learn that trade than the boat-yard. There's nothing much doing there just now. And they say newspapers are always the last to feel a slump and the first to notice an improvement. I'd like to see you secure." He stared again at me over the top of the book, aware that something was wrong. He seemed to be trying to convince himself he was right in his decision and was seeking confirmation from me. "Don't you want to or something?"

"Dunno." The problem seemed to be far too big for me just then. I'd never thought much of earning my living. Money hardly had any meaning for me. I was decently clothed, well fed and all my amusements seemed to cost me nothing.

"Had you a fancy for something else?" Dig watched me anxiously as though afraid his fumbling might turn me against him. "I managed to use a bit of influence for you. They think highly of me, you know."

His lie didn't deceive me any more than it did him. I knew as well as he did that he had no influence at the newspaper at all. But, I suppose, in choosing a career for me he'd hoped I might take up where he left off and carve out a living for myself as a journalist or something.

He'd persevered for a long time trying to interest me in it, and to a certain extent he'd succeeded. I knew all the words even if I couldn't string them together in the flowing manner Dig fancied. But I often wrote other people's letters because I could do it quicker than they could, and could think of things to say when they'd chew a pencil to splinters trying to sort out something interesting.

But that was only because Dig had taught me the know-how and the minute he let up on me I always dashed off to the river and borrowed a dinghy or bummed a lift on the ferry that ran over to St Clewes. I'd even worked the beaches with Old Boxer during the summer or taken holiday-makers up-river...

I saw the look of disappointment on Dig's face as I frowned. He must have seen I didn't want to work indoors.

"Good openings, Jess," he said cheerfully – more cheerfully than he felt, I knew. "Make something of yourself. Nothing blind-alley about it. And jobs aren't easy to get these days. What do *you* think? What's *your* idea?"

I was silent. I was awed by this tremendous decision that confronted me. There seemed to be only one career I could think of that I'd ever seriously considered.

"Wun't mind being a sailor," I said, and Dig whirled and stared at me.

"What?" he said, and his eyes were startled and hurt.

"You know," I said. "Go to sea."

Dig turned on his heel suddenly, more quickly than I'd ever remembered, and stared through the window across the drab little street.

"I'd just as soon you went to the Devil," he snapped.

three

The dying sun was casting pink rays across the evening sky like a great open fan when I managed to escape out of the house at last and make my way to the river. Over in the east, where the last of the sunshine fell, St Andrew Light shone like a bright pencil as the glow fell on its whitewashed surface. Beyond it was the steely sheet of the evening sea.

I sighed with relief as I put the Atlantic Street area behind me. I always did. Every other alley seemed to have an iron-railed swing bridge at its end, or a level crossing. In its crowded shop windows you could always find a cat dozing on the cards of patent medicines. Yelling kids played like moths round the gas-lamps long after dark and shabby men and women hung about outside the pubs – the Mariners' Rests, the Chain Lockers, the Anchors, and the Starboard Lights, one on every corner, one at every passage end.

In the quieter streets up-river near Wiggins' boat-yard the buildings seemed less oppressive and the patches of sunshine were wider. The town was quiet in the evening stillness, and the shadows that crawled across the roadway had begun to paw their way up the opposite walls.

As I made my way past a sagging wooden fence to a gate that bore the faded words, "Horatio Boxer, Boats for Hire", I got a whiff, in the smell of desolation, of salt water and sea-weed, that curious scent peculiar to the coast which includes in it everything that ever came from the sea or went to sea: pitch, canvas, wood, steel and steam.

The gate was unlocked and creaking in the light breeze and, pushing it open, I passed through a maze of lopsided planks that had once been stacked one upon another but had long since fallen down in mouldering jigsaws through neglect, rotten, worm-eaten, and draped with the mildewed canvas that bad been thrown out of the sail-loft when Old Boxer had made it his home. A rat scampered among a pile of rusty fittings and tangled cordage in a gaping doorway that hadn't seen a door for years.

Beyond the old-fashioned crane with the drunken boom, and down at the sagging wharf, the scent of seaweed grew stronger round the bones of an old ship that reared starkly from a caved-in deck. Grass grew from the piles of ash and cinders on her timbers and her mooring-ropes were rank and festooned with weeds.

Alongside her, Old Boxer's boat lifted gently to the lap of the water. She was a small craft and old-fashioned, but sturdy-looking. Out of sight below the gunwale, Yorky was whistling "Shenandoah" in a mournful off-key note that was interrupted from time to time by the clink of his tools. He was kneeling on the bottom boards, one foot half submerged in the oily bilge-water, podgy and unshaven, in grimy dungarees and singlet. He was wiping the old converted car engine with an oily rag he seemed more to lean on than use as a cleaner. His plump tattooed arms and shoulders were white and un-burned, a pale fish-belly white that never darkened despite its constant exposure to the weather.

I leaned on the black wood of the wreck and called to attract his attention.

"Hello, Yorky," I said.

He looked up, smiling, and pushed his paint-smeared cap back on his sparse hair. Then he went on wiping, a stub of scorched cigarette between his lips. " 'Ello, me old flower," he said in the North-country accent that had given him a name at sea which had stuck to him for ever and become the only one he seemed to acknowledge.

Yorky had turned up in the town from a ship paying off in the docks years before and had met Old Boxer drunk in the High Street. He'd helped him home and put him to bed, and since then he'd been to sea only in fits and starts.

He was now supposed between voyages to work at the ramshackle boat-yard that seemed to cower, shabby and ashamed of itself, alongside the glossy, efficient premises of Wiggins' where Dig was employed. His duties were as catch-as-catch-can as his wages, and consisted chiefly of servicing the broken-down boat that was really Old Boxer's only source of income, with parts begged and wangled from Wiggins' at no expense to either of them.

I watched him poke with a stubby forefinger into a dismantled carburettor and wipe it on the seat of his trousers.

"Well?" he queried. "Wot 'appened? Tell us all about it. I suppose 'e lost 'is temper and made a bloody fool of 'isself?"

I nodded. "They sent him to prison," I said.

He appeared not to have heard, and I repeated the words.

"Ain't the fust time," he said. "Always one for spittin' into the wind." He spoke in a monotone as though starting out of a daydream. "Shouldn't worrit. Ain't nothink you can do. 'Ad it comin' to 'im for a long time."

"I bet he's fed up," I said.

Yorky spat into the water. "Just another one of the various sorts of private 'ell 'e treats 'isself to from time to time, lad," he observed. " 'E's allus been the same – sourer'n the smell o' tomcats. Like my old Dad back in 'Ull. Never spoke except to fetch you one across the kisser." He threw aside the rag and heaved himself up to sit on the gunwale. Slowly he lit his cigarette-end, turning his head sideways to avoid burning his nose. Within a couple of seconds it was out again.

He threw the still-burning match with a sizzle into the water and stared across the sparkles towards St Clewes.

"Them cops'll stand so much and no more," he said. "Jeeze, the number o' magistrates 'e's upset with 'is bloomin' jaw. Mouth like a parish oven 'e's got when 'e wants to be awkward."

He scratched himself vigorously, his face troubled.

"More'n three weeks 'e got, didn't 'e? That ought to just about finish the stupid old clot. Ain't got two 'a'pennies to rub together. Next thing you know, 'e'll 'ave the bums in. This little lot'll be sold to Wiggins' an' old 'Orace'll be movin' 'is ditty-box up to Ma Fee's lodging-'ouse. And what'll 'e do with the money 'e gets for it?" he asked bitterly. "Pour the lot down the drain and come up next day brisk as a bishop at a bunfight wonderin' where it's gone. An' then where is 'e? 'Ave to go to sea again to keep body and soul together. Burgoo and bloody ticklers 'stead of a tiddley little outfit like 'e's got 'ere."

He spat the cigarette-end out viciously. "Christ, the things 'e could 'a' done with 'isself! 'E could 'a' made this place pay easy. The man's a sailor if nowt else. But I been doin' all the ruddy work an' 'e's been drinkin' all the profits."

His eye fell on the engine he'd been tinkering with, and he stared at it gloomily.

"Bleeden engine," he said sourly.

"What's wrong with it?" I asked.

"What's *right* with it?" Yorky countered. "Wants a new 'un. That's what. This 'un's finished. Done. Napoo."

I stared into the water, struggling for ideas that might help them out of what seemed to be insurmountable difficulties.

"Can't he *ever* make the boat-yard pay?" I asked. "Sell things for instance?"

'E oughta, I suppose," Yorky said. "Only 'e never will, Ain't got it in 'em. 'E'll sell enough to buy 'isell a bellyful of rum and then 'e'll lose interest. Ain't never done any more."

I listened in silence. I'd heard Old Boxer's history before. If it hadn't been for Yorky, Old Boxer wouldn't have kept his head above water as long as he had. Everybody knew that. Yorky did all the boat-hiring and repairs and sold the things Old Boxer was too lazy to sell; even cooked his food for him when he was too drunk to do it himself.

We were both silent for a while, thinking of Old Boxer and his troubles, then Yorky spat into the shining water.

" 'E came 'ere first," he said bitterly, "nigh on twenty year ago, I reckon. You was no more'n a gleam in yer Ma's eye. Reckon it was some ugly business somewhere 'cos 'e'd been on the move for years afore – wanderin' around like a flippin' graveyard ghost."

I tried to decide just what sort of ugly business it could have been but Yorky broke in again, obviously anxious to share his troubles. "Within a week, 'e'd 'alf the waterfront upset with 'is sarcasm. Within a month, there wasn't one as would lift a finger to 'elp 'im. 'Course 'e tried to kid 'em on 'e didn't care, but 'e did. I know old 'Orace. 'Im and me's been shipmates a long time. 'E makes a lot o' noise – plenty o' bluster an' that – but it's all rattle – just like when you bang an empty oil-drum. All noise, but 'ollow – 'ollow as you please."

I didn't really understand what he was getting at – not then, anyway – but I kept quiet, for he clearly wanted to talk. He paused to light a fresh fag-end, then went on in his picturesque, blaspheming way.

"Drinkin' 'eavy, too." He sighed. "Ever sin' I known 'im there's been summat wrong with Old 'Orace. Like a – like" – Yorky's brow wrinkled as he sought in his inarticulate way to give expression to an idea – "like summat was biting 'im inside. That's why 'e snaps people's 'eads off like 'e does. Got a rare chip on 'is shoulder, 'e 'as." He paused, then slapped the old engine with the oily rag. "Gawd," he said, "what we worritin' about *im* for? 'E wouldn't be grateful. 'Ow about you? What did yer dad say about bein' fetched up in court?"

"I've got to start work at the newspaper on Monday," I said gloomily. "I'd sooner work here."

Yorky stared. "You'd never git paid," he commented.

"I bet it's more fun."

"Depends what you call fun," he said. "It don't exactly make me wet me britches a-laughin', puttin' Old 'Orace to bed of a night when 'e's three sheets in the wind and 'is steerin' gone. 'E's a big chap. Takes some luggin' about. Once round 'im, y'know, twice round the gasworks. I've 'ad to chin 'im many a time to sort 'im out a bit." He wagged a fist at me, and continued. " 'Sides, think *I* like tryin' to flog a bit o' gear for 'im to some nance with a glass in 'is eye and a yachtin' cap from St Clewes, or stoppin' the stupid old fool from puttin' 'is 'ead in a gas-oven when 'e's feelin' down in the dumps? 'E's like my Aunt May in Denaby for that. Jeeze, the number of times she tried to do 'erself in! We got sick of cuttin' er' down from the banisters.

"There ain't a penny-piece 'ere." He flung out an arm to indicate the wreckage around him. "No tools. Ain't a plank o' wood worth using. Kep' 'im out of debt more'n once, I 'ave, takin' a boat-load o' junk out there" – he indicated the yachts in the river – "and floggin' it 'alf price. 'Oo looks after the place when 'e's blindo? Billy Muggins. Joe Soap. 'Oo ain't never 'ad a penny-piece for all the trouble 'e's 'ad with this swine?" He gave the engine a vicious swipe with the cloth. "Yours truly. 'Oo's even bought parts for it when *'e* couldn't?" He looked at me under one eyebrow. "Well," he said, "not exactly bought 'em. Bummed 'em from Wiggins' storeman.

"It's all right," he went on in aggrieved tones. "But all of a sudden 'e'll lock up the place and off we go off to sea with 'im owin' me 'alf a quid for booze and swearin' blue murder 'e'll pay me back at the end of the trip. First 'e goes as a mate. Then 'e goes as a bosun. Next thing you know, 'e'll be a flaming galley-boy. They won't 'ave boozers these days, kid.

'E'll be down to stevedoring or fish-loading afore long, you see. Gawd, 'e gives me the Jimmies. An" – he jabbed at me with a fat forefinger – "an' when 'e comes ashore wi' the money 'e's earned, does 'e pay me back? Does 'e 'ell as like. 'E drinks 'isself silly and goes on owing. Never thinks about my ten bob. Not 'e. Not 'im." He spat into the water again. "An' where's it fetched 'im to? Bitin' 'is nails in clink. That's where."

He heaved himself to his feet and cocked a leg over the gunwale on to the tumbledown wharf. "I'm goin' to make meself a cup o' tea," he said. "Want one?"

I nodded and climbed after him.

"Won't be ten minutes," he said, clumping across the broken timbers. "Then maybe you'll knock me off a letter to my old Ma. We can tell 'er I've cut me 'and again."

I nodded and, as he disappeared, I stared at the water for a while. I could hear the slap of the wavelets that washed the seaweed to and fro like long brown hair around the piles, and the soft bumping of the boat as the river caught her and elbowed her against the wharf. I felt a bit depressed just then, what with knowing I'd got to start work where I didn't want to and Old Boxer being in prison and, according to Yorky, likely to be in worse trouble as soon as he came out.

All my life I seemed to have lived among unhappiness. I'd watched Ma growing daily more careless about her appearance as she nursed her grievance and her imaginary ill-health, and Dig growing by degrees more silent, the hurt look in his eyes like a kicked dog's. With a sudden feeling of maturity, I realised I was lonely. I'd often been lonely. I'd not spent much time in the company of youngsters of my own age. Most of my leisure had been spent with Old Boxer.

And you never knew where you were with *him*. He was bitter, sour and sarcastic, savagely cruel one minute and the next tender and thoughtful, but always unreliable, drunk or sober. It was only Yorky's vast zest for life, his enormous

interest in everything that went on around him, that made
Old Boxer bearable at times.

I wondered for a moment if Old Boxer would *ever* sort out
the tangle of his financial affairs, and if Ma would ever speak
civilly to Dig and grow out of her imagined grievance. The
relationship between them, like their relationship towards
me, was always a bit distant. With Ma, I was unfriendly, I
suppose, always just beyond her reach. With Dig, I was
willing to be friendly but it always broke like a wave in an
anti-climax when I realised his attention had wandered to a
book.

Perhaps this was why I liked Old Boxer in spite of his
sulky moods. Sometimes he'd give you a grin of flashing
brilliance that charmed the heart out of you. At least he was
never gloomy and dull in the way that Ma was gloomy and
Dig was dull. You could always reckon on fireworks,
whatever his temper, and I'd always preferred the shambling,
rambling, tumbledown old boat-yard, as ramshackle as Old
Boxer's life, to No 46 Atlantic Street, which had no more
happiness about it than a graveyard.

Staring unseeingly along the wharf, busy with my
thoughts, I gradually became conscious of an erratic splash
of oars behind me that disturbed the even whispering of the
river. Turning to squint into the last of the sunshine, I
recognised Pat Fee in a skiff.

I knew the girl with him. I'd cherished a bosomful of sighs
for her ever since I'd first met her, in spite of the fact that she
was three years older than I.

Pat pulled the boat to the end of the wharf and leaned on
his oars as it drifted slowly on the tide.

" 'Lo, Jess," he said. "You know Minnie, of course."

" 'Lo, Pat," I said, and nodded to Minnie.

Pat was smoking and he took the cigarette from his mouth
with a confident gesture.

"Yer Pa mad?" he queried.

"Yes. Got to start work on Monday, he says."

"So've I," said Pat. "Got to 'elp the old lady with the lodgers. And I've got a job as barman for Minnie's Ma in the pub at night."

Minnie sat back in the stern of the boat and preened her hair as though she were enjoying my staring eyes and Pat's admiration. She'd a mature figure, plump in a tight summer frock that didn't leave much to the imagination, but there was something about her face that just missed being pretty.

"Ma says we only need a chucker-out now," she pointed out to me. "Fancy the job?"

I blushed, knowing she was only mocking me.

Pat struck one thumb in the armhole of his waistcoat and grinned. "You don't need no chucker-out, Minnie," he said cheerfully. "The Steam Packet's a well-be'aved pub."

Minnie's Ma had kept the Steam Packet Inn at the end of Gibraltar Lane, a spit and a jump from Atlantic Street, ever since her father had broken his neck falling down the cellar in a drunken daze. It was a dark little place down by the waterside, with nut-brown rooms, floored with flag-stones and smelling of stale beer. Its backyard was a stone jetty where dinghies were moored. Once it had been a coaching house of some importance where merchant skippers and ship-owners met their crews for the first time with signing-on papers. But now its customers consisted of deck-hands, donkeymen and greasers out to enjoy themselves on the proceeds of a long voyage home, and the dockside touts with their greasy betting slips and fag-ends.

"You *got* to work, Pat?" I asked, uneasy at the absence of conversation and Minnie's bold stare.

"No." Pat shrugged. "Only Ma says if I can go poachin' I can go out to work. Still, I've 'ad a good run." He chuckled suddenly. "What you think of Old Boxer, eh? Proper old boy, ain't 'e? The things 'e said to that old Mayor. Enough to make yer 'air curl, it was, Minnie."

"Bad enough being sent down the line for stealing," Minnie said primly. "Without fighting in police-courts."

Pat grinned easily and held out a packet of cigarettes to her.

"Fag?" he asked.

"Don't mind," Minnie said, taking one.

"Should be able to pick up a bit in bets at the Steam Packet," Pat observed to me. "Sailors is a bit free with their money. 'Specially if they've been a long time comin' 'ome." His eyes suddenly had a faraway look. "Wouldn't mind startin' a book of me own if I'd got the cash."

I was silent before all these mysteries of adult life of which Pat spoke so glibly. I couldn't have afforded them even if I'd been interested.

Pat was squinting saucily at Minnie. "Would you marry me, ducks, if I started to make some ackers?"

"Wun't mind." Minnie was non-committal, and Pat put an arm round her waist and deposited a smacking kiss on her cheek. It set the boat rocking crazily and Minnie squealed and shoved him away.

"Minnie and me's goin' steady," he informed me. "Aren't we, Minnie?"

"People don't want to get too cocky," Minnie warned him.

"Where are you going?" I interrupted, suddenly remembering that Pat was a long way from home.

He grinned slyly. "It's not so much where we're goin' as where we've been," he said. "In the woods along the river. 'Ired the old barge 'ere. Bob an hour. Feeling flush. Come up on the two-thirty today."

"What you been doing in the woods?"

Pat winked. "Go on with you," he said as Minnie smoothed her thin frock over her ample thighs. "What we been doin'? A bit of the old kiss and cuddle, fat'ead. What's a chap take a girl in a wood for? Play marbles with 'er, or something?"

I felt I was on the edge of something unpleasant.

"Like a romp in the grass, don't you, Minnie," Pat said, laying his hand on her knee.

"Go on with you, Pat Fee," Minnie said coyly.

"Well, young Jess..." Pat suddenly realised they'd drifted away from the wharf and the conversation was being conducted in shouts. "...got to be off. Got a date at the Odeon, then a meal and a pint to finish off with in Minnie's back kitchen. Come on, ducks. Don't want to be late."

"People wouldn't be late," Minnie pointed out, "if they didn't stop gossiping to people."

"Oh, come off it," Pat grinned. "You wasn't so much on your 'igh 'orse this afternoon."

He bent over the oars and, splashing badly, they went slowly and erratically up-river, the sun picking up the splashes and the ripple at their stern in diamond points. Pat had never been much good in a boat, but he was cutting a bigger dash than me just then in his pearl-grey flannels. Minnie had had her hair frizzed for the occasion, too, and her skirts were short, adult beyond her years. I watched them out of sight, full of uncomfortable, jealous ideas. Maybe I was growing up.

I wished until it hurt that *I* could take Minnie to the pit stalls of the Odeon, wished *I* could sit beside her at one of the scrubbed tables of a chip shop beneath the garish light of an unshaded bulb and drink beer with her afterwards. I wished *I* could take her in my arms, warm and vital and desirable, and make love to her.

The blood mounted to my face and neck, and there was a sudden choked feeling in my throat. I stopped short, ashamed of my thoughts.

I shoved my hands into my pockets, a bit bewildered with myself, and turned my back on the murmuring river. From the sail-loft the thin wheeze of the concertina that Yorky had carried round the world and back with him was grinding out the nostalgic notes of "Shenandoah". Unaccountably, I felt miserable inside.

four

The Weekly Gazette and News Letter, where I started work the following Monday, was called "the Local Bible" round our way, and its news was accepted as gospel. Not that it carried much news, mind you. Just the police-court and town council stuff, and that was about the lot except for accidents. It was mostly jammed full with company notices and shipping movements and drapers' adverts, and yards of three-line ads. Secondhand washing-machines and ten-foot dinghies. Shipchandlers' wares and farming implements. Old clothes and scrapyard cars. All bundled together in a heap with the births, marriages and deaths. The news pages seemed oases in the deserts of small ads that sprawled unrelieved wherever there was room.

The front office in the High Street was an imposing affair – white stone and gilt letters and windows full of photographs – but the rear end finished up in a maze of grubby alleys among the secondhand bookshops and the auction sale-rooms and the rabbit warren of the solicitors' quarter. They put me at this end – in a room that was as far from light and air and breathing space as they could make it, a dusty little closet next to the works manager's room and looking out on to the courtyard where the newsprint was delivered.

It was a bleak and empty life I lived there, and I hadn't been there two months before I thought of looking for another job. I rejected the idea in the end because of the hurt, unhappy look I knew I'd see in Dig's eyes.

I did my best for him, but I never liked it. They employed me chiefly, as far as I could see, to fetch snuff or cigarettes, and sandwiches on Fridays, the day the paper went to press. Not what you'd call an exciting job. And I had three years of it. Three years! Each one of them as long as centuries. Each one of them a lifetime to me. My face as I went to work in the mornings must have given Dig a few heartburnings. I knew from things he said that he thought often about me and worried in case he hadn't done the right thing. I think he knew he'd made a mistake sending me to the printing works instead of the boat-yard. It was his dislike of the sea that had made him turn down that idea. There'd always been at the back of his mind the fear that Ma's connection with the sea and her admiration for ships and seafaring men had had something to do with her mental sickness. I suppose he thought it might affect me in the same way.

Poor old Dig, he never knew of the time I wasted sitting in the lavatory whistling tunes or reciting "The Shooting of Dan McGrew" over and over to myself to pass away the time, or staring from the window of the store-room where I could lock myself in and enjoy in peace the dirty strip of river that flowed nearby. It was a dull enough strip, fringed by tall buildings, but it was the river nevertheless, and I knew it flowed into the sea and its water was blown by the wind over the horizon.

When I could, I slipped away to the wharfside, down to Old Boxer's boat-yard for a mug of strong tea with Yorky and a sniff at the dark water or a glance at the horizon. But these trips were few and far between. I never seemed to have time for them, what with overtime and night school and errands for Dig, and even they came to an end eventually, for Old Boxer sold his property to Wiggins' as Yorky had predicted and went off to sea.

With him when he left, carrying his concertina and a brown paper parcel that held a couple of clean collars and a clean singlet, went Yorky, continuing his blasphemous martyrdom as Old Boxer's servant and protector. After that, during the three years I worked on the newspaper I saw Old Boxer only occasionally and then he was invariably so drunk he could only concentrate on getting to the dreary room he rented at Ma Fee's lodging-house. Shabbier than ever he was and, strangely, with no time for me. As Yorky had prophesied, the money he raised on the sale of his property went in one terrific bender that landed him in gaol again with the magistrates' instructions to the police to see him safely off to sea when he came out. He shambled down to the docks a fortnight later, dragging a kit-bag, shabby and dull-eyed, and followed by Yorky and a watchful bobby.

It was then I lost touch with them. Even Katie Fee, who was growing into a tall, dark-eyed young woman, helping her mother in the time she could spare from Wiggins' boat-yard, where she'd started in the office, could never tell me when they were likely to be back...

I remember studying that bare, dusty little office where I worked one day, the grubby desk covered with the works manager's snuff and the stubby chewed pencils and scrap-paper, and deciding I wasn't going to live and die there, doing a job I detested until I faded away, just as Dig had been doing for twenty-five years or more. I looked at the windows and couldn't recall when they were last open. I squinted at the bare light bulb which took the place of the daylight that never quite managed to get into the room, and listened to the clattering machines beyond, and I nodded and said out loud: "Not likely. Not much more of this, Jess, me boy."

With three more years on my shoulders, the determination to get away from it had grown to a hard little knot at the back of my mind. But I still hadn't the courage to put it behind me. It takes a lot of doing, throwing up a good job, even if you don't like it. And I'd always got that miserable hurt look in Dig's eyes to think of...

Yet, while it takes some doing to throw up a good job, it also takes some doing to hang on to it when you detest it. It takes all the sparkle out of life and makes it dull and drab and monotonous. When Old Boxer and Yorky went, there was nothing left, nothing to relieve the dreariness of it. And, Lord knows, I was young enough to want a bit of excitement.

There was nobody to lend me a boat or give me a trip to sea. Wiggins' turned over a dinghy to me occasionally – on the strength of Dig working there, I suppose – and I did odd trips on the ferry at weekends when they were short of a hand, or helped with the fishing in summer. But Dig never liked that. I used to come home tired out and falling asleep on my feet, and then I never heard the alarm next day and it used to worry Dig when I was late. I don't think he'd ever been more than a minute behind time at Wiggins' all the time he'd worked there – even with Ma to look after.

But what suited Dig didn't suit me. I'd just about had my bellyful of printing and words and paper. I remember standing in the doorway of that office that day and having a rare old sorting-out of my thoughts. It had been raining, and the sky was dull and the room dark and the dust on the windows had been splashed by the drops that had fallen off the roof and blown against the glass. The grey light in the room reflected my thoughts.

Just when I'd decided I couldn't see any way out, a tap on the window made me jerk my head up.

"Now then, sonny!"

I looked round to see Pat Fee's face pressed to the glass, his nose a bloodless triangle against the pane.

"Got some paper for you, youngster. Better come and get it unloaded or someone's goin' to cop it. Come on, now, or do you want me to take me strap to you? Just 'cos the boss's across at the Crown knocking back his lunch-time pint, it's no excuse for slacking."

I gave him a dirty look and, picking up my receipt-book, followed him outside.

He was leaning against the wall, whistling to himself, the same old Pat, confident to the point of getting on my nerves, a cigarette dangling from his lips, another behind his ear.

He'd long since ceased to work for Minnie's Ma at the Steam Packet. The pittance he received as a barman had soon become too small for his maturing tastes and even the attraction of Minnie hadn't held him there for long.

He'd tried his hand at various jobs – a bookie's runner, a pawnbroker's clerk; even, it was rumoured, a little bit of fraud. Finally, with his winnings from a day at the races, he'd scraped up enough to buy himself a small lorry and had gone into business as a carter at the station and was doing well at it. In addition, he helped his Ma at the lodging-house, *his* part of the business being to make sure that the old rag-tags who inhabited the place paid their rent on the dot or went out into the street.

Despite all this, though, his tastes were such that he was always short of cash and not above borrowing five bob from me when I had it, a loan that had something of a threat in it for me, being younger and smaller,

As I went out into the sunshine of the court, I treated him to a scowl.

"Got my money yet?" I asked.

"What money?" Pat pushed his cap to the back of his head and stared. "I got no money of yourn."

"What about that half-crown I gave you to put on a horse for me. It won."

"You never gave me no 'alf-dollar," Pat said nonchalantly. "Come on, now, kiddo, let's get this paper off. I got another job at the gasworks in a bit."

"I gave you half a crown," I said, mad as a bluebottle in a window. "I wish I hadn't now, and I wouldn't have if you hadn't been at me for half an hour saying it was a cert."

"You're imagining things. Come on. 'Urry up. Think I've time to argue with a kid?"

"I wasn't such a kid you couldn't pinch half a dollar off me!" I shouted.

"Listen!" Pat put a thumb in his waistcoat pocket and with the forefinger of his other hand tapped me weightily on the chest. "I got no half-dollar of yourn. Put that under yer little smock, son. Now let's get this paper off my lorry or I'll just 'ave to sort you out a bit. See?"

He was taller than me by several inches and muscular, and he leaned over me and scowled.

"Just 'cos I was a pal o' yourn once, you don't go accusin' Pat Fee o' bein' a thief nor a liar. Get me?"

I swallowed my anger and turned towards the lorry backed up against the swing doors that led into the works.

One day, I promised myself, Pat Fee would pay for this. And for the half-crown he hadn't paid back. *And* for all the others. *And* for all the times he'd baited me.

All my life I seemed to have been under his thumb. He'd pinched my belongings as a kid and bullied me everlastingly. He'd walloped me at school and jeered at me after I left because I worked in an office. Everywhere I went, Pat seemed to turn up, too, claiming friendship till it suited him to become threatening.

"Come on," I said sourly. "Let's get on with it."

"OK. That's better," Pat commented, pushing his cap over one eye. "Pat Fee's not the one to stand for cheek, mister."

"Oh, shut up." I said angrily.

Pat grinned confidently, contemptuous of me. I only came up to his shoulders in those days.

"Gettin' cocky all of a sudden, ain't yer?" he queried. "Proper saucy little bastard."

"I'm an honest little bastard, anyway," I said furiously, goaded beyond endurance by his smooth smile and the jaunty air that couldn't hide the fact that he'd swindled a hard-earned half-crown out of me.

Pat turned at the words, his hands on his hips, his fingers like thick sausages over his leather belt.

"Gawd," he said, "you're a cheeky little customer, ain't yer? Two more words out o' you and I'll 'ave you over my knee."

I glared at him, and I could feel my distrust and dislike growing. Once I'd been proud to feel that Pat would include me in his poaching forays, but we'd grown up along entirely different ways. Perhaps because he'd once condescended to call me a friend, I disliked him all the more – and still more because Pat, who'd got a way with him, could twist Minnie round his little finger, while on the only occasion I'd shyly offered my heart to her she'd laughed at me and called me a "saucy little monkey".

My jealousy was like a scar on my mind.

"Got that?" Pat was saying. "And don't burst into tears, kiddo, 'cos you can't 'ave yer own way. Blimey, you'll be offin' it up to Wiggins' any time now and yellin' for ole Ferigo to come and sort me out."

"You know jolly well I won't."

"Wouldn't be much good if you did," Pat grinned. "I expect he'd be about as dangerous to me as he was to yer dad."

I didn't get what he said at first. I thought I'd not heard him right. Then, when I realised I'd made no mistake, I stared at him uncomprehendingly.

"What do you mean?" I demanded.

"Go on," Pat said contemptuously. "Don't tell me you ain't got the truth of that yet? When you arrived on the scene, old Ferigo just quietly shuffled off and said nothing. Somebody'd got a belting from me if it 'ad 'appenened to *my* wife. *I* wouldn't 'ave 'ad nobody playin' cuckoo round *my* missis."

The inference of his words staggered me. I still couldn't believe I'd heard them correctly. But, even so, I knew somehow there was truth in them. I stared at him, my hands limp at my sides.

"What do you mean?" I repeated. There was a chilly stillness inside me.

" 'What do yer mean?' " Pat mocked me in a high-pitched voice and pranced in a half-circle with his hand on his hip. "What do yer mean? Don't you know no other words, sonny? Ain't you learned the facts of life *yet*? If *you* don't know that old Digby Ferigo ain't yer dad, then you ought to. Everybody else does."

As he spoke, the words burst like an explosion inside my brain. Until he had actually uttered them, I'd been numb, almost stupid, but now that they were said, without waiting to weigh up chances I flung myself on him.

" 'Ere. 'Ere." He picked me off like a troublesome fly and held me at arm's length, my overall bunched in a great fist.

"You don't want to go off like that when you 'ear things," he said, "or you might get 'urt. If you want to set about somebody, pick somebody yer own weight. Give me 'alf a mo,' and I'll get our Katie down 'ere to spar a couple of rounds with you."

He gave me a shove that sent me reeling away, to land on my behind in a puddle of muddy water among the cobblestones, feet sprawling, papers scattered, smouldering with resentment.

Dismissing the incident, he turned and walked towards the swing doors that led to the works.

"Now, come on," he said over his shoulder. "Let's get this job done, or I'll 'ave to take yer pants down."

He'd just put one hand on the door-handle when I got him. I flung myself with all my power at the jaunty, sneering figure that completely disregarded me as a potential source of danger.

As the doors burst open under our weight the two of us stumbled through into the machine-room, crashing into the compositor at the nearest linotype. His chair promptly skated away and deposited the lot of us on the floor.

Pat scrambled to his feet, more startled than hurt, and rounded on me. I was just as dazed and more startled than he was at what I'd done.

"You little twerp!" he yelped furiously. "Put yer fives up."

I scrambled to my feet, my receipt-book and papers forgotten, and closed with him while the compositors left their work and crowded round.

"Back there," I heard someone say. "Give 'em room."

"Fists up, little 'un," a voice bawled in my ear. "You'll not do much good with 'em down there."

I'd never been much of a scrapper and Pat was having a rare old time with my face. Blood was running down my chin from a split lip, and he was dancing round me, well on his toes, with all the airs and graces of the Fancy, tapping my nose repeatedly with his left hand. I couldn't have stopped him any easier if he'd been Joe Louis.

"Come on, Jess. Let's 'ear from yer."

" 'Es down! By God, 'e's down!" The excitement welled up to a crescendo.

I didn't notice much of it. I was sitting in a litter of wastepaper half underneath one of the benches. I shook my head, dazed by a crack between the eyes and barely conscious of the din going on around me.

"Up, Jess. Up, you little devil, and give 'im the old one-two."

"Shut yer row!" Someone was yanking me to my feet and his voice was shouting in my ear. I could feel his breath on my skin. "You'll have the boss round in 'alf a shake."

The noise penetrated gradually into my dizzy brain, and as my eyes began to focus once more I faced Pat again, fists well up. But my legs were wobbly and I was squinting through only one good eye. The other was already closed.

I moved more cautiously this time, watching Pat warily. But all the time that great brown fist of his was right in front of my face and, no matter which way I dodged, I couldn't get past it.

" 'Ad enough, young 'un?" Pat grinned.

"No. Not likely," I said. But I didn't feel half so hearty as I sounded. I wanted to sit down and cry.

" 'Ark at 'im. 'Ark at 'im talk." Some wag pushed forward with a bucket. " 'Ere, do the job proper. 'Ow about some sawdust to soak up the blood?"

There was a guffaw from the crowd that hurt me as much as Pat's fists. No one was taking the fight seriously, and to me just then it seemed a matter of life and death.

"Seconds out!" shouted the Wag, thoroughly enjoying himself watching me getting a hammering. "Come on, Butch. Let's be seein' yer!"

It didn't take long to realise I'd get nowhere trying to box. Pat could do the job twice as well as I could. So I decided to make a rush and take a chance on getting in a few blind swipes before I was stopped. One would almost have been enough. One good one, with my arms whirling the way they were.

"Whoa, mare!" shouted the Wag, and if I hadn't been too occupied with Pat I might have had a go at him, too. "Sails away like a flippin' Derby winner."

I'd forced Pat backwards between the benches and we were brought up sharp by a galleyful of type which teetered and overbalanced. It landed in a shower on the floor and was immediately scattered by the shuffling boots.

"God!" someone yelled. "It took me all the bloody morning to set that lot up!"

"Never mind, mate," said the Wag, having the time of his life. "Small price to pay for a fight like this!"

"Oh, my word, 'e's tapped 'is claret!"

More by luck than judgement, I'd started Pat's nose bleeding. He wiped it away with the back of his hand and stared at it, startled, just long enough for me to land another one.

"Again, Jess, lad! Again!" Everybody was enjoying himself but me. "Don't stand looking at him!"

Pat was backing away hurriedly now, the sneer of contempt gone from his face. I followed him, hitting out wildly, blind with rage, able to see from only one eye.

"Now, lay off, young 'un," he was muttering as he pushed me off. "Don't be so soft. It was only my kid."

His words ended abruptly as I sent him sprawling to his knees among the scattered type. The crowd yelled.

"Now, Jess. One in the eye as he gets up."

As Pat staggered to his feet again I landed another wild swing at the side of his head that sent him reeling back. He was still more startled than hurt.

"Leave off, young 'un," he panted. "Can't you see I was only joking!"

I was too berserk with rage to hear him, and I landed one or two more on his head and shoulders that jarred my arms more than they did Pat.

He was becoming irritated, by this time, though. At first he'd regarded the fight as exercise, but now that the blood was running from his nose he was ready to stop. He wasn't hurt, but his dignity was suffering. As for me, I was aware of only one thing – the desire to knock seven bells out of him, and Pat began to get furious.

"Leave off, you little fool," he roared, "or I'll give you one!"

He shut his rattle sharp enough as I clipped his mouth to with one full on the jaw just as he was backing away. I must have caught him off balance, for he staggered back against a bench and sprawled there for a second. As he groped to regain his feet I saw his fingers close over one of the rollers the compositors used for pulling proofs.

"Look out, Jess!" a voice screeched in my ear. "Lookout!"

From my one good eye I caught a swift glimpse of the roller coming over Pat's shoulder and I ducked. The roller missed me and flew over my bent back. It got the Wag right in the bread-basket.

"Christ!" he gasped, changing his tune. "Everybody's gone bloody barmy!"

This was a new and vicious shift of events. But I was as good at it as Pat. I grabbed for the nearest thing to my hand. It was a tub of printer's ink that had been upset on the steel bench.

"Look out, boys!" The onlookers scattered. "It's getting dangerous!"

Just then the door opened on the works manager. He was back from lunch and sniffing like a bloodhound to discover the cause of the shouting that had disturbed him.

Pat ducked.

"Oh, Gawd!" someone muttered, the awe in his voice tempered by ecstatic delight. "Smack in the clock!"

The uproar died as suddenly as it had started. The flush went out of everybody's cheeks. There was a sudden hurried scuffling and the crowd melted away like smoke in a breeze. The waste-basket was righted and the scattered type was hurriedly kicked out of sight under a bench.

Pat and I stood staring, struck dumb, gaping at the works manager. He was staggering and spluttering and spitting by the door, groping with grimy fingers at the sticky ink that dripped from his face and over his waistcoat. Then Pat had vanished, too. There was a crash of gears and the roar of an engine outside, and I was alone, panting, my lips bleeding, one eye closed, my knuckles raw, still staring at the clawing figure in the doorway.

Then someone held out a piece of waste rag and slid away hurriedly. That helped a bit but not much. All you could see were two wild white eyeballs and a face livid with fury underneath the coating of ink.

Suddenly the breath filled my lungs with a rush. I'd been standing paralysed, and movement came into my limbs. While the Old Man was still glaring round for me I walked calmly past him towards the office. There was no feeling of panic in me. I wasn't hurrying from anybody's bad temper. It was just that I knew suddenly that my life at the printing works had ended – completely and utterly, as if it had been cut off with a knife. Silently, and without a flutter of hesitation, I took my jacket from its hook and left the building.

five

I must have walked for hours. I'd no idea where I was going. I was unaware of any feeling except freedom. I only knew I was never going to the printing works again. I was finished for good and all with newspapers and type and ink. I could have been forgiven, I suppose, in spite of the enormity of the crime, but, somehow, something inside me told me my life among the grimy buildings and the narrow streets with their hurrying crowds was finished, that there was no longer any place in the town for me.

I walked slowly through the light rain that was falling. I had my head down, trying to sort out the jumble of thoughts that were racing through my mind, my hands deep in my pockets, my hat on the back of my head.

"Hello, youngster." A friendly bobby stopped me as I passed. "Been in the wars?"

I stared, unhearing, then, as I realised what he'd said I shook my head and pulled my arm free.

"It's nothing." I said.

I'd forgotten my split lips and my closed eye and raw knuckles. I never noticed the pain in them – any more than I noticed the people around me. I made my way slowly through the shopping crowds, never feeling the baskets I joggled or seeing the vans and buses that nearly ran me down.

I was shocked and dizzy. Not so much because of the walloping Pat had given me, nor the sight of the boss clawing the air as he struggled to free his eyes of the ink, as Pat's words. Back there, before the fight started, I'd known there must be truth in them. I don't know why I bothered to start the fight even. I knew Pat wasn't lying. As I thought about it, I remembered a thousand and one things which had seemed in the past to have no explanation but which were laid bare in one second by Pat's insult: Dig's vagueness towards me; the shy relationship that was never quite fatherly; Ma's sullen grievance against life. All the questions that had never been satisfied in my life seemed to have found their answer in the rough challenge Pat had thrown out.

I suddenly felt lonely. It wasn't a solitariness but a loneliness of the spirit. The streets seemed oddly unfamiliar – as though I were in a strange town. Even the crowded mariners' shops, jam-packed with oilskins, seaboots, soap, needles and everything the sailor needed, appeared to be different. The hurrying traffic, the sailors ashore in dungarees, the few Lascars in tarbooshes and a shuffling Chinee, all seemed to be something from another life that gave me a sense of unreality, a sense of being in a dream.

Straight down the High Street I walked, down towards the river. My eyes were on the pavement, and I was conscious only of a desire to throw off the cheerless memories of the printing works. Straight on I went, scowling to myself, having a fine old sorting-out of things.

I don't know how long I'd been walking when a familiar voice caught my ear and I halted reluctantly. "Now then," it said, "what you been doin', eh? Giving people a fright with a clock like that."

It was Minnie, and I realised I must have walked miles. I was outside the Steam Packet and Minnie stood on the front step, polishing the brass handles of the swing doors.

"Hello, Minnie," I said. I was grateful for the unaccustomed kindliness in her voice. It was a tone she'd never used to me before. There was compassion in her words. It must have been my bruises and the blood that still smeared my face that did the trick.

"Better come in and wash yourself," she said. "You'll be gettin' run in else."

"Yes, I will, Minnie." I suddenly felt the desire to talk to someone, the desire to confide.

She put down her cloth and led me through the empty bar into the back kitchen. Her Ma, a plump, wheezing little woman, with a florid face and orange-coloured hair that didn't look quite natural even to me, gave a shriek of horror as she saw me.

"My Gawd!" she said. " 'Ere, 'e been run over?"

I stared at her, trying to make my one good eye focus. I could see her only as a vague, blurred shadow by the fireplace.

"No, mam," I said. "Fighting."

" 'Oo was it? King Kong?"

"Was it Pat Fee?" Minnie queried, her hands on her broad hips.

"How did you know?"

"It's been comin' to him for a long time," Minnie laughed. " 'Sides, he called in here half an hour ago. He had a split lip and a thirst. I think he'll have a black eye by tomorrow."

I grinned, wincing at the pain from my bruised lips.

"Left my mark on him, anyway," I said.

"He left his mark on you, too," Minnie's Ma said, her great red arms akimbo. She was running water into an enamel bowl.

" 'Ere, shove your 'ead in this."

I pulled off my jacket and began to sluice the water over my face and neck. I hadn't realised till then how hot I was or how much my eye hurt.

" 'Ere," Minnie's Ma said when I'd dried myself on the damp grey towel Minnie held out for me, "put this inside of you."

She handed me a pot of beer and I downed it at a gulp.

" 'Ere," she said – most of her remarks seemed to be prefaced by the word – "where did you learn to drink beer like that?"

"Shut up, Ma," Minnie said placidly, still standing with her hands on her hips. "Leave him alone."

Minnie's Ma clucked her tongue and disappeared towards the bar, lifting a glass of gin from the sideboard as she passed with a dexterity that indicated there'd been many earlier glasses.

"What was it all about?" Minnie asked, unexpectedly warm and friendly.

"Pat said something to me," I said, and all the bounce went out of me suddenly.

"Always at it." Minnie nodded understandingly. She'd felt the lash of Pat's tongue more than once, I expect.

"So I went for him," I boasted.

"Good for you." Minnie nodded again. "He'a saucy one, that."

The unexpected praise made my head swim. I sat on the horsehair sofa rubbing my knuckles and staring at Minnie. Though she was only three or four years older than I she was completely a woman, with a full, well-fleshed body and an adult face beneath the piled hair. Her frock was a little too tight as usual, so that it couldn't hide her curves. She saw me staring and my mouth closed with a click of embarrassment as she grinned.

"Growin' up, aren't you?" she said. "Lookin' at people like that."

"A bit," I admitted.

There was a strained pause for a moment, then she spoke again, breaking the silence in the dark kitchen sharply.

"Hadn't you better be getting back?"

I stretched luxuriously, suddenly feeling better. Minnie's concern for me had made me a man. I felt big enough now to face up to the discovery I'd just made, big enough to sort out the problems it had raised so unexpectedly.

"I'm not going back," I said cheerfully. "I'm never going back."

"My word!" Minnie commented. "Quite the young gentleman, aren't you? Don't need to work for his living."

She sat down at the other end of the sofa and I flushed as she gazed at me. Her eyes were violet and big and bright.

"What are you going to do?" she asked.

"Dunno." The question brought me back to earth with a jolt.

I stared round the kitchen. It had a blackleaded fireplace, untidy with airing clothes that hung from the mantelpiece where two great ornaments towered away into the shadows.

I realised I'd never been inside Minnie's kitchen before. Not many of her admirers had, and I drew a deep breath, feeling a man. It wasn't a particularly prepossessing place. It had a gloomy wallpaper, stained nut-brown by the smoke from the bar, and a cracked ceiling. And heavy woven curtains that kept out what little light the dark walls outside allowed to filter past. Even the picture of Minnie's father, a moustached man in a stiff collar, looked a bit flyblown and faded. Stockings, dingy towels and more intimate things that made me stare hung about everywhere. Under the sideboard and the sink were old, curling shoes with the toes kicked out of them, and an elderly and mangy-looking cat snored noisily in the hearth on a towel. Underneath the towel there was a plate with the remains of the cat's dinner on it.

The heat from the glowing fire where black saucepans simmered like witches' cauldrons was overpowering. It made me wilt but Minnie didn't seem to notice it. She lolled on the end of the sofa, staring at me, lazy and voluptuous.

I drew in my breath sharply at the intimacy it suggested.

"If you aren't goin' back to the *Gazette,* what are you goin' to live on?" she queried suddenly. "Can't just sponge on people."

"Think I'll leave the town," I said slowly.

"Leave the town?" Minnie stared at me as though I were mad. "Where'll you go?"

"Dunno." I shook my head. "Something'll turn up, I suppose."

"Where you goin' to live?"

I was stumped. "Couldn't say. I'll be all right, though."

I paused. Then I looked at Minnie and I felt daring and rakish.

"Will you miss me, Minnie?"

Minnie stared at me, startled by the question. "Suppose I will," she said carelessly. "I've seen a bit of you on and off."

My thoughts were plunging ahead along a new and romantic track. "*You* wouldn't like to live in this old town for ever, would you?" I asked, preparing the way for the next question. "Not for always?"

"Wun't mind," Minnie said placidly, and I didn't bother to ask the next question. I felt deflated.

"Expect you'll be all right," Minnie murmured. "After all, you're a man now." She hesitated. "I'm glad you gave that Pat Fee what for," she went on savagely. "My Gawd, I'd do it meself if I wasn't a girl! Gets me down, he does, with his rattle. Like a rooster on a muck-heap."

"What's he been doing, Minnie?" I asked, bold and protective as you please.

"Stringin' people along the way he does," Minnie spat out. "Only comes to a see a girl when he's spent all his money on the horses. Only comes when he wants a free drink or two. Oh, he can hold a girl's hand over the bar all right. He can squeeze her fingers when she slips him half a quid. But he can't come and see her when he's flush. Oh no! It's one of them flash pieces that hang round the docks then."

"Not really?" I scowled. Young as I was, I'd been stopped more than once by the women who made a practice of loitering by the dock gates for sailors fresh from sea, and I was wild that Minnie should have been spurned for one of them – even by Pat Fee.

"Tarts, they are," Minnie said bitterly. She was working herself up to tears of self-sympathy. "And him after 'em like a dog after a bitch."

"Minnie!" I gulped. "You aren't in love with Pat Fee, are you?"

Minnie swung round on me furiously. "In love with him? Me? That's a good one. Not likely. Not me. Not with Pat Fee."

I sighed with relief. I never noticed that the vehemence in her tones carried no conviction. I opened my mouth to speak, but just then the clock struck and Minnie stared at it.

"My Gawd!" she said. "Ma'll be after me soon. Isn't it time you was going?"

I scowled at the clock that had interrupted us.

"Suppose I'd better be off," I said gloomily, depressed at the thought of leaving her. Just when we seemed to be getting to know each other. Just when Pat seemed to be disposed of.

I suddenly felt the need for friendliness, something to take the place of the love I'd never had from Ma. I felt bitter against her as I thought about her. She'd brought me into the world, wide open to Pat Fee's insults, and had never given me any kind of affection to help me on. I needed Minnie's kind words just then, not merely because she was Minnie whom I'd always admired despite the absence of any encouragement, but because she was a woman. Because she was warm and kind and I needed some gentle word – now that I'd decided to leave – to take away with me.

"I'll miss you, Minnie," I said.

"Will you?" Minnie was flattered. She smiled and smoothed her frock over her knees.

"Minnie!" I gulped and blushed down to my collar. "Minnie, I'm going away, probably a long way, and I might not come back for a long time. Will you – will – Minnie, will you kiss me goodbye?"

Minnie stared, then she laughed softly.

"Gawd," she said, "you're a bit of a one, aren't you?" But she smiled. " 'Course I will," she added. She'd never been mean with her favours, according to the stories I'd heard.

She leaned over and laid her lips on my cheek. "There, how's that?"

I went a flaming red. "No, Minnie," I said. "I mean a proper one."

Minnie laughed again, uproariously, her head back so that I saw her teeth and her white throat. "You're a saucy one, you are," she said. "All right, me lad, I'll give you a kiss to curl your hair and turn your toes up. Stand up and take it like a man."

I rose, awkward and gauche, feeling as though I'd left my pants behind. Minnie smiled at me with veiled eyes, her lips moist and full.

"Come on," she said, "put your arms round me proper."

I took hold of her clumsily, but she took my hand in hers and put it on her breast, then she clutched me fiercely, kissing me till I was breathless. Her full rich body pressed against me, moving. Her lips were parted, and my stomach seemed to fall away from me as she held me to her, her thighs against mine, her full bosom warmly pressing on my chest, her eyes closed.

I staggered when she released me and almost fell down.

"There!" Minnie seemed pleased with the effect of her embrace. "How's that?"

My eyes must have been bright, for Minnie stared.

"Now don't go and burst into tears," she commanded.

"No, I'm not going to, Minnie." I gasped the words breathlessly.

I stared at her for a second, then abruptly I picked up my cap.

"I'm going now, Minnie," I said firmly, though my feet were yards off the floor. "But I'll be back – one of these days."

Outside, I stood on the pavement, my arms still feeling the pressure of Minnie's body. I stared down at my hand, the hand that had cupped her breast. It still felt warm with the touch of her and I grinned awkwardly. Then I slapped my cap on, cheerfully kicked a piece of orange peel skidding along the gutter, and began to walk away, whistling.

As I passed the front door of the Steam Packet I caught a glimpse of Minnie leaning over the bar talking to her Ma and a few words floated out to me.

"...kid going away," she was saying. "Wanted me to kiss him goodbye, if you please... An' him with the marks of the cradle not off his be'ind..."

I stopped dead, my ears burning, the flush coming back to my face.

"...'a proper one,' he said. A proper one, eh! Gawd, I gave him one to make him wet his britches..."

Minnie's Ma laughed, a high-pitched shriek that made me go hot with shame. Kid going away. Kid. The word burned into my brain.

A couple of men across the narrow street were leaning at the door of a blacksmith's shop and, as I turned away, one of them spoke, bringing laughter from the other.

I moved away hurriedly. They seemed to be laughing at me. There seemed to be jeers even in the sound of the hurrying traffic.

s i x

By the time I got home I felt I wanted to break something.
Dig hadn't come in, and I stood in the hall and stared round
the shabby living-room with the table he'd set for tea before
he went to work. I glowered at the neat, old-fashioned
ornaments on the mantelpiece and the row of cheap
leatherette classics on the sideboard, hating them for their
neatness and their cheapness. I wanted to smash and tear the
lot. I felt frustrated and cheated.

I scowled at the photograph of Ma that showed her as I'd
never known her – young and lovely, only a sulky mouth
spoiling an attractive face. It still had the place of honour on
the sideboard – as though Dig still hoped to rescue her from
the chaos of her mind by the reminder of how she was once.

I hung up my cap, Minnie's words still in my ears, echoing
in my mind with great dull sounds that numbed me. A kid
going away. I could still hear the casualness in her tones, the
indifference.

I mounted the stairs slowly to the bedroom I shared with
Dig and pushed a few of my personal possessions and a little
clothing – the first I could lay my hands on – into a small
cardboard suit-case. Then I left the room again, tiptoeing as
I noticed the door of Ma's room was ajar. I had a feeling for
a moment she was listening, perhaps even watching me. I
toyed with the idea of going in to her and demanding an
explanation of Pat's disclosure, then I realised she wouldn't
even listen and certainly wouldn't help. She'd hide behind

bitterness and harsh words, probably bursting into a flood of tears of self-sympathy. I suddenly felt a feeling of revulsion for the musty-smelling room where I'd had to stand so often as a child and recite my lessons to Ma, who'd never been interested anyway.

Then, oddly, remembering Pat's words, I felt a twinge of sympathy for her, left with a child she'd perhaps not wanted, and an unsatisfying husband who probably couldn't understand her more physical passions.

But, as I considered, my sympathy changed to anger again. She'd never given me any love or affection or tried very hard to understand Dig. She'd done nothing in all her life but dramatise her tragedy, nursing her grievance and allowing herself to grow ugly, and miserable with a misery that was infectious.

No. To hell with her, I thought, and grasped my case tighter and made my way downstairs.

As I reached the bottom I realised Dig was watching me through the open door of the living-room.

"Why aren't you at work?" he asked. "Surely you shouldn't be home yet?"

"I've left," I said.

"Oh!" Dig considered this for a moment but his expression showed no sign of disappointment. He must have been half expecting it for a long time. "I see," he said. "What are you goin' to do now, then?" His eyes had travelled to the case in my hand.

"Dunno yet." I shrugged.

"Where are you going, Jess?" he asked quietly, and there was a hint of apprehension in his voice.

"Away," I said. "I'm leaving home."

Dig looked at me for a moment, then his eyes fell and, in doing so, dropped on a magazine on the table. It was some piffling publication that Ma read, but instinctively he picked it up and began to turn the pages.

"Why, Jess?" he asked.

"Just got to!" I told him of the fight and the accident to the works manager. I was feeling pretty depressed with reaction by this time and the words came wearily.

Dig stared silently at the magazine in his hand, then he lifted his head slowly to meet my eyes.

"I suppose," he said, "you'll be needing some money?"

"No." I felt secure in my newly found independence and maturity. I wanted to show all these people – Pat and Minnie and the whole lot of them – that I wasn't a kid any longer. "I've got a bit saved up."

"It won't be enough." Dig fished in his pocket. "Here," he muttered shyly. "You'll need money if you're going away. This's all I've got. Not much, but it'll help."

He pushed a few bob into my hand. Then he fumbled again and produced threepence-halfpenny in coppers and a stamp.

"Here. Might as well take the lot." He hesitated, staring at the stamp, then he pushed it at me. "Better have this. Might be useful. You can drop me a line."

He dropped his hands to his sides, wordless, and we stared at each other in a silence that grew until it was strained. I saw his eyes were moist, and I wanted to cry at the thought that he'd pressed on me his few shillings spending money.

He was studying me, his eyes blinking rapidly. "Won't you tell me, Jess?" he asked. "Surely, you're not leaving home just because of a fight at work? There must be more to it than that."

I stared at his feet for a moment, then with a sudden intake of breath the things that Pat Fee had said burst out:

"He said things about you. He said you weren't my father."

Dig stood very still for a moment, still fiddling with the magazine. He appeared to scan it from cover to cover before he spoke, then he looked up at me with that habit of his, over the top of the page, and as he did so his grey-flecked hair and moustache and the dandruff that was always on the collar of his shiny suit made him seem dusty and neglected, something that had been forgotten and allowed to collect cobwebs.

"I'm not your father, Jess." He spoke quietly. "I've been afraid of this for a long time. It had to come some day."

I'd been hoping against hope he'd deny everything Pat had suggested, though all the time, deep down inside, I knew – almost as though I were acting and had played the scene before – that he wouldn't. As he spoke I caught my breath, like a kid disappointed in its wishful thinking.

"I thought – I thought perhaps he must be right," I said. "Things you'd said – and Ma – and, oh, all sorts of things."

I shrugged helplessly and took another grip on my case.

"There's no need to go, Jess," Dig said. "It needn't make no difference."

"Who is my father?" I asked, and Dig jumped as though the question startled him.

"I dunno, Jess." He looked away as he spoke, and I felt he wasn't telling the truth. "It all happened during the war. I was in France at the time. You'd arrived when I came home. I tried to forget all about it. But" – he shrugged, suddenly pathetic and small and drab – "your Ma didn't seem to want to forget."

"Would *she* tell me who it was?"

"I don't think so." Dig turned a page of the magazine with a sharp crackle of paper. "She's never told me. Whoever it was, he made an impression on your Ma. She's made it a grievance ever since because I wasn't like him. I don't think she'll ever say who it was now."

I nodded. Suddenly I didn't care, anyway. After all the years of indifference towards each other, after all the years of coolness between us, Ma and I couldn't indulge in intimate researches of this sort.

There seemed nothing more to say. We stared at each other for a moment, then I turned away.

"Well, I'll be off," I said. Oddly, I could no longer think of Dig as my father. There seemed a great width of loneliness between us already.

"Must you, Jess?" he said. "Must you go?"

"Yes," I answered shortly. I felt a stranger in the house all at once. There was suddenly no longer any place for me there.

"Can't I help?" Dig's voice was unsteady, as though he was blaming himself.

"No. I'll be all right." I put on my cap and turned to the door.

As I reached the hall Dig called again.

"Stop a minute," he said.

"I tried," he mumbled, and his cringing humility made me want to soothe him like a crying baby. I was bigger than he was. Perhaps that's what did it. "I'm sorry, Jess. I always regarded you as me own." He became engrossed in the magazine again, embarrassed. "But there's still a home for you here if you want one. There'll always be one."

The sight of his drooping, unhappy figure almost brought me to the point of turning back. I very nearly dropped the cardboard suit-case on the spot. Then I remembered the printing works and Minnie's words.

I scowled and gripped the bag tighter.

"Thanks," I said. "Thanks. I'll remember that."

I turned away. I could see Dig had put the magazine down and was following me with his eyes, and I was glad to put the door between us.

seven

It was late evening by the time I reached the riverside, and the rain was falling heavily. I stood in the doorway of a shabby, down-at-heel shop for a moment, drawing in the scent in the air. It was a strange yet familiar scent, a scent that had always fascinated me. I put down my case on the wet pavement and stared at the shop lights reflected in the glistening streets, and sniffed as I rested my stiff fingers. There seemed a peculiar magic in the air all of a sudden.

Then, at that moment, I knew where I was going, where I'd been heading all my life. In spite of my troubles I grinned with a sudden delight.

A dreary, drenched old Bible-thumper with a dewdrop on the end of his nose, who was shuffling past with a placard bearing the words, "Jesus is Virtue, Sin is Death", must have caught my grin, for he suddenly shoved a collecting-box at me.

"How about a copper for God, brother?" he said in a hopeless voice.

I pushed a penny into the box – all I could spare – and the old man shuffled off, leaving me still excited. I was on the threshold of something new. There was a violent pulsing of emotion in me, and all the bonds that held me to home dropped away. I felt scourged of all meanness and misery.

" 'Ere, move on, there!" A voice jarred me back to the present, and I became aware of the shopkeeper prodding me in the small of the back with a shutter. "Ain't goin' to stand there all night, are you?" he queried. "Ain't you nowhere to go?"

I stared at him for a second, almost too ecstatic to speak, then I hurried off into the darkness, hardly noticing where I was. Eventually, however, the scent that had caught my nostrils seemed stronger again, and I made my way down a dark alley to where I could see the sparkle of light on water.

In the blackness, I collided with a soft body that stank of cheap perfume, and a heavy drawl came out of the shadows.

"Look where you're goin', shipmate," it said.

"Fetch 'im one, Jackie," said a woman's voice, and I hurried on down the alley towards the water, flushing with embarrassment in the darkness.

Dropping my case underneath a spluttering gas-lamp, I stared over the river, suddenly filled with a fierce exultation. Above me, the gas-lamp was veiled in a circle of mist as its light caught the slanting rain, and all around me there was the hiss and trickle of water. My shoes were only thin, and my feet were wet, but I never even noticed. Unable to restrain my feelings any longer. I thrust my hands deep in my trousers pocket and laughed out loud.

Away over the water I could see masts and a web of rigging. Almost in front of me was a small freighter with a lanky funnel, placid on the calm river, its lights reflected in glittering diamond points on the oily blackness of the water.

"Ships," I said out loud. "Ships."

Then I knew what I'd been wanting more than anything else in the world – more than security, more than Minnie, even – what I'd been reaching out for all through the past. Suddenly the future seemed buoyant with hope, and all the doubts and difficulties that go with youth fell away from me.

"Ships," I said again.

A grimy little figure in a high bowler hat, who'd stopped to light a pipe nearby, turned as I spoke. " 'Course they're ships," he said. "What did you think they was, mate? Blue-bells?"

I turned towards him as he blew a few puffs of smoke into the damp air.

"You new 'ere?" I was asked.

"No," I said with a grin. "Not really."

"Thinkin' o' goin' to sea, mate?" The little chap's false teeth were loose and jiggled in his mouth as he spoke.

Even then I hadn't thought of any such thing. I'd been glad to see the crowded shipping in the river, but I'd still no intention of becoming a sailor. But the little man suddenly put into words what I wanted, what I needed, even.

"Yes," I said eagerly. "Yes, I am."

"Then Ernest Nanjizel's the boy for you," he said enthusiastically, becoming an agitated, energetic, bustling figure in a second.

He sidled closer and, taking off his bowler, brought out from the hat-band inside a bundle of cards. " 'Ere you are," he said. "Trelawney's for yer sea-boots and oilskins. Best in the town. Platt's for yer dungarees. Can't be beat. And if you feel like spendin' a bit of cash in a blow-out afore you leave Old England's shores, try the Anchor Inn. Joe Plant, proprietor. Licensed to sell ale, beer, wines, spirits, cigarettes and tobaccer. Looks after yer like a little baby when you've 'ad one too many. Never takes advantage of yer and keeps yer change when yer blotto. An' me – now me – "

Obviously we were only just coming to the real point in the rigmarole.

" – Ernest Nanjizel! That's me. Put that in yer card-case." He shoved a dog-eared card at me, brushing off the fluff and the rain as he did so with a grimy hand.

"What's the matter? Ain't you got one?" he said. He stared at me as though it were a crime. "Nemmind, then. Shove it in yer 'at. I always do. Go on," he urged. "Read it. Ernest Nanjizel. That's me. Now, where you goin' to kip for the night? Got a bed laid on? Ernest Nanjizel's the man to look after you if you ain't." He paused just long enough to squint up at me. " 'Smatter? Can't you read? Ain't you goin' to look at yer card?"

I was breathless by this time. I'd been too fascinated by his patter to notice the card. I started and squinted at the grubby pasteboard in my hand. By the light of the gas-lamp I read his name, "Ernest Nanjizel", then, cryptically, "Agent".

The card was snatched out of my fingers almost before I'd finished and disappeared once more into Mr Nanjizel's bowler, which was then slapped back with a thump on to his little bullet head.

"No 'at. Nowhere to put it. Ah, well. Better give it me back. Use it again. Know me now, anyway. Ernest Nanjizel. That's me. Agent." His teeth seemed as if they were trying to jump out of his mouth at his briskness. "Now, where you goin' to kip?"

"I dunno," I said. This was one of the things that hadn't occurred to me when I walked out of Dig's front door.

Off came the bowler again and out of it appeared another card. " 'Ere y'are, then," he said, reading from it. "Beds for men. Threepence a night. Suppers extra. Fee, 14 Bodmin Road. That's the place for you, young man. Everything laid on. 'Course, if you're flush we can go to a 'otel. I know just the place." Another card appeared as though by sleight-of-hand. "Mrs Carey. Apartments. 27a The Parade. Four and six the night. Dhobeying thrown in. Nice woman. Girls, too, if you want 'em." He clicked his tongue and dug me in the ribs with a bony elbow. "Just the ticket for a matelot."

" 'Ere." He squinted up at me again. "Let's go somewhere we can talk. A chap can't chew the fat in the piddling rain, can 'e? Come on, let's go an' 'ave one."

He picked up my case, felt its weight carefully, thoughtfully clucked his tongue and smiled, then hurried off along the waterfront, with me close behind.

"In 'ere." He made a sudden right-angled turn just when I was least expecting it and bolted into a courtyard like a rat up a drain. I followed him through a maze of alleyways and dark passages, just managing to keep track of him before he disappeared into an open doorway.

I found myself in a crowded bar, where the low roof shut down on me like a weight, trapping the smoke so that it hung about my head in a thick fog. The floor was sloppy with spilt liquor and more than one of the men in there appeared to be awkward with drink and throwing his weight about. A big man with a beard, who had a buxom woman in high boots tattooed on his arm, was calling for drinks for the house at the top of his voice.

"Come on, landlord," he was roaring. "Set 'em up! There's six months' wages to pay for 'em!"

Nanjizel seemed startled to see me still behind him. "Oh, 'ello," he said. "Well – er – 'ere we are." He seemed a bit upset and hurried into more of his patter! " 'Ow about a drop of the old rum to warm you up? Nelson's blood. That's the stuff for a matelot. Yo ho ho and a bottle of it, eh? Got any money? Good. Well, keep it in yer pocket, son, I'll pay. Ernest's the boy to look after you. I know this lot. They'd pinch the gold out yer teeth if you'd let 'em. 'Ere y'are, shove in 'ere and lay alongside the counter." Using the case with considerable skill he barged his way to the bar and began to thump on it.

"Come on," he yelled. "Let's 'ave some service."

I hardly heard him. I was too excited. Although I'd lived in a seaport town all my life I'd never been in a waterfront bar-room before at that time of night. All I'd seen of them were glimpses through open doorways on warm evenings. I'd seen these men around me before, though – or their doubles – and the women, too, near the docks or outside the mariners' shops or back-street pubs. When I thought about it, I even remembered seeing Nanjizel on occasions, hanging round the shipping offices. But somehow, in the glare of the lights and with an atmosphere of noisy laughter, they all seemed different – coloured men, Chinee or Englishmen, whether in dungarees or going-ashore rig.

All around me was the evidence of the sea. Ships in bottles and glass cases. Mummified sea-horses, hanging from the low ceiling with stuffed sword-fishes, pickled to a ripe teak colour with tabacco smoke. Brass-bound rum kegs, cutlasses and pictures of windjammers and ships-of-the-line in Good Hope storms or gales round the Horn. The whole shooting match. Curios from all over the world from Singapore to 'Frisco.

In a corner by the door a prostitute was shamelessly haggling over a price with an Asiatic, and a tipsy sailor was telling a long-winded yard of a storm at sea. But I saw no sordidness. Only an atmosphere of excitement that made me think of tropical scents and peacock-blue seas and waving palms such as I'd only read about but had always had vividly in my imagination.

I grinned, unable to hold back my happiness. Then I realised there was more than one shifty-eyed individual around me, and I remembered Nanjizel's warning. I placed one foot solidly on my suit-case and waited for my drink.

Nanjizel suddenly interrupted my thoughts.

"Just got to go to the necessary," he said. "Be back in a moment. Don't move or you'll lose yer place." And he melted away, almost from under my elbow. Even as I was searching for him, a jerk at the case under my foot almost threw me on my back. I bent and saw Nanjizel's ferrety face at the level of my knee, both hands on the bag. His false teeth were even and shining in an awkward grin, as symmetrical as a row of gravestones.

"Just moving yer whatsaname," he explained. "In me way, sort of. Thought I'd best put it where it was safe. Didn't know you 'ad yer foot on it." He grinned foolishly, patted the case and disappeared. Then I became aware of someone addressing me from over the counter.

In a daydream by this time, I stared round at the barman. He was huge, red-faced and with arms as massive as his belly, covered with tattooed anchors and scrolls bearing the word "Mother".

He was pushing forward two rums. " 'Smatter? Don't you want 'em now?" he said. "You was shouting loud enough a minute ago."

I indicated the door. "My pal's paying," I said. "He'll be back in a minute."

"I've 'eard that one afore, too," he said, and he was just going to waltz the drinks away when I stopped him.

"Here, half a tick." I flushed and fished in my pocket for my money...

Almost before I'd received the change Nanjizel was back, smiling and oily and friendly, his shabby coat shining in the electric light. " 'Ello," he said, staring at the counter in surprise. "Drinks 'ere already? Well, I'll be bust. An' me goin' outside just when they was on their way. Never mind" – he slapped me on the shoulder – "I'll pay next time."

Next time, though, he was deep in conversation with the man next to him and couldn't be drawn away. " 'Alf a mo'," he said over his shoulder. "Won't be a tick." In the end, I paid again.

By the time I'd finished the second rum my head was beginning to whirl, and the noise and the bad ventilation and the overheated atmosphere of the smoky room didn't help to steady it. Dimly, I became conscious of Nanjizel's voice by my ear.

"Don't forget," he was saying. "Whenever you're ashore in this port, just ask for Ernest Nanjizel. It's not a 'ard name to remember. I'm the man to get you out of yer difficulties. Everybody knows Ernest Nanjizel. Ask a copper. Ask the mayor. Ask the parson. They'll all tell you the same. Go to Ernest Nanjizel."

"Yes, Mr Nanjizel," I said. I was worried by this time by the way his face had started to grow blurred in patches and swing up and down. "I will. I'll remember."

"And look after yerself," he impressed on me. "Don't waste yer cash when you go ashore. Don't get drunk. Drink and the Devil had done for the rest, as the sayin' goes. Don't spend yer wages on idle things. Always think of my advice. Ask for me any time you're in the town. Only too pleased to 'elp. And keep away from the girls. They don't do it for love, y'know," he urged. "They only want yer ackers. And, by God, they're sharp, too. If you want a nice young lady, see me. I'll put you right. Feather in 'er 'at and plush drawers."

"Righto, Mr Nanjizel." I said, focusing my eyes with difficulty by now.

"Women," he said. He wagged his head and clucked his tongue disgustedly. "Keep off of 'em. No good. Bad lots. Tarts," he ended, "they 'ave you so you don't know whether you're comin' or goin', I know. I been married four times." He was getting a bit noisy himself by this time, too.

Another rum was added to the first two, together with two more for a couple of shifty-looking chaps who were introduced as Nanjizel's pals. Nanjizel drew closer again.

" 'Course," he said, "I can always put you on to a place or two if you're interested. 'Ere." He fished in his bowler hat and fetched out his cards again before replacing it over his wispy hair.

He flipped through the pasteboards like a whist player, and selected one or two. " 'Ere's a nice one," he said. " 'Mademoiselle Dupont. Guide to Marseilles. Pleasant Company. Intimacy.' See that?" he said. " 'Intimacy.' That's the stuff, eh?"

He dug me in the ribs with a bony elbow again and cackled. It was a low, lecherous sort of chuckle. I stared at him, mystified and bewildered. I must have been young then.

" 'Ere's another," he went on and passed the grubby card over to me.

"Visit the Café Matsala," I read. "For Soft Lights. Liqueurs and Wines. Lovely Girls."

" 'Amburg, that one," he said. "All right. I know. Been there. Ernest's the boy for fun."

Almost before I'd read the dancing words he'd whipped the card from my fingers and, stuffing it back into his hat, he began to offer me the addresses of half the bawdy-houses from Gibraltar to Suez.

"They all know Ernest Nanjizel," he said. "All of 'em. I been around. I know the ins and outs. I know all that goes on. Everything that opens and shuts. Let's 'ave another drink." He thumped the bar. "Your turn to pay, I think."

I tried to object but the words wouldn't come. My tongue seemed stiff and clumsy and Nanjizel interrupted me. "I paid for the last one," he said severely, as if I were trying to pull a fast one. "Don't you remember?"

I could have sworn he hadn't, but I was too dizzy by this time to know what was happening. I fished in my pocket for my money. Nanjizel seemed to scoop his teeth to a place of safety in his cheek with his tongue and stared at me anxiously as I fumbled.

"What's up?" he said. "Lost something?"

My mouth had dropped open and I was trying to make my fuddled brain function as I was suddenly shocked into a dreadful realisation.

" 'Smatter? No money?"

"Only a bob."

It was Nanjizel's turn to be shocked. "Looked such a smart, well-rigged young man, you did, too," he said bitterly. "Thought you was out for a good time. Thought you wanted some fun. A bob! Can't have much fun on a bob." He appeared to be thinking hard, then he picked up my case. "Come on," he said sourly. "Got to get you somewhere to kip afore you spend all your bloody money. Got to get you all sorted out and parcelled up." He paused for a moment, brought out his cards from his hat and consulted one before returning them.

" 'Ere y'are. Apartments for men. Just about do you. Cheap. Clean. You can 'ave the bed next to mine. Come on. We'll 'ave a tripe supper, then 'ome. Just about do it on a bob."

He pushed me through the door into the darkness of the alley.

"There y'are," he said. "Straight on, then 'ard-a-starboard."

Fuddled with drink and dizzy in the sharp night air, I groped my way towards the nearest gas-lamp to wait for him. For a minute or two I leaned there, trying to make my head stop its whirling.

Then I began to panic as I realised I'd forgotten my bag, and I started off up the dark alley again. Blundering my way into the bar once more, dazzled by the light, I stared round widely for Nanjizel.

I hurried to the counter and searched there for the bag, groping around between the customers on the sawdusted floor.

" 'Ere, 'Oo're you shovin'?" someone demanded.

A woman's voice joined in, way up above me, harsh and strident. "My God, the little pimp! Clip 'is ear'ole. 'E's after my legs!"

A hand on my collar jerked me upright and I stared into the angry face of the bearded sailor and the hard eyes of a woman who looked like a prostitute.

"What the hell are you fiddling at down there?" I was asked.

"I've lost my bag," I said. I was panting and a bit desperate. "It had all my clothes in it. All my belongings."

"That's right," the woman said, her tones more friendly. "I saw him come in with it, now I think on. What was it like, sonny?"

"It was a brown one," I explained. "With my name on it. Jess Ferigo."

"Blimey, yes, I remember. Yer pal took it."

"My pal?"

"The little bloke you come in with. 'Im with the rat face and the teeth like off a corpse."

I stared round wildly. "Where is he? Where did he go?"

The man waved a glass of whisky at a door on the other side of the bar. " 'E went through there. A bit sharp 'e was, too. Didn't waste no time."

I hardly looked at him. "Thanks," I said and darted through the door he indicated.

I found myself in the main street where the gas-lamps glimmered wetly in the mist. A prowling cat stared at me from an alley-end. But that was all.

eight

The rain hadn't slackened much as I made my way round all the addresses I could remember from the cards in Nanjizel's hat-band in the hope of finding him. By that time I was in a panic-stricken haste that made me heedless of my saturated clothes. But I could have saved my breath. I hadn't a hope in hell of finding him. At most of the addresses they'd never even heard of him. In fact, by the look of them they didn't run to visiting-cards at all.

At one of them, a dingy two-up-and-two-down, the door was opened by a slatternly woman with a cigarette drooping between her lips and I stared at her for half a minute before I realised she wore nothing under the dowdy kimono that covered her.

"All right, son," she said good-naturedly. " 'Ave a good look, then tell us what you've come for."

When I mentioned Nanjizel, though, her hair nearly stood on end with fury. "Just let me get 'old of that little swine, she said, "an' I'll screw 'is neck round. The last beggar 'e brought 'ere tried to break the joint up."

I trudged from one dreary reach-me-down to another. Almost without exception, they lolled over the narrow streets as though they were tired, with brown-papered windows and no lights beyond the dirty glimmer that showed the entrance. Full of weary old men they were, the human debris of the dockside. The sharks and the old mariners whose cash had gone on drink. The street touts and the wharfside lags. The match vendors and the bootlace hawkers. The newspaper sellers and every variation of seaport hotchpotch. Men without hope for the most part. Old men and men with a load of care on their shoulders, but none of them the shuffling little rat in the bowler hat I was after.

I stumbled back to the docks, dog-tired with the tramp round the town, still not quite sober after the rum, angry with myself and everybody else…

The fury I felt against Nanjizel had died away by the time I reached the waterfront again. Inside me now there was only a sullen, impersonal resentment. I was kicking myself for a fool. I'd lived within sight of the docks all my life, and I'd seen sailors in every stage of drunkenness relieved of their money by every dodge and fiddle there was under the sun. And yet I'd been caught by a shifty little rogue like Nanjizel, whom I ought to have spotted for what he was as soon as I saw him.

I stopped, dog-weary, and leaned on a row of iron railings beside the dead, heavy-looking water that was lit fitfully by the reflection of the riding lights of shipping. Something inside me was nagging at me like a physical pain, something that urged me to get away over the horizon that stretched, rolling and mysterious, beyond the curtain of darkness. Everything about me strengthened it into a hard knot of determination – the bowed shop windows, with their uneven panes, full of oilskins, dungarees, knives, belts, chests, patent logs and binnacle lamps. *The Africa Pilot* and *The Manual of Seamanship*. Everything the mariner needed. The cobbled streets and the few hurrying figures that had the smell of the sea about them. The brine that coated everything when the wind blew and whipped up the water to a fine spray. Even the floating patch of garbage where half-a-hundred gulls would wheel and sweep in the morning, picking up refuse in their beaks and soaring away to circle the neighbouring vessels before swooping to dive for more.

Out on the river a ship's siren sounded. It was heavy and lonely, mourning on the night air that struck coldly through my clothes. I turned up my collar, suddenly conscious of weariness, and, stuffing my hands into my pockets, moved away along the docks. I'd only the prospect of a hard bed in a park shelter before me.

As I turned a corner towards the main road my feet caught the sprawling figure of a man. He lay face down on the cobbled pavement, one arm half round a bollard. At first I thought he was dead, attacked for his pay by one of Nanjizel's pals, then I realised he was moving, kicking feebly to regain his feet.

I knelt down beside him and turned him over, searching for an injury. But instead I received a blast of stale liquor in my face that turned my stomach over. He was drunk, not dead. Stinking. Canned as they come. Ripe as an old kipper.

"Drowning," he said thickly. "Drowning in a bloody puddle. Couldn't lift a hand to save m'self."

Then, by the light of a neighbouring gas-lamp that roared as the breeze caught it, I became aware of a sea-chest on its side nearby, and a deep-sea kit-bag lolling as drunkenly as its owner in another puddle. Horatio Boxer was the name painted across it in black, the words written in a bold, strong hand, starkly on its side. Horatio Boxer.

I laughed – a bit light-headedly.

"Well, fancy meeting you," I said. "Fancy bumping into you tonight."

I suddenly felt I was among friends and the docks seemed less oppressive. Yorky wasn't far away, I knew.

I helped Old Boxer to a sitting position in the puddle. It wasn't easy. His legs and arms seemed almost boneless.

"Sea tomorrow," he said, his voice heavy, and I struggled to hold him upright as he sagged again. "Little celebration. Gets me legs." He choked suddenly, fished in his mouth and brought out a set of false teeth which he stuffed into his pocket. "That's better," he said, and he was trying to concentrate sufficiently to see me. In spite of the physical effort he put into it, though, he could obviously see only a few blurred lights and someone attempting to get him on his feet.

He heaved himself up, trying to help, but his legs and arms refused to work properly. He spat out grit and rain-water from his mouth and tried again to see what was going on. But I could tell from his eyes that his vision was out of balance.

He managed at last to get to his feet. I was trying to button his coat against the rain.

"Avast there!" His angry mind seemed to tell him he was accepting charity in the form of help and he shoved me away fretfully. "I can do that. I've got two hands, haven't I?" he said sarcastically. He spread them in front of him. "A right and a left. Each with four fingers and a thumb. See?"

He fumbled hopelessly with the buttons, then, giving up in disgust, he staggered to a doorway where he sat down on the wet stone steps. They must have struck cold through the seat of his trousers for he tried to heave himself up again, then he sketched a shrug and gave up. His hat over one eye, he stared at me owlishly.

"S'maritan," he mumbled, his tongue getting round the word with difficulty. "Good S'maritan."

"Been having a bit of a drink?" I asked brightly. I was collecting the few odds and ends that lay scattered about – a brown paper package of soap bars, a packet of needles, a pencil and some cheap notepaper, a tin mug.

Old Boxer squinted as he struggled to take in the meaning of the words. "Only one," he said. "Lasted all week."

"Where're you goin'?" I asked.

"*Archibald Harvey.*" His tongue stumbled a bit over the name. "Starvation bastard she is, too."

"Those your bags?" I queried, indicating the luggage in the roadway.

Old Boxer gaped dully round him. He was focusing his eyes now but with a lot of trouble. He nodded and moaned softly to himself. "My God!" he said. "My God!"

He dragged himself to his feet with the help of the bent iron railings on the steps and stood swaying, huge in the gas-light.

"Boxer's the name," he announced suddenly, and it was clear he hadn't recognised me. "Horatio Bloody Boxer."

For the first time in three years I was able to study him closely as he swayed there. He was gaunt, with his bedraggled appearance and rain-soaked muddy suit, and as he took three hurried steps backwards to keep his balance the light caught his face and I saw the years had worked hard on him. He'd been good-looking in a weak sort of way that had nothing to. do with his heavy features, but now he was an old man with a hollow, creased neck. And I knew there couldn't be much difference between his age and Dig's.

Old Boxer glowered as he realised I was watching.

" 'Smatter?" he asked suddenly. "Never seen a man drunk before?"

I noticed that shabby grandeur of his again as he spoke. I'd noticed it once before, the day we were all up in front of the beaks. It seemed pathetic, but it was magnificent, and there was no trace of shame.

"You'll see me drunk again," he said. "On the *Archibald Harvey*. Bottle Boxer, the Boozer's Gloom, they call me."

We stared at each other in the lamplight. I didn't know what to do next. Then Old Boxer swung out an arm in a gesture that almost put him on his back again.

"My bags," he said grandly. "Get me aboard. Give you a bob."

I grinned. "Right you are," I said.

I lifted the sea-chest by its handle and stuffed the kit-bag under my arm. "Come on," I said. "Let's have you."

"My God!" Old Boxer growled. He lifted his face to the sky and the rain. "A deck-boy who sounds his aitches! Praise be to God, a deck-boy without a snotty nose!"

I was just going to protest when he went on:

"Go home, young man," he said. "Go home to your mother."

I shook his arm, annoyed that he hadn't recognised me. "Don't you know me?" I asked. "Don't you know who I am?"

He stared owlishly at me, then shook his head so violently that his hat fell off. I put it back again.

"No," he mumbled. "Never seen you before."

"Go on," I smiled. "Of course you have."

"You accusing me of being a liar?" He was indignant immediately. "Never, I said. Not once."

I decided to let the matter drop since he was obviously drunk and he went on:

"Don't go to sea, my boy," he said grandly. "Never go to sea."

He held out a hand to indicate the shipping nearby.

"Ten days on one of those hookers," he said, "and you'll have learned all the pornographic wit that's ever been scraped up out of all the sewers in every corner of the world. Set a course home to your mother before it's too late."

As he finished he tottered forward unsteadily. I caught him by the arm and began to lead him in rolling, generous curves along the cobbled wharf. The bobby at the dock gate stared at us through the rain that ran down the windows of his shelter but didn't attempt to stop us.

Following Old Boxer's vague gestures and vaguer directions, I helped him along the wharfside. It was dark in the shadow of the warehouses, and we stumbled between the railway lines and under the towering black bows of freighters that were thrown into silhouette by the lights above their decks. Here and there a steam winch was clattering noisily as stores were hauled aboard and a few shabby dock workers huddled in doorways out of the rain near the giant cranes that reared like gibbets above us. A corrugated-iron sheet high on the side of one of the warehouses clanged and rattled as it swung in the wind that whipped the rain away.

Once we fell as Old Boxer lost control of his feet and they got between mine. We sprawled on the puddled cobbles and the kit and the parcels went rolling away into the shadows.

"Pardon me crossing your bows," he said gravely as I hauled him to his feet. "Me steering's shot to hell."

I was getting tired and angry by this time. At first it had been a joke, but now it had ceased to be funny. I hurriedly brushed the mud from my clothes and, hoisting Old Boxer's kit into position again, we set off once more.

I was more than glad when I found myself alongside an ugly black ship with a single, gaunt smoke-stack. The deck lights that glistened in reflection on her salty sides made the wet rigging a shining spider-web of ropes, and threw the cobbles of the wharf into sharp relief. High on her bows I could see the name, *Archibald Harvey,* in shadowy lettering.

"Come on," I said to Old Boxer, who had lapsed into a coma. "Nearly there now."

Together we stumbled up the gangway, Old Boxer's feet bumping behind us, and half fell on to the narrow deck that was crowded with tangled mooring-ropes and heaped tarpaulins. Aft, coal was roaring down a chute into the bunkers and a heavy cloud of dust was settling on the wet decks. The noise was deafening.

Forrard, in the shelter of the forecastle, were crates of hungry chickens and pigs, and they were all setting up a din of their own in rivalry.

The watchman, who was smoking at the head of the gangway, glanced once at us, but he said nothing.

"Forrard," Old Boxer mumbled. "Forrard, lad. Full speed ahead and damn the torpedoes."

We found the forecastle with difficulty and stumbled up the alleyway. The deck smell of tar and oil grew stronger here, and finally I found myself in a cramped space in the eyes of the ship, hard beneath the forecastle head, in a tiny triangular cabin that smelled of paint and grease and hot oil.

Yorky was there, wearing a stiff collar and a blue suit with a gold watchchain big enough to hold a prize bull. He got up from a scrubbed bench where he'd been sitting holding his head and disinterestedly thumbing through a copy of *True Love Stories*.

"Old 'Orace, is it?" he queried dully, and he, too, failed to recognise me. "Shove 'im in 'ere, mate."

"My name's not 'Orace," Old Boxer mumbled. "Confound you, Yorky, give me my proper tag."

"Ain't no time to call you 'Oratio," Yorky said, rising and stumbling over the concertina that was between his feet. "Ain't got all day. My Uncle Bill was called Osbaldestone, but nobody ever called 'im owt but Bill to 'is dying day. 'Orace should be good enough for you."

"Ach, shut your rattle!" Old Boxer snapped. "Yap yap yap! You're a windy old flea-bag!"

"Am I, 'Orace?" Yorky said wearily. "All right. Now. come on, let's 'ave you nicely tucked up and in bed, see."

"Thank you, Yorky." Old Boxer was meek all of a sudden. "Always look after Old Horace, don't you?"

"You're welcome, I'm sure," Yorky pointed out. "Now, come on, get your 'ead down. You'll be as right as rain after a bit of a kip and yer bowels moved in the mornin'." He nodded to me as he shoved Old Boxer's legs into the bunk with a deference that belonged properly to a manservant. Then he tucked a blanket round the old man's sprawling figure and sat down and held his head again.

Then he looked up sharply. His dulled eyes were staring, "I'll be jiggered!" he said. "Rat me if it ain't young Jess!"

He grinned at me, then winced as it appeared to make his head throb. "Fancy seein' you," he said. "Fancy you findin' Old 'Orace."

He shook his head dejectedly.

"I told 'im not to go ashore tonight, kid," he went on. " ' 'Orace,' I said. 'You'll get soused again. You know you bleeden will. You allus do.' Didn't know where to put 'isself. Didn't know what to say. But 'e went all the same." He let his words trail away dismally and began to scratch himself. "Don't know why I bother with 'im," he ended.

Neither did I. Neither did anyone else. People just did bother with him, even the police. He had the manner that made people take trouble on his behalf.

Yorky reached under his blankets and produced a bottle of whisky. He took a swig and held it out to me. " 'Ave a mouthful," he suggested.

He indicated Old Boxer. "Scuttles 'isself with booze every time 'e goes ashore," he said. "Fair creases me, 'aulin' 'im about when 'e comes back. Told 'im so often, I 'ave. ' 'Orace,' I've said, 'you're a dirty old drunkard.' "

He took another swig from the bottle. "You ain't comin' to sea with us, are you, lad?" he asked, and he looked anxiously at me.

I shook my head. "No," I said, "but I wouldn't mind."

Yorky studied me silently. " 'Ave a gasper," he suggested.

He pushed a packet of cigarettes along the bench towards me. Then he produced a tin of tobacco and began to roll one for himself. He stared at the smoke that curled upwards as he drew the first puffs from it. " 'Ard life," he said. "Live in 'ere; y'know. 'Ell of a place in 'eavy weather. Like a bloomin' oven in the tropics."

"I'd manage, I suppose," I said eagerly. I stared round at the forecastle. It was tawdry despite the white paint. There were comfortless iron bunks covered with sacking mattresses, and piles of kit lay about, dumped down by its owners before their last jaunt ashore.

"Meself, kid," Yorky said, "my tastes run to a chip-shop or a small-'olding and a few chickens when I gets the cash saved up, but there's no accounting for tastes."

"I never knew *you* wanted to leave the sea," I said. I was surprised, knowing Yorky's habits.

"Always did," he said. "Only time I managed it, though, was when I worked ashore with 'Orace, Allus do me wages in the first two nights ashore."

"What on?"

"Same as 'im." Yorky indicated Old Boxer, who was snoring now. "Same as all sailors. Booze and women."

He pulled on his cigarette and stared at the deck between his feet for a while, then he spat into a box in the middle of the forecastle.

"It's easy to get to sea, Jess, me old flower," he said. "Make no mistake. But it's flamin' 'ard to get shot of it. I've tried. Fancied a job shoving a broom round the gutter once. But what did they tell me when I went to sign on at the Labour Exchange? 'Says "seaman" 'ere on yer card, mate,' the bloke said – snotty as yer please. 'Seamen's wanted down the docks – bad – and we ain't no openings in the road-sweepin' profession just now. Orf yer go.' I didn't – not then – but a fortnit on the dole changed me mind. Besides, it gets 'old of you. Make no mistake about it." He spat again. "Perhaps it's as well in the long run. Once you've been a sailor you never settle ashore. There ain't a town big enough to 'old you."

He grinned suddenly, cheerful again. "You can't change it, mate. You never will. Just like you'll never stop the tide comin' in and going out and never stop the sun risin' and the moon shinin'. When you think you've managed to get away from it for a bit you find yourself watchin' a old 'at floating in the river, and you start calculatin' which way the tide's goin', and afore you know where you are you're off after it again.

"Tell you the truth, lad, I was glad to get away from that ruddy boat-yard. If I'd stayed much longer I'd 'ave looked like a flippin' oilcan. I was that miserable for a ship. I never realised it till I got on one again. Since then," he said cheerfully, and he'd obviously forgotten his reference to a chip-shop and chickens, "I ain't never fancied a shore job."

He stared at the glowing end of his cigarette for a while, then he suddenly turned his head and looked at me. His black eyes were bright and shrewd beneath his shaggy brows and he seemed to know exactly what I was thinking.

"Well?" he said. "Still want to go to sea, kid?"

I paused and drew a deep breath. Then I grinned and answered without hesitating.

"Yes," I said, "I do."

"And yer dad?"

"It's nothing to do with him."

Yorky tossed his cigarette-end into the box on the floor and rose to his feet. "Come on, then. What are we mucking about at? Let's 'ave you along to the skipper's cabin and get you signed on. We need a deck-boy. You're a bit 'efty for cleanin' closets since you growed up, but we ain't choosey, and you might as well ship to sea among pals if you're goin at all."

The following morning when the *Archibald Harvey* headed for the open sea, chivvied port and starboard by tugs, I was on the foredeck in a pair of dungarees borrowed from Yorky.

Around me, as the town fell astern, was the banging of the winches and the rattle and whistle of blocks as the gangway was hauled inboard. As a newcomer I was told off to lend a hand with the stowing of the mooring-ropes, a humping, back-breaking, boring job that made my arms ache with the unaccustomed labour.

Yorky was on the forecastle head in singlet and dungaree trousers, more his old recognisable self with his blue suit stowed safely away for the rest of the voyage. Old Boxer *was* with him, silent and morose. His face was grey and gaunt and had a ravaged look about it. His expression was pinched and haggard, and he looked as though he'd a headache and a sour stomach. His eyes were glazed and taut lines were etched across his cheeks.

The rain had stopped and the skies had cleared. The day was bright but with a cold wind whipping the top of the bow wave to a feathery spray. The ship began to feel the first of the open sea as she butted her nose past the white pencil of St Andrew Light that gleamed in the sun on the bluff of headland, then she began to dig her nose into the waves. The water coming over the bows was blown by the salty gust into glittering fans of rainbow hues. I made a hurried grab at a stanchion when the decks canted unexpectedly, and my ears were filled with creaks and groans as the old ship began to pitch. Like the cries of a living creature they were.

Above and around the mastheads were the gulls, shining in the morning sunlight, wheeling shapes against the cold blue of the sky. Their wailing cries cut sharply into my brain like music I'd been hearing all my life, a symphony made up of birds' calls and the wind's song in the rigging, the rush of water and the sighs from the framework of the ship. A symphony that had the steady thump of engines amidships as its bass accompaniment.

Gradually the town grew smaller, but still clear and bold and white in the sunshine. I turned my face towards the open sea that stretched rolling and mysterious from where I stood to the very limits of the world.

I drew a great breath full of salt air and cleanness, and felt suddenly free of the sordidness of Atlantic Street and the drab squalor of the docks. Behind me was the meanness of people like Nanjizel and the narrow life of the printing works. I felt a queer tug at my heart for a second as I thought of Minnie, soft and warm and seductive, Minnie with the veiled eyes and the suggestion of all sorts of promises. Then I swallowed sharply as I remembered the words that had come to me as I stood outside the Steam Packet. "A kiss to make him wet his britches." A kid going away.

Well, I'd finished with that life now. I'd thrown them all off, Dig and Ma and Minnie and Pat. I was heading for a new life, a harder life, standing on my own two feet, dependent on no one and responsible to no one.

I looked round at Yorky and Old Boxer drawing grateful puffs at their cigarettes in a pause in their work. They seemed cleaner, stronger, more wholesome men as the staleness of their port debauch was blown away by the wind. Their dulled eyes had grown brighter, and the sourness had gone from them, as the keen breeze cut into them, blowing away the cobwebs of their shore leave.

Old Boxer spoke suddenly to Yorky as they leaned on the bow-rail and stared ahead at the grey, heaving sea. "Ha!" he said. "We've shaken off the scent of the sewers and the stale perfume of harlots again..."

"I been with no 'arlots, 'Orace," Yorky commented. "You speak for yourself."

"...the odour of public lavatories and the dock pubs' stink, and the touch of the filthy shysters who'd have a sailor-man's soul. Yorky, we're men again."

I grinned at Yorky's puzzled frown. He was an unsubtle soul, and Old Boxer's high-flung sentiments were wasted on him.

"Ain't ever been anything else," he said.

Old Boxer turned away cheerfully then and, turning, caught sight of me down on the foredeck. He stared for a moment, his eyes peering, then he brushed a hand across his face and stared again.

I grinned at him.

He swore suddenly and came bounding down the iron ladder in two or three strides. He stopped in front of me, huge and imperious. his eyes furious in the great dark hollows that encircled them.

"What the devil are you doing here?" he demanded.

I was startled by the fury in his words.

"Working for me living," I said. "Same as you."

Old Boxer turned to Yorky, who'd come hustling after him. "Yorky, get hold of the pilot and tell him there's a passenger to go ashore with him."

"Passenger my backside," Yorky said. " 'E's the deck-boy."

Old Boxer whirled back to stare at me again. I was still startled by the power of his anger.

"Get back to your mother!" he snapped. "This is no life for you."

"Don't be daft," I said. "I'm going to sea. I *want* to go to sea."

"Oh, gi'e o'er, 'Orace," Yorky said angrily, pulling at his arm. "What's bitin' yer? Can't the lad go to sea if 'e wants, to, without a song and dance from you? 'Sides, *you* brought 'im aboard."

Old Boxer stared at me for a moment longer, then he went to the ship's side and threw away his cigarette.

"Sure," he said, laughing as though it hurt him. "That's all right. What am I talking about?" He squinted round at me, his face heavy and sardonic, then his features, which had been distorted with anger, were softened by a smile. It was a smile that explained Yorky's devotion to him and made me realise why I'd always liked him in spite of his drunkenness and his weakness and his insults. A smile of sheer charm it was.

"Come on, then, lad," he said gently. "We'll make you into a real sailor – if you've got guts enough. And, by God, I suspect you have."

BOOK TWO

one

The tumbled white serpent that was the *Archibald Harvey's* wake, that long, seething trail of phosphorescence through the dark nights, made me more of a man with every tumbling wave it covered, with every turn of the screws that caused it.

That first week aboard ship was a nightmare of scraping and chipping. The tap-tap of hammers and the screech of steel on steel seared into my brain until it became as much a part of it as the rustle of cockroaches in the forecastle and the glory-hole and the thump of engines amidships. My hands were blistered within twenty-four hours, raw with weals that sent the blood running on to my wrists and made me wince with pain every time I moved them. I painted until my hair was plastered with it, and did every stinking, filthy job there was on the ship, to say nothing of running errands for everyone who chose to ask me.

Bullying and jeers, foul language that made my ears stick out like chapel hat-pegs, and fouler reminiscences that turned my stomach made me grow up overnight. The forecastle was a dripping, heaving, groaning hell-hole when the old ship was in heavy weather, a steaming dive where the water dripped off the bulkheads as I lay shivering on my narrow bunk and watched the newly greased oilskins and dirty clothing swinging by my side. Backwards and forward, backwards and forwards they went, in jerky monotonous arcs to the pitch of the ship. It became an oven in the tropics so that we lay gasping for air in our hammocks on the deck, and the moisture burst through our bodies in beads of sweat as fast as we put it in as tea, or ran down our legs into our boots whenever we went below for a gasper. And an ice-box in winter it was, so that my clothes were never dry, and I prayed beneath my two miserable blankets for warmth and swore blind I'd never go to sea again.

But one forecastle followed another over the years as the only home I knew, beyond the lodging-houses and sailors' hostels we used whenever we were in port. Ship after ship we tried, good and bad, according to how we'd spent our money ashore and how desperate we were to earn more. Banana boats there were, tankers out to Abadan and Curaçao, molasses ships or timber freighters. Grubby old tramps foul with the stink of guano or stuffed full of coal that crept with a sickening insidiousness into the forecastle and the mess deck and made your blankets black and left a dirty ring under your eyes.

We were caught by touts who signed us on for trips in weekly boats where the skippers wore bowler hats and the rest of the crew consisted of a boy and a dog and when we were flush enough to pick and choose we tried the fashionable liners that touched at New York and Sydney, and bobbed our heads and said "Yes, sir," and "Certainly not, sir," every time some pompous ass out of the first-class bar started throwing his weight about concerning the ships he'd sailed in.

I couldn't hope to recall them all now. Only a few. The *Ekaloon* for instance, that took a hammering when Jerry caught the *Jervis Bay* convoy. The *Mill Hill*. She was a beauty. Sailed like a lady, she did, for all that she was only a freighter. Sweet as a bird she went. The *Singaree*. She twisted a warp in her on the Goodwins before they could pull her off. The *Abraham Landor*, whose skipper they broke for drunkenness. And dozens of others, with nothing to recommend 'em or condemn 'em, ships that just took you

there and brought you back without an incident to remind
you of them.

I couldn't even remember the storms they carried me
through now. I know I sampled them all. Typhoons in the
Pacific that put the fear of God into you; Western Ocean
gales where the waves came at you big as houses, grey and
forbidding and ugly; and that particularly dirty kind of
weather peculiar to the coast of England, the stuff that butts
up the Channel and gets you cold and wretched and wet and
makes you wish to God you'd never seen the sea.

I had it all. And not only the weather, but all the fights and
all the fun that go with seafaring. It took four of us once –
on the *Singaree,* I think it was – to pull the Fourth Mate off
the Chief Cook, after a fight on deck. They'd been at each
other throughout the trip over the grub, and it came to a
head at last after they'd been ashore in Port Said. And there
we were, the First Mate and the Donkeyman and Old Boxer
and me, dragging them apart. A fat lot of good it did, too.
The Chief Cook tried a carving-knife on the Fourth the
following day and got a bang on the swede from a spanner
as long as your arm for his trouble.

We touched at Penang, where the lighted doorways along
the waterfront were noisy with the babble of voices and the
grind of loudspeakers, and the heavy air was blue with
smoke. We called at Saldanha with its few houses
tumbledown with dry-rot and its glaring white sand that hit
you between the eyes like a hammer-blow when you came
out into it from the bars; at Port Suez on our way into the
oven-hot Red Sea, and Panama, a steaming jumping-off spot
for half the riff-raff of the world; at Rio, and Havana, and
New Orleans, and San Domingo – oh, everywhere you can
think of, everywhere you can get a ship in without going
aground.

There were South Sea Islands, too, I remember, where
Polynesian women came aboard and prostituted themselves

with the crew without turning a hair, as unconcerned about it all as they were about the peacock-blue skies above them and the lazy gulls and the clear water that showed the sand and the coral fathoms down below.

But all that came later. Long before the *Archibald Harvey* turned her bows for home, her mastheads scrawling circles across the sky as they rolled and swayed to her pitching, I was a man. I went aboard her a lean youngster with no more luggage than I could stuff into my pocket, worried stiff because I hadn't a bean, but I grew broad and sturdy, with the tan of the sun on me, and my face burned nut-colour with the nip of salt winds.

Placid seas that reflected the sun's glare and howling south-easters off the Cape of Good Hope that drove the spray parallel with the tormented wave-tops left their marks round my eyes and at the corners of my mouth, the stamp and trademark of any sailor. It's something they all have, even the longshoremen who poke about up rivers with small craft. You can spot it a mile away.

I grew in knowledge as well as in strength and size. Under the coaching of Old Boxer and Yorky, I became self-reliant and reliable, able to do anything that was asked me, from maintenance to stowage and back again, until eventually *I* was the one who went as bosun and had to push Old Boxer around.

Not that it was *all* plain sailing. Seafaring came easily to me, but there were days at first when, between them, they made me want to weep with weariness as they made me sew and splice and reeve until my fingers ached.

Old Boxer unearthed navigation books and *Africa Pilots* that hadn't seen the light of day for years and had the green of mildew on them. Up from the bottom of his sea-chest they came, ripe with that damp smell of old books, for him to hammer the principles of navigation and maritime law into my head until it whirled. He taught me morse and the stars and how to read a sextant, how to shoot the sun and lay a course. He taught me stowage and flags and, when the rest of the crew were yarning on the forecastle in the evening sun, haggling about beer and women and ships, he'd have me sweating below deck, struggling with the curve of the earth's surface. While I was content to be part of the deck crew, he was chasing me inevitably in the direction of the bridge and the officers' saloon.

"God damn it!" he stormed when I protested. "You're not going to end your days like me, rotting in the forecastle. You're not going to sweat your time out chipping rust and hauling ropes, and going ashore after the booze and the women. You've chosen to go to sea but, by God, I'll see you go to sea like a gentleman!"

Yorky was behind him in everything he bullied me into, and that odd friendship that had always existed between us grew. It withstood all the pornographic comments of the forecastle wits, a curious link that bound us together: me, a raw youngster; the fat, white little Yorkshireman with his blasphemous affection; and the corpulent, grey-haired, prematurely old man whose words varied with the days from bitterness and pent-up anger to an odd tenderness that was sometimes even embarrassing. Between us there was an unspoken understanding, despite Old Boxer's sarcastic tongue and the chip on his shoulder that made him difficult to get along with.

He was a curious enigma. Education was manifest in every word he spoke. At sea, he was as different as chalk from cheese from the man we knew ashore, and as the days progressed on that first voyage and the *Archibald Harvey* put the long miles between us and England, all the raw bitterness dropped away from him, all that melancholy sense of wreckage that clung to his huge frame. Into his drawn features came a spark of life and interest as he taught me navigation and forced out of me an unwilling promise to sit for a mate's ticket. His great shoulders straightened, and he seemed to draw in his sagging belly and become a giant of a man, sure-fingered and confident, capable and reliable.

But, as port followed port, and the North Star gave place to the Southern Cross, I watched him drink himself stupid in God-forsaken dives where no self-respecting sailor went. Whether it was Marseilles or New York, Cape Town or San Francisco, whether it was some huddle of clay dwellings with biscuit-tin roofs or a group of charcoal-smelling wattle huts under a fringe of palms, Old Boxer always came back aboard drunk. As drunk as he could possibly get, with whatever money he could lay his hands on. The cheaper the stuff the better, it seemed. Arak in Abadan. Palm wine in Freetown, Vaauwjaapie at the Cape. If he couldn't get ashore he bribed bumboatmen or the crew of a water-boat to bring the booze to the ship's side or got a dock worker to smuggle it aboard. Every time he touched civilisation he seemed to set out methodically to soak up all the sense in him with rum.

I dragged him out of Port Said cafés where half-naked Arab girls danced to a barbaric tune with clicking anklets of jingling coins. Out of smoky waterfront dives in Singapore where wailing wind instruments and gongs made the music for Balinese dancers. From Cape Town shebeens and from Honolulu huts. From reach-me-down holes-in-the-wall in Freetown where the vultures waited like rusty old spinsters on the corrugated-iron roof-tops outside in the glaring sun, and the women were as black as the ace of spades.

I dragged him back to the ship weeping with drunkenness, the two of us staggering and stumbling in and out of the railway lines all the way along the docks. I fished him out of the harbour in Freetown when he fell out of the launch that had ferried us out to the old *Cherrapunji* that was lying up the Bunce, and he was so canned he'd have drowned, surrounded by his floating parcels and hat and a pumpkin he'd picked up from somewhere.

I fought off a naked black harlot in Valparaiso where he was trying to booze some strength back into him after a murderous trip round the Horn where the sea had whipped two men off the deck of the *Ballymena* clean as a whistle. She'd threatened to carve his heart out, and I had to tap her over the noggin to get him away. But all the same I spent the night with him in the calaboose there, among the lice and the cockroaches, among the beachcombers and bums and good-for-nothings, and the shining buck niggers who sprawled on the floor, their clothes under their heads for pillows. I helped him next morning out into the sunshine, trembling and ashamed of himself, his face grey and hollow in the glare.

The years and his furious, bitter mind inevitably began to leave their mark on him. As one trip followed another, and ship took the place of ship, he grew more careless of his appearance and his moods grew more violent – whether it was soured bad temper and vicious sarcasm, or the overwhelming tenderness for me that made it so difficult to leave him to stew in his own juice when he was drunk. London or New York, he always ran out of cash long before his leave was over and had to pawn something or borrow to pay for his digs. Or at the very worst leave his kit behind as security for a debt he never paid.

It was an accepted fact in the forecastle that he had a secret, but whatever it was he kept it securely locked away. It never saw the light of day and brought down a curtain of silence in front of me or Yorky whenever we unwittingly nudged some unhappy ache. It was something that shut us both out and cut off laughter like a knife.

"Closer'n a duck's be'ind, old 'Orace, when 'e's like that," Yorky complained. "Gives me the creeps, it does. My old Ma's like that sometimes. Mopes round the 'ouse like she's 'ad 'er 'ead fast in the mangle, and everybody wonderin' 'oo's to blame."

Whatever it was, it was like an inflamed wound and drove Old Boxer back inside himself, inside a hard shell we couldn't penetrate, and made him cold and angry and bitter. It drove him, abject and inhuman, into all the evil corners throughout the Levant and the Far East; even, it was said, to opium.

There were papers in his chest and belongings in his ditty-box that no one ever saw. Papers we argued about and puzzled over and would have stolen just for the chance of a squint at them, but for his size and the weight of his fist or the cold bite of his tongue that could lacerate you like a whiplash when he was roused.

When the drink had worn off, though, there was the sea in his very bones and marrow. In the way he wore his clothes. In the way he walked and spoke and looked at us. In the cock of the jaunty grey beard he grew at sea and the glint of his eye. Old Boxer was a sailor to his fingertips, who could run rings round the rest of us, and always would be. In spite of the misery that made him sour in his moods of black depression, in spite of the bitterness that made him drink himself silly whenever he was within reach of liquor, in spite of the weakness that made him swear over and over again he was going to leave the sea and yet had never let him get beyond the first shabby hotel, there was something magnificent about him. There was something awful in his debauchery, but something more, too, something I could never put my finger on, that made me as loyal to him as Yorky, whatever his mood and whatever his condition.

It was a grey November day when I first saw familiar streets again. The *Archibald Harvey* was long behind me and long forgotten in the procession of ships I'd made my home, and when I first saw the St Andrew Light again I was in the *Mossulu* that found her grave in Tobruk harbour.

There was something vaguely oppressive in the air that day as we approached to tie up, and it didn't come entirely from the dark surroundings. The news those days was enough to give anyone the pip. For months there'd been uneasiness in the air. Germany was scooping up great areas of land – Austria, Czecho-Slovakia, Sudetenland – and was goose-stepping all over the place, terrifying people with the armaments she was building. Italy had made a grab at Albania and was making anything the excuse to set about someone. There wasn't much peace in the world just then, in spite of old Chamberlain's recent visit to Hitler.

The sky was heavily overcast and low clouds mingled with the smoke and steam when the *Mossulu* came alongside. We sent heaving-lines ashore with her mooring-ropes, and she was winched into the quayside by her clattering donkey engines. Overhead, the grey gulls wheeled and cried. Alongside, the oily water was lashed to a muddy foam by the screws that churned over and over again the matted debris round the stern – all the oil-smeared boxes, the paper and the sticks, the usual old hat.

I stared through the flurries of rain at the tall buildings along the river bank, and the shining roofs of the dark warehouses and the cranes and the coal-chutes. There was an odd feeling in my stomach. This was my home – but I was a different person. For the first time in my life I had money in my pocket to spend in the town, and I felt mature enough to withstand any buffets it could hand out to me.

In the forecastle, the deck crew were rolling up their gear and cramming it into sea-chests and bags and trunks. Yorky, an old cap over his ear, was in the bow, trying to make a brown-paper parcel of all the odds and ends of worn-out clothing that made up his kit. He was swearing and cursing, excited by the prospect of shore leave and money in his pocket.

"Just let me shake the dust of this old cow off me feet," he was saying, "and they'll never catch *me* at sea again. This lark puts years on a chap, and I've 'ad enough of it. I'm goin' 'ome to my old Ma. No more sea time for me. Not this kid. Not yours truly."

"We'll swallow the anchor together, Yorky," Old Boxer said, though his voice was flat and had none of the excitement in it that showed in Yorky's eyes.

I leaned on the bulkhead, watching them, knowing that neither of them meant what he said, and that they knew, too. Both Yorky and Old Boxer had lost the ability to sleep soundly away from the cry of the gulls and the smell of the sea.

I stared at the litter of paper and old clothes on the deck – discarded rubbish left for the ship-yard workers to pick over – and I had that sense of chilly loneliness that came on me at times. All the little hand-made curtains that normally decorated the cold ironwork of the bunks had disappeared. All the personal bedding. All the oilskins that swung on the bulkhead and rubbed a half-circle of dirt on the white paint. The forecastle looked bare and bleak in the light of the guarded bulb in the deckhead and the cold grey glow that crept timorously in through the portholes. The bunks had a queer, comfortless look about them, yet there'd been times when the place had seemed homely, when there was the fug of pipes in it and the wind was cheerless outside.

Abruptly I went to my own bunk and started to pack.

" 'Omesick, Jess?" Yorky queried, glancing round at me. "No," I said. "I'll be at sea again as soon as you."

Yorky grinned. And his grin was his admission that he was a liar. He'd threatened to leave the ship in Sydney after a free-for-all with Old Boxer, but before she was due to sail he'd come back along the waterfront, shuffling and penniless, stale with booze and dodging a moneylender...

An hour later we were ashore and I was staring at the familiar buildings almost as though we'd come to a foreign land. The streets seemed shorter and narrower and far more crowded and dirty than I'd ever remembered. I began to wonder how I'd ever managed to live in the place, and why I hadn't choked with the nearness of the walls.

Our first call was to drop our luggage in one of the shabby establishments near the docks.

"How about a hotel?" I suggested. "It's the first night ashore, after all. Let's sleep in a comfortable bed."

"The Grands and the Royals," Old Boxer said soberly, "have never welcomed seafaring men."

"Thank Gawd I'll 'ave a feather mattress to bounce on," Yorky said gleefully. " 'Stead o' them flea-pits Ernie the Weasel 'ires out. I'm goin' 'ome, mate. Sleep in me own tiddley little bunk in 'Ull tonight." He flourished the ticket he'd bought at the railway station as we passed, then shoved it in his waistcoat pocket. "Tomorrer night I'll be in the local with me Ma and me old Auntie May – me with me pint o' dark and them with their Guinnesses."

He chuckled. "Jeeze," he said, "the number o' times I've set off for 'Ull and got no further than the first pub. Well, I've got me ticket this time. Safe as the Bank of England."

He tucked his concertina tighter under his arm and picked up his parcel. "Come on; 'Orace, let's get yer established afore I go. Ain't only one last thing I got to do. That's see yer settled. 'Ow about Ernie the Weasel's, same as usual? It's not much cop, and Ernie's a bit of a bloody Crippen, but it'll do yer, I reckon."

I listened to them arguing, wondering if I ought to go home. I was itching to see the shabby house in Atlantic Street, yet I had a feeling I might not be wanted. Over the years I'd spent growing into a man I'd studiously avoided home, leaving the ship in London when necessary. I'd even spent my shore time between ships there, when they were paying off in my home town, lonely in a Salvation Army hostel while Yorky and Old Boxer took digs near to Atlantic Street and Minnie's Ma's. I'd been dodging something for years, it seemed, but now that I was home at last the thing I'd been avoiding was suddenly no more frightening than a shadow.

Eventually we found a drab lodging-house next to a tripe shop, a place with a dark, bare hall that smelled of cabbage; it had brown patches of damp showing in all the corners, and its stairs were as bare of carpet as its windows were of curtains.

"Ernie the Weasel's." Old Boxer waved a hand in an ironic gesture of welcome. "Welcome to Poverty Mansion." He raised his voice and called imperiously down the echoing hall. "Ernie! Come and book us a berth."

Yorky wrinkled his nose. "Pooh! Stinks o' tomcats," he commented. "Ernie, you old flea-bag," he bawled at the top of his voice, "your doss-house needs a rub of the old carbolic!"

A door opened as he was shouting and Pat Fee, of all people, appeared in his shirt-sleeves, his waistcoat open.

"Upstairs," he said shortly in answer to Old Boxer's question. "First floor. And don't make so much row."

"The bloomin' reception committee, Jess," Yorky said sarcastically. "Look after yer 'ere, they do."

I saw Pat peering at us in the gloomy hall, then he burst into a laugh. "Blow me down if it ain't little Jess Ferigo growed up," he said. "How's it goin', kid? 'Eard you went to sea."

He'd grown fatter and was florid and prosperous-looking despite the dinginess of his surroundings.

There was no enthusiasm in my reply, though. I'd no love for Pat. I began to mount the carpetless stairs that were noisy with creaks behind Old Boxer, while Yorky sat on the doorstep and lit a cigarette.

"Ain't comin' in," he said. "If I see a bed 'ere I might be tempted to stay the night, and if I do I'll never get 'ome."

Pat watched us climb the steep staircase, then he suddenly tossed aside his cigarette and followed us.

"Ain't you goin' 'ome?" he asked me. "Or 'ave you decided after all you don't belong there any more?"

I said nothing. The old fierce dislike for him burned inside me like a pain.

"Reckon I'm doin' better nor you now, Jess," he went on cheerfully. As he spoke he lit a cigar with a flourish, almost as though he wanted to demonstrate his prosperity. He drew deep puffs at it as he talked, claiming an easy friendship. "Running a book now. Paying game, bookmaking. Only run this joint as a sideline. Took it over when Ma died. It's bigger'n the one she had, and it's just the job for making money out of matelots when they come ashore, or blokes as don't fancy goin' 'ome. Costs me nothin'. Ernie the Weasel runs it for me in return for 'is keep. Wun't be 'ere now only I 'ad a bit of a to-do with the bit of fluff I kip with. Got to wait till she's been got out of my flat."

We'd reached the landing now, and Pat leaned on the banisters, still chatting, slyness dripping from his words.

"Me sister Kate works with your old man now," he said informatively. "Got too big for 'er boots and left 'ome after the old lady died. Thought she might 'elp me run this place, I did. Just the job for a woman. But not 'er. Too bloody clever she was. Scholarships and that. Secretary at Wiggins'. Works late at night sometimes," he said in tones that were immediately suggestive of unpleasantness.

I paused with my hand on the knob of a door on the landing, waiting for him to say something more.

"Gawd knows what she gets up to there," the drawling voice went on. "Work late often, they do, I've 'eard. Work! That's a new name for it. I know what I'd be doin' if I was in an office at night with a girl."

I dropped my bag and turned on him. "Shut your trap!" I said, and I meant every word I was saying. "Shut it or I'll knock you backwards down the stairs. I mean it. I'll knock you straight to the bottom."

Pat retreated hurriedly down two or three steps. "OK. OK," he said, changing his tone. "Only my bit o' fun. Nothing to get snotty about. Any more of yer carry-on and out you go. This is a respectable lodging-house."

He started down the stairs, jauntily as ever, and I itched to land a kick on his broadening behind.

"Give me love to Kate when you go an' see your old man at the boat-yard," he said. "I ain't seen 'er for six months."

I turned back and followed Old Boxer into the room we were sharing, a bleak little closet almost devoid of furniture and darkened by the wall of a warehouse outside. Old Boxer, unconscious of what had been happening on the landing, had tossed his bags on to one of the two shabby beds.

"The old familiar places," he said bitterly. "God, I hate 'em as I hate the thought of the hell that surely awaits me."

There'd been a lordliness about his words as he called for Ernie, but now they seemed lost and friendless and bewildered.

Yorky appeared in the doorway then, his stiff collar lopsided already, his cap in its usual place over one ear, his brown paper parcel safely tucked under one arm, his concertina under the other. "Come on," he said. "Shake a leg. Let's go and find some young ladies and push the boat out."

"Yorky, my lad," Old Boxer said, cheering up a little, "you look like some lecherous Lochinvar, some rampant Romeo roaring for his Juliet." He spoke as he always did to Yorky, as though he were a friend, but in a way that suggested subtly that he was an inferior.

He heaved himself from the bed to a chorus of jangling springs.

"Come on, Jess, let's go and find him some painted little slut who'll swop him a kiss for a drop of booze."

"Now, look 'ere, 'Orace," Yorky said indignantly. "That's no way to speak. You don't find young ladies amiss yourself."

"I detest 'em," Old Boxer snapped. "But I've human instincts like anyone else. Come on, let's go and get a drink before we pay off." He looked at me. "Only an eyeful, Jess," he said half-apologetically, as we thumped down the bare stairs. "Just one to keep me going. We've got to kill time."

The Town Hall clock was booming as we went outside into the damp air again, the deep notes echoing among the grey stone buildings. Knots of men whose clothes stamped them as sailors, for all that they wore the blue suits and hats of shore leave, suddenly came to life. They heaved themselves from the corners where they lounged, smoking, and headed for the pubs like a flock of pigeons at feeding time.

Old Boxer dived into a dark little inn I remembered, whose courtyard had once been used as a meeting-place for duels. Pirates on the way to the gallows had stopped in it for a hot toddy. Inside, the rooms were full of noisy men whom he jostled imperiously to one side. He was soon in earnest conversation with the landlord and offering his watch as security.

"Just a couple of quid," he was demanding. "To keep us going. We pay off at three, and a sailor's got to have a drink before then."

Yorky came in, a paper in his hand, and flung himself into a seat beside me.

"Jeeze," he said. "It's good to see an English paper again instead of them fuzzy-wuzzy efforts you pick up in Freetown."

He stared first at the racing results. "Chase me Aunt Fanny," he said. "Starlight won at Doncaster last time out.

Lost 'alf me wages on 'er when I was 'ome last trip, the bastard. Thought she'd only got three legs the way she run."

He opened the paper, his mouth working as he read. "Bloke 'ere been a bigamist six times runnin'," he went on. "Gawd, six of 'em all fightin' for 'im when 'e comes out o' clink."

He squinted over a pair of bent tin spectacles. They were lashed to one ear with a loop of sail twine.

"You know, Jess," he said seriously, indicating the paper, "these 'ere Nazzies are goin' to cause trouble afore long." He was suddenly grave. "Wantin' this and wantin' that. You can't go off like that, y'know, kid. Sooner or later the bloody balloon's going to go up. I was torpedoed three times in the last lot, and I don't want no more. Munich. 'We 'ave snatched the nettle, Danger,' or summat, old Chamberlain said. Stand up to 'im, I say, and give 'im the old one-two on the ear-'ole."

Old Boxer was shouldering his way through the crowd towards us with a tray of drinks. His breath announced out loud he'd already had a rum. "Here we are," he said. "A drop to keep us on an even keel till tea-time."

Yorky grabbed for his glass. " 'Ere's 'ow."

"Praise be," Old Boxer said fervently. His tones were light but there was a hint of seriousness underneath his gaiety. "The first thing that always occurs to me when I get ashore," he said, "is what an old bum I am."

"Oh, dry up, mate," Yorky said, glancing up from his paper. "Always so cheerful, you are, when you're out on the razzie. Why don't you smile and give yer face a joy-ride, 'Orace?"

"Damn me, my name's not 'Orace, you old grannie. I was called after Nelson. Nelson, you old windbag, do you hear? What do you think he'd have done if Hardy had called *him* 'Orace?"

"If you're called after 'im," Yorky said, "I'll bet 'e spins in 'is grave like a bloody 'ummin' top every time 'e sees you ashore. Blimey, fancy a bloke like you leading the Royal Navy into action!"

Old Boxer sat down. His face was bitter and that inexplicable curtain of silence had fallen on him.

"Cheer up." Yorky grinned. " 'Ere, let's 'ave another and I'll carry you to the Board of Trade for paying-off meself. Come on, you ain't goin' to see yer ole shipmate turn 'is back on the sea without a fiddlin' little drink to see 'im off, are yer?"

Old Boxer's depression had disappeared entirely by the time we reached the Board of Trade building. We were signing off there and drawing our pay in the drab rooms where the names of ships and the times of their arrivals and departures were scrawled on blackboards. But he wasn't alone in his mellowness, for the rest of the crew had been hanging around the bars killing time as well and they were now propping up the walls and corners, their eyes dull, their voices noisy. The old endless, pointless forecastle argument was going strong, as it had been ever since Drake sailed to meet the Armada:

"She does, you know."

"She doesn't, you know."

"She bloody does."

"She bloody doesn't."

"Just one to see you away, Yorky," Old Boxer said as we trooped outside again, "and then you can shove off."

"I wouldn't mind something to eat myself," I pointed out.

"Eat!" Old Boxer stared. "Leave that to the little men. The years are creeping up on me and I've only a short time left. Let's enjoy ourselves." He was gay again. It was that gaiety that was usually followed by foul temper or maudlin stupidity. You could always tell. Once he started using fancy words he was well on the way. "Tonight, I feel a giant. I'm the Emperor of Rome. I'm the King of Spain. By God, I do believe I'm the Pope!"

"You'll be a flamin' nuisance afore the night's out," Yorky commented dryly. "I know you, 'Orace. I've told you afore. I told you last time we was ashore in Jamaica that you were a dirty, drunken old man. 'E didn't know where to put 'isself," he ended in an aside to me. "Did you, 'Orace?"

"Ach, you muling ninny," Old Boxer said cheerfully. "You self-centred, pot-bellied old windbag."

Yorky wagged his head, unmoved by the insults. "You're always the same," he said. "Allus start off on me. Allus open yer big trap and try to talk me down. Cunning as a doss-house rat, you are."

Somehow, we found ourselves in a dark place full of aspidistras and marble-topped tables.

Old Boxer gaped round in disgust. "My God," he said, "it's as cheerless as a workhouse fire. Call up the liquor, Yorky, before the chill gets into my bones."

That drink became two and eventually three. Within the hour Yorky had fished his concertina from under the seat. " 'Ow about a tune, mates? 'Shenandoah'? 'Old Bull and Bush'? 'Tararaboomdeay'? 'They're Shifting Father's Grave to Build a Sewer'?" Within another hour we were on the street again, with Yorky swopping insults with the landlord, who glared at us from his front steps.

"Go on, get away with you," the landlord said, "before I call a bobby. Picking fights with a chap's customers!"

As the day drew on and the grey damp night shut down the three of us dodged from one dockside dive to another. It was nothing new. We'd repeated the same procedure every time we'd touched port in the past few years.

We swaggered down dripping alleyways that re-echoed with our noise, splashing through the puddles, oblivious to the water that spotted our trousers. From parlour to tap-room we went, from fun fairs where the loudspeakers made your head ring to fish-and-chip queues or coffee-stalls for a bun or a cup of tea.

Old Boxer led the way. One moment he was noisy and hilarious, magnificent in his superb contempt of everyone around him, the next shuffling and bowed and sour. Yorky's eyes were dull by this time and he'd acquired a second parcel, a new suit and a pair of braces. One end of the braces hung through a tear in the paper.

The time was a noisy nightmare of clattering traffic and taxis: a sailor's not the one to argue about the price of transport on his first night ashore. One smoky room followed another, and note after note changed hands as the party grew wilder and bigger with the addition of a Latvian greaser and the donkeyman off one of Yorky's former ships, to say nothing of a couple of Yorky's young ladies, brazen-faced harpies in cheap jewellery, the sort who'd do their own grandma in for a glass of gin and a drag at a ship's Woodbine.

There was a restless hour at the cinema which I'd just begun to enjoy when I was hauled away again to a bar-room harsh with bright lights and gilt mirrors. There was an argument with a bobby and a brawl with a coster, a shoving match that ended in maudlin embraces.

Eventually, long before closing time, I had to drop out of the party. "I'm going home to bed," I said. "I've drunk enough to float a battleship. I'm sick of it."

"Sick of it?" Yorky said, and his drooping eyes opened. "The night's young, kid. Use yer loaf!"

"You can't go away like that, dearie," one of the women said, clinging to my arm. "We was just getting to know you."

"Such a nice, well-be'aved young gentleman," the other smirked. "Full of fun, I bet." And she winked archly at me.

"Let the lad go!" Old Boxer broke the chain of linked arms and thundered the words unexpectedly. "He's had enough. Let him go and sleep it off. He's not like the rest of us with a sponge for a stomach and a spirit keg for a nose. Ought to have gone long since, if the truth were known, instead of trailing through these damned alleys after us. If we'd had any sense we'd have sent him. Go home, Jess. And sleep well. Get to the devil out of here to where it's decent and clean."

He turned to Yorky and the others, and the two women hurriedly let go my arms as he glared at them. "And one word out of any of you," he stormed. "And I'll drive it back down your throats with this." He flourished a half-empty rum bottle and they shuffled off slowly and unwillingly. I stood in a dark archway out of the drizzle and watched them move unsteadily away, shepherded by Old Boxer, then I turned away, suddenly dog-tired and sleepy with drink.

And as I did so I stumbled and almost fell into the arms of Kathleen Fee.

Katie Fee had grown into a tall, frail-looking girl with dark eyes and a pale face that belied the strength in her.

She must have had a heart as big as the King George the Fifth Graving Dock, for she'd lifted herself by sheer willpower out of the dark streets and the drab, vicious environments where she'd been reared, clean out of the farthest backstreets of Dockland, where the long, straight rows of terraced houses ended by the river in crazy alleyways and dark courts. I'd had letters from her, so I knew.

As a child she'd seen the corners of these courts filled at night by amorous sailors and their painted lady-friends, and festooned with strings of shabby grey washing during the day. She'd seen her father bring home every kind of dockside tart he could find when he came from sea. She'd seen him beat her mother stupid, and in every sort of drunkenness, and finally watched him die of injuries received in a dockside brawl. She'd seen her mother work herself to a standstill trying to keep going the lodging-house he'd left her with, a tall tenement with a ladder of a staircase, where she'd never charged enough.

When her mother had died, her heart broken by overwork, Kate had cut herself clean away from Pat and found a home in lodgings at the other side of the town, a cheap place, all she could afford. A homely enough place, I suppose, but one where she was often lonely.

And maybe she was extra lonely that night, for when I bumped into her she seemed to clutch eagerly at my conversation as though it were an oasis of friendliness. I knew she was glad to see me. I could always tell what she was thinking. Her face was too honest for her to hide her feelings.

"Jess," she said when she saw me. "Jess Ferigo."

I raised my hat clumsily and tried to make my eyes focus on her. But they were dizzy with drink and for a moment I thought she was just another dockside tart trying a pick-up.

Then I realised that her neat figure had none of their blousy tawdriness, and I held my hat unsteadily to my chest and frowned, struggling with the vague familiarity of her pale features.

"Sorry, miss," I said. "Can't seem to place you."

Then Kate must have seen I was far from sober, for she spoke more slowly, like a teacher to a daft child.

"My name's Kathleen Fee, Jess," she said carefully, as though she were afraid I wouldn't remember her. "Surely you know me?"

I stared, then I smiled as I managed to get her features into focus.

"Sure, yes," I said. "Now I can tell. Got a bit of a headache," I added by way of explanation. "Making me a bit dizzy."

Kate smiled. "You need a coffee," she said quietly. "Come on. You could do with sobering-up before you go any further, Jess."

I grinned. I couldn't help it. It was so naive and frank.

"Yes, I could," I said. "I've had too much. I've been trying to get away from the docks since midday. Still" – I shrugged – "it's the first time I've been in the town for donkey's years. A chap feels like celebrating."

She took no notice. "In here," she said, turning into a small tea-room hard under the lee of a ship-yard wall. "Have you been home yet?" she added.

I sat down, conscious of my unsteadiness. I was trying to kid her I wasn't drunk, but I was just a bit too precise in everything I did to be convincing. She didn't seem impressed, anyway.

"Hadn't thought of going home," I admitted, and I felt a bit of an oaf as I spoke. "Only likely to be here for a short while. Going up to London to sit for my mate's ticket. Officer, y'know. Back to sea in a day or two."

This wasn't strictly true. I'd more than three weeks at my disposal before I'd got to present myself for examination, but I felt that Kate wouldn't be interested in my reasons for preferring Pat Fee's lodging-house to Atlantic Street.

Her voice was gentle as she replied, and her eyes were wide and dark. "Of course you must go home," she said. "Your father would be upset if you didn't."

"Would he?" I asked, frowning. Somehow I'd imagined that Dig, with his shy, aloof manner, would have learned to do without me. I'd thought he'd have taken refuge in his books and managed to put me aside, clean out of his dusty life. I'd had a few letters from him at first but I'd never answered them.

I stared at Kate's pale, earnest face. The café was warm and the drink was making me dizzy again so that her features were more often blurred than not. I opened my mouth to explain a few things to her then I shut it again with a click. The words I wanted just wouldn't come in the right order.

Besides, I told myself, she wouldn't be interested in the fact that Dig wasn't my father. Obviously she imagined he was.

"Do you think he'd like to see me?" I queried, more for conversation, and because the simple words were all I felt I could trust my tongue to form just then, rather than because I was really concerned.

"Of course he would," Kate said. She pushed my coffee towards my shyly, and she seemed suddenly and oddly happy to be doing things for me.

I began to smile at her. I was feeling steadier after the coffee and a little more sober. Suddenly, in the bright, gaudy café, the afternoon and evening I'd spent with Old Boxer and Yorky, hanging round the dark taverns of the dock area with hard-eyed harpies and drunken hangers-on for pals, seemed a dream that was miles away below the surface of my consciousness, somewhere down a deep well that sent confused echoes up to me. For years I'd done little else ashore, whether in England or abroad, nothing apart from chasing Old Boxer in and out of pubs. I suddenly realised how much I missed conversation, how much I missed delicacy in the forecastle, and just how much Kate's cleanness and decency and her shy words fulfilled the need.

"How is Dig?" I said awkwardly, fiddling with my spoon. "How is he? And how's my Ma?"

Kate told me and, as I thought of Ma, I wondered if I'd been a good enough son to her. But my concern was only the remorse of a sick visitor who hadn't made his calls. Ma had never given me the chance to be a good son.

Kate must have seen me frown, for she laid her fingers lightly on my wrist. "You *will* go home, Jess, won't you?" she said. "I don't know why you went to sea. I suppose it was some quarrel that's none of my business. But you must go home. He needs you."

As she spoke I felt ashamed of myself for my treatment of Dig, who, throughout the years, apparently hadn't lost faith in me.

"He's never ceased to wait for you, Jess." Kate was still speaking in a low, earnest voice. "He's a good man, Jess, and he deserves kindness."

"I'll go home," I said seriously. "I promise you I'll go, Kate." I frowned and rubbed my hand across my eyes, feeling stupid and oafish. My mouth was sour and my stomach queasy with drink. "I've been a bit of a damn' fool one way and another, I suppose." I looked at her and grinned and Kate smiled back at me. "And I'm sorry I'm a bit bottled. Perhaps I'll see more of you. It'll encourage me to slam the hatch down on the booze."

Kate nodded in a vague sort of way, as though she hadn't quite heard what I said. I felt she liked me, but I could see she wasn't trusting herself to like me too much. I knew what the trouble was. I was a sailor, and her father had been a sailor. And she'd learn to distrust sailors when they came home from sea. She'd seen her father in action ashore too often, and I suppose she thought I might be just another of the same sort. It upset me a bit when I realised what she was thinking and whom she was comparing me with, but I caught on in the end and saw her point of view. And, anyway, she smiled and finally agreed.

As we rose to go I saw an agitated figure in the window of the café. It was Yorky, pale-faced and sober, waving his arms and pulling faces to attract my attention, his nose pressed to a white splodge on the glass that was steamed inside with the heat. I grabbed Kate's arm and hurried her to the door.

"Oh, Christ!" Yorky seemed to be trying to draw his breath and speak and put the parcels and the concertina he was carrying out of his way all at the same time.

Then he realised Kate was with me and he pulled himself together.

"Sorry, me old flower, if I've interrupted yer," he said. "I didn't notice your young lady." He raised his hat to Kate with a clumsy gesture that was impeded by a ruptured parcel and the concertina, then he burst out as though he could contain the words no longer: "Jess, come an' bail 'im out. They've got him in the bloody lock-up."

t w o

I got him out. I argued with the police sergeant for an hour. The old old story: sailor in his home town for the first time in years. Fortunately, the sergeant was new to the district and didn't know old Boxer.

"Well," he said – he was a bit doubtful at first – "I'd like to help you, son, but you know how it is. Regulations are regulations. 'Sides" – his voice rose indignantly – "who's he think 'e is, anyway? The way 'e spoke to me, 'e made me feel like a bloomin' butler. Not nasty, as you might say, but sort of 'aughty. If I 'adn't caught 'old of meself sharp, I'd 'a' been feeling proud to look after 'im."

I worked hard on that sergeant. I spun a yarn as long as my arm about Old Boxer's wife waiting at home, and about his kids who were breaking their necks to see him. In the end he gave way.

"Well, blimey," he said. "I got a son in the Merchant Navy and I wouldn't like to think I might 'ave shopped one of 'is pals. 'E's a bit wild 'imself, if the truth's known, when 'e gets 'ome. Fair worries 'is Ma."

In the end we got quite matey, especially when we found I'd been to the same school as his son. I even struck up a friendship with the lad to suit him, though I didn't know him from Adam. It pleased the sergeant, though, and he finally agreed to let Old Boxer go if I didn't say anything to anybody and saw that he behaved himself.

"Don't worry," I said. "I'll see to it."

Old Boxer was lying on a bunk in one of the cells, his face pressed against the whitewashed wall, so that his mouth was pushed all askew. He looked pathetic and old, but there wasn't much sympathy in me for him just then. I was angry at being dragged away from Kate.

I got him on to his feet, one arm round my neck, and sent Yorky for a taxi.

" 'Alf a sec'," the sergeant said. "Just let me 'ave a squint round to make sure the inspector's not about. Then we'll nip 'im out. I'll give you a hand."

Between us we dragged Old Boxer out of the police-station and shoved him into the taxi, on to the leather cushions that smelled partly of mildew and partly of polish. He leaned against me on the way back to Pat Fee's until I gave him a shove, then he rolled over to the other side and Yorky had him for the rest of the journey.

Finally we lifted him out at the other end and heaved him up the stairs at Pat's lodging-house, the whole fifteen-odd stone of him. Miles of steps there seemed, every one bare and squeaky like the last, and Old Boxer's boots clattered on them enough to wake the dead. There wasn't much ceremony about the way I shoved him into his room and let him bounce on to the bed.

It was early morning when I finally got him tucked in and got rid of Yorky. Then I lay down on my own bed for half an hour and waited for him to come round.

The sun was well up and the kids were in the streets when I woke up. Old Boxer was sitting on the edge of the sagging bed, staring at the floor with empty eyes, a dreadful weariness in the curve of his back. His thinning hair was dishevelled, and his suit had streaks of mud on it. I climbed off the bed and leaned near the window, smoking a cigarette, glad for once that Yorky wasn't there with his chatter. I'd packed him off home, bundled him unceremoniously away to the station, protesting, apologising, and with half his pay already spent.

"I told him, Jess," were his last words. "I told him over and over again until he didn't know what to say."

I drew on my cigarette slowly and watched Old Boxer, half-resentful against him for dragging me away from Kate. She'd gone quickly, with nothing more than a brief goodbye, leaving me disappointed at the suddenness of her going, and I'd turned savagely on Yorky, full of recriminations I knew weren't really deserved, but angry that they should drag me back just when I was beginning to feel sober and intelligent again.

Over my head on the faded wallpaper in a patch of grey morning light hung a Biblical quotation, one of Mrs Fee's furnishings that Pat had taken over, I suppose.

There is no peace, saith the Lord, unto the Wicked, it proclaimed in ornate gilded letters, and I felt there was no apter description for the torment of the wretched old man in front of me.

There was no peace in his soul, no peace in his mind. Only turbulent thoughts, cynicisms and bitterness that wouldn't let him rest. When he wasn't majestically drunk, there was only a shabby, shuffling old creature left, only the shell of a man.

Old Boxer looked up at me unexpectedly.

"I'm sorry, Jess," he said. "I always do it. But I can't sit in these awful places and sniff at the cabbage that drips off the walls."

"What's wrong with getting a good meal under your belt?"

"And coming here sober and tasting the cheerless joys of the tomb?" His shoulders shuddered. "I can't do that. I've done it too many times already. It's a slow poison that gets into your system."

"Why don't you try a decent hotel?" I suggested, staring round the drab room and at the street outside crowded with screaming kids.

"It's all the same," he said wearily. "I'd still have to sit alone in the damn' places."

"Haven't you a home anywhere?" I queried, and as I asked the question I was startled to realise I didn't know the answer – even after all the years we'd spent together.

"Home?" He gave a short sharp bark of laughter. "Only a ship's forecastle." He lit a cigarette with trembling fingers and drew hurried puffs at it.

"Haven't you any relations?"

"Plenty."

"Can't you go and stay with them?"

"Hah!" He laughed. "They'd drive me mad with their sanctimonious pi-jaw – if they'd ever have me near enough to let me listen to it." He seemed to be cheering up a little as the glint of anger brightened his dull eyes and warmed his gaunt features. His bad temper was always more bearable than his depression. "They wouldn't be seen dead in my company," he said.

"Why not? What's there to be ashamed of in a sailor?"

"According to my family there are no sailors outside a Royal Navy Ward Room."

I stared. Old Boxer caught my eye, and tossed his half-smoked cigarette into the untidy fireplace.

"And you didn't fancy the Navy?" I asked.

He hesitated a long time before he replied. "I was more than ten years in the Royal Navy," he said slowly.

"And you left?"

He suddenly stood up and began to pace up and down the small room, in the old familiar habit of walking on a short deck for exercise, backwards and forwards, backwards and forwards, monotonously. It seemed ages before he replied.

"They asked me to leave," he said eventually.

"Oh!" I felt I'd turned over something unpleasant that Old Boxer had been trying hard to hide.

He looked at me. "That's what they always say when they find out. They say 'Oh!' just as you did, and their faces look as though they'd just put their foot in something dirty."

I stared out of the window, unable to look at the bitter, twisted smile on his mouth. He leaned at the other side of the window and stared intently at a milkman delivering his goods on the far side of the street.

There was a silence in the room for a while. Suddenly a lot of things about Old Boxer were explained – the obvious culture, the breeding that proclaimed itself in spite of his shabby clothes, the gaunt good looks, the education. It explained also why he'd bought a decrepit boat-yard and never had the interest to make a business of it. He lit another cigarette and reseated himself on the bed to the tinny accompaniment of springs.

"God knows why I'm telling you all this," he said. "I haven't told it to any man before." His eyes were narrow as he went on speaking, as though he were peering back into the past, forcing himself to stare into places he'd never dared to re-explore before. "I was court-martialled," he said quietly. "Two men were killed because I was drunk, and a good ship broke her back."

I waited for further explanations but he seemed to prefer to leave the incident buried. Outside, the milkman was calling his wares, and I could hear his voice, melancholy and monotonous as a fog buoy, above the sound of the traffic. Inside the house, someone was clumping about the landing, clattering buckets on the bare stairs.

Old Boxer sat on the edge of the iron bedstead, his hands limp, his head deep between his shoulders, then he suddenly reached out and drew towards him his long deep-sea kit-bag from the end of the bed. He untied the cord at the top and drew out a sword and scabbard. I'd seen it before for brief instances. Everybody in the forecastle had always known he had it. We'd often wondered about it, but he'd never seemed to want to tell us anything, and nobody had dared ask or steal a gander at it, even when he was on watch.

"See that?" he said, holding it up and indicating the tarnished gilt and silver. "That was my dress sword. That's all I've got left now."

I felt the slender weapon in my hands and handed it back to him with a feeling of embarrassment. He took it reverently. "It was my father's," he explained. "It was *his* father's, and probably his grandfather's. I don't know. It would have been my son's only – "

He stopped dead and, tossing aside his cigarette-end, ground it out with the toe of his boot.

"And there you are," he said with forced cheerfulness. "The story of my life. How to be an old bum known to half the barmen in the world. How to become a doss-house ghost. How to end up on the rubbish dump." He seemed brighter and even appeared to be enjoying his bitterness. He always did, I think. I suspect he got a malicious pleasure out of his cynicism.

Then he turned round to me and said wryly, "That's why I can't sit in these cabbage-smelling rooms thinking of things such as I've told you."

I said nothing. There didn't seem to be much I could comment that would be any good to him.

"It isn't a pretty story, is it, Jess?" he said, and the bitter cynicism was fading, and depression was settling on him again.

"There's not much more to it," he went on sourly. "Only a history of pawnshops and shabby lodging-houses like this, and one dreary ship after another." He rubbed a hand across his face suddenly. "You know where I'll end up?" he asked. "In the forecastle of a Greek steamer, or out on the China coast. That's where they all go. Nobody else'll have 'em. People like me are the only ones who'll stand the racket.

"God," he said, "it makes you wonder sometimes what *might* have become of me. Once there seemed such a lot of hope. And now" – he indicated the sword on the bed where he'd placed it – "that's all I've got left. And even that's getting shabby and old and tired like me. The only thing that's holding it together's tradition."

He stood up and stretched himself, gaunt and grey-faced, his eyes red with booze.

"But they'll probably be glad of me yet, Jess." He indicated a newspaper on the bed. Its front page carried a photograph of Hitler. "If that madman heads the way I expect he will, they might have me back after all. Cheer up, lad," he said suddenly. His mood of black depression seemed to have transferred itself to me.

I hurriedly shrugged off the feeling. There was more to Old Boxer's story, I knew, I'd heard only half of it. Some inner knowledge told me he'd left things still unsaid, but I felt in no mood for more bitter confidences. I was suddenly dreadfully tired. I'd been up all night sorting out his affairs, and I felt I'd had enough of them.

I pushed myself upright and threw my fag-end out of the window. A small boy picked it up and began to draw at it in hurried puffs, waving to me as he did so.

"You're on your own now," I said, "I'm going home. God knows," I went on in a fit of anger at myself, "I've wasted enough time. If you're in trouble again you can stew in your own juice."

He stared at me with a hurt look, like a kicked dog.

"I shan't worry you, Jess," he said quietly.

He began to unpack his kit-bag, then, as though losing interest, he threw it under the bed and flung himself down on the hard mattress.

"I'll stay here," he said. "I always stay at Ernie the Weasel's. You can forget you ever knew me." His voice was suddenly gentle. "If I see you with anyone I'll pretend not to know you."

His self-abasement and humility, his utter degradation, touched me and I felt like a lout.

"Oh, don't be a bloody fool!" I growled.

I moved towards the door. "I'll be seeing you," I said. "I'm going to enjoy my leave here in my own way. If you want a trip up to London, you can come with me when I go up to sit for my ticket. We can have a bit of a run round the pubs."

Old Boxer lay on the bed for a moment, watching his cigarette smoke curl upwards to the cracked plaster of the ceiling. He thought I'd gone, and his face suddenly looked old – old and dried up, like a withered apple, and he seemed devoid of feeling and emotion.

The door opened gently as I looked at him and Yorky appeared, clutching his brown-paper parcel, still with the braces dangling, his concertina in the other hand, his made-up bow-tie adrift, his cap on the back of his head. I was behind the door, and he never saw me as he entered the room.

Old Boxer had turned a dull eye towards him, and his depression seemed to have deepened at the sight of Yorky's moon smile.

"Missed me train after all, 'Orace, me old flower," Yorky said cheerfully. "The chickens and that'll 'ave to wait a bit."

He tossed his parcel on to the bed.

"Come and 'ave a drink, cock," he went on. "They've just opened."

Old Boxer licked his dry lips as though he were conscious of the sour taste in his mouth.

"God damn you, Yorky!" he said, half under his breath. "God damn you to everlasting hell!"

"That's the stuff!" Yorky grinned cheerfully and bent to help him off the bed. "Come on. You sound more like yer old self now."

I slipped outside and dodged silently down the stairs. I wasn't going to get mixed up in anything more. I suddenly felt I'd had a basinful of Old Boxer. I wanted to get away to people without care, young people, people with hope.

I paused on the landing below as I heard Old Boxer speak.

"Only an eyeful then," he said. "No more. Just one till you can get another train. And, for God's sake, if I get bottled, don't fetch Jess again. I'll stew in my own juice this time."

The words came down to me through the cage the old-fashioned banisters made.

"OK, 'Orace," Yorky was saying, as I set off down the next flight of stairs. "As soon as you start getting awkward, I'll chin you and call a cab."

three

Dig was in the hall when I arrived, poking at an old pipe with a feather, a scarf round his neck against the cool air, his carpet slippers on his feet.

He was in a restless mood. He'd been writing and he had a pen over his ear and a wad of paper stuffed into his pocket. There was a hole in his sock, I noticed, and he looked a bit neglected in his frayed jacket and trousers. He wasn't very well-shaved, either, and I saw that his whiskers had flecks of white in them.

He was by the stairs when the door opened and as I stared down at him he seemed to have shrunk a little. He was greyer and dustier and stringier than ever, his long neck stretching out of his loose collar, his suit more rumpled than I remembered it.

His mild eyes looked up, startled, almost as though he thought I was an intruder.

"What do you want?" he said. Then his eyes widened and he lolloped across the hall like a great shaggy puppy, one slipper flapping off, his pipe and feather dropped to the floor and forgotten.

"It's Jess!" he shouted in his high-pitched, reedy voice. "It's Jess come back!"

There were tears in his eyes as he held me at arm's length and studied me.

"Jess," he said. "Jess." And he seemed to be rolling my name round his tongue. It made me embarrassed and ashamed of myself. "You've grown. You've put on weight proper. Where've you been? What you been doing with yourself?"

He dragged me by the arm into the kitchen, talking faster than I believed him capable of.

"Singapore. And Australia. All over the shop. I heard about you through the shipping office. I followed your ships." He sighed then and said simply: "I've missed you, Jess. It's been like a tomb here without you."

He suddenly noticed one of his slippers was missing and jumped up. "Funny," he said. "How long I been without that?" He glanced round him, anxiously, and I realised just how much he'd grown older and vaguer.

"I had it when you come in," he said. "I coulda sworn."

He hurried out of the room, just a little fussier than I remembered him, just a little more unsure of himself, just a little more absentminded.

He reappeared in the doorway a moment later, a smile on his face. He held his slipper in his hand but made no move to put it on. He sat down, bombarding me with questions. How long was I staying? What were my plans? Then his face fell suddenly and he blushed.

"You home for long, Jess?" he queried.

"Don't know," I said. "Don't suppose so."

I could see he was disappointed. "Thought you might be staying for a bit," he said. "Even wondered if you might be thinking of settling down here."

"Shouldn't think so," I admitted. I tried to be as non-committal as possible. I could never have told him that Atlantic Street would be a prison to me after my years at sea. It seemed ten times smaller than the smallest forecastle I could remember. It must have been all the things on the wall that did it – all the ornaments where Dig put his pipe cleaners, all the gilt-framed pictures, all the crowded furniture. It seemed no bigger than a rabbit hutch.

And it wasn't just the size of it. It was the stuffiness and the darkness that came from the nearness of the warehouse opposite and the narrowness of the street. Either that, or I'd grown bigger, in the way you can grow bigger than your surroundings.

"Ah, well!" Dig did his best to make his smile cheerful. "We've got to remember you're a sailor now. You've got your living to earn. P'r'aps we'll be seeing more of you, though?" He ended on an anxious, questioning note.

"Yes," I said, and I meant it. "I'll be coming home more often."

Dig grinned, then his grin died and a look of weariness crossed his face.

"You ought to go and see your Ma, Jess," he said. "She's always asking for you. She's often wondered how you are. Slip up and see her."

As I left the room I had the feeling that he'd suddenly become conscious of that thing that separated us, that relationship which bound me to Ma despite our differences, but was denied to him. His eyes had an unhappy look and the excitement had gone out of them.

"Don't be too long, Jess," he said, then he hurriedly added:

"But don't worry about me. You can see me any time. Your Ma's fairly well just now and she wouldn't want to see you if she had one of her spells."

Ma's room was in its usual semi-darkness and as I entered I found myself wondering with amazement how anyone could live in such self-entombment for so long. Dimly, I saw the figure in the bed, swathed round with clothes; cheap magazines on the floor and on the eiderdown; dead flowers in vases. Ma was always too occupied with her grievance to empty them.

I edged into the room, half-suffocated by the stale, warm smell of it.

"Hello, Ma," I said loudly, half hoping she was asleep so that I needn't disturb her. "It's Jess."

The interview was a difficult one. I was as uncomfortable as usual before her. There was no longer any love left in her for anything except herself.

"Been long enough making up your mind to come home," she said.

"Never had a chance before," I lied cheerfully. "Never paid off here before."

"Forgotten your old Ma," she complained. "Now you've grown up you've no time for her. Expect it's girls and that. They always say boys soon grow out of wanting their Ma."

"No, Ma," I said. "I haven't forgotten you. See, I brought you a present."

I passed over a silk shawl I'd bought in India years before. As a matter of fact, I'd bought it for Minnie, then decided she wouldn't like it, and it had been in my kit-bag ever since. I'd remembered it at the last minute and dug it out for Ma.

I needn't have bothered, though. She hardly looked at it.

"Shan't ever need it," she said. "Never get around to sitting up these days. Proper bedfast, I am."

I knew she was lying because half her magazines and a bowl of fruit were on the dressing-table out of her reach, and the knowledge that she was putting on a show for me destroyed what little sympathy I had left for her.

"Bedfast," she repeated. "And nobody comes near me half the time. And me unable to help meself. That Dig never bothers these days."

It made me angry to hear her talk like that. I knew Dig was wearing himself to a frazzle running up and downstairs for her, doing the shopping and the errands, getting up practically in the middle of the night to clean the house before he went to work. Besides, I could tell she pottered about the bedroom in her aimless fashion, because her bedroom slippers were under the bed and her dressing-gown was over the chair. I suddenly wondered whether I was just the result of a night out on the spree, or whether Ma had once been intelligent and attractive – sufficiently to make a man want to take her in his arms.

"What's the matter?" Her voice interrupted my thoughts suddenly. "Gone quiet, haven't you? Never a word for your Ma."

I struggled on for about a quarter of an hour, trying to make intelligent conversation with her, but she wasn't interested in the ships I'd been in or the countries I'd seen. I could see she was trying to read a magazine out of the corner of her eye and I gave up in disgust.

Outside on the landing I listened to her while she gave me a list of instructions to be passed on to Dig. I felt I'd like to go in and shake her out of her silly self-sympathy.

Once, I suppose, I'd regarded her with affection – as a child, I must have done, because she was my mother – but now there was nothing left to love. Even the dreary whine that came through the door irritated me. I found I couldn't feel anything for her but anger for the misery she'd caused Dig. I felt almost that there was no kinship between us; that she was nothing more than a disembodied illness, and even that largely imaginary. There were half a dozen questions I'd been intending to ask her for a long time but I knew they'd always remain unanswered now; part of the past, far beyond the dark wall of bitterness she'd erected between herself and the rest of the world.

That autumn the weather was mild and sunny for a spell, with warm, bright days full of light breezes. Old Boxer and Yorky seemed to have disappeared into some back-alley haunt of their own and I rarely saw them. When I did, they were grey-faced and stale with liquor, only out in the daylight for food.

I moved my belongings to Dig's on one of Wiggins' barrows and, with Dig's aid, borrowed one of the dinghies from the boat-yard to make full use of daylight far out beyond St Andrew Head. I drifted idly in the sunshine as I trailed a line over the stern for pollock, just as I had as a boy, staring deeply down into the dark waters, forgetful of troubles, and the restlessness that made me itch to be off to sea again.

Often Kate was with me, her thin suit covered by one of my jerseys, the wind in her hair, her cheeks glowing, her eyes bright with happiness. She'd been unwilling at first. She was afraid of the sea and disliked the motion of a boat, but she'd agreed in the end.

"How long are you going to be home, Jess?" she asked me as we lolled over the gunwale. We were idly holding fishing-lines. Our hair was tousled with the breeze and our feet were in the bilge-water that sloshed around in the bottom of the boat.

I was non-committal. I was enjoying myself at home – more than I could have imagined. Life was better than I'd felt it could be. "Dunno," I said cheerfully, keeping my eyes on a snarl in the line I was untangling. "Got another week or so before I must go to London to take my ticket. After that I might come back here again. Or I might go straight off to sea. Depends how the money spins out."

I saw her look at me with a sudden fear. In the past few days we'd drawn closer than I'd believed she'd allow.

"Do you want to go back, Jess?" she asked, and she seemed to be hardly daring to anticipate my answer.

"I don't know," I grinned. "Sometimes I do."

My eyes must have had a faraway look as I spoke, for Kate suddenly seemed cold and she shuddered. But it wasn't the nip in the air that caused it. It was the old trouble. The trouble that had made her hesitate when I'd asked to see her again that first night I was home; that thing that was always popping up between us. It had caused more than one odd moment of coolness in the past few days. She was fighting against her own emotions, reminding herself persistently that I was a sailor with a sailor's instincts. Ashore I was unreliable, untruthful and restless. God knows, she must have realised I was a bit different from the shifty-eyed rat who'd fathered her, but that didn't help her. Every time she saw that look in my eyes – and it's a look that comes to every matelot's eyes occasionally, even though he doesn't know it's there – she was telling herself that the town couldn't hold me, that I'd more wandering to do before I could stop.

There was something powerful pulling at me, she was saying to herself, and in a way she was right. It was a strong pull. It had all the weight of the seven seas behind it and all the world besides. There was too much of the sea in me now for the narrow ocean that lay beyond St Andrew Light to satisfy me.

When a man's been washed by spray from half the oceans of the world and blown by half its gales, it puts something into his system that can't be thrown off overnight.

"Couldn't you settle here, Jess, if you wanted to?" Kate asked suddenly, and she looked as though she were probing a wound, as though she didn't want to hear my reply.

"Might," I smiled. I couldn't lie to her. She'd have known straight away. "But not yet. The place seems so small."

I was thinking of the width of ocean that gives a man a feeling of freedom from all the chafing ties that bind him to a landman's life, just as they'd held Dig to home – an office, a sick wife, his friends, all those things that held him tight to the dark town I could see rising and falling over the bow of the dinghy. I remembered suddenly the tall, shuttered houses of Copenhagen, the hot oven-draught of Kissy Street in Freetown, with its stale-smelling bars set on the edge of the sizzling red road that ran to the bush through the beaten-out-tin dwellings, and the soft beauty of blue Table Mountain rising sheer above Cape Town.

"There's such a lot to see in the world, Kate," I said, slowly. All the desire to stay in England was slipping away from me again. I felt I'd only touched the fringe of travel and must explore further before I stopped.

There seemed a shadow between us now, as though a cloud had crossed the sun, and the soft wind that blew from the south had taken on a chill. I pulled in my line and hauled the brown lugsail up so that it fluttered in the light breeze, shook itself out, then swelled and filled. Kate watched me silently. Her expression seemed to say something had been stolen away from her.

It was growing dark as we drew silently alongside the wharf and neither of us had spoken. I made fast the painter and jumped ashore, heaving Kate after me. Still in silence, we unstepped the mast and lashed the sails and carried them to the shed where they were kept.

The place was dusky with evening as we put away the canvas and turned towards the door.

"Kate." I saw her jump as I spoke suddenly out of the darkness.

I was conscious of the difference in her demeanour. The liveliness had gone out of her. "I'm sorry, Kate," I said. "I don't know what I said to hurt you."

My hands were at her elbows now, and I could feel her warm through the thickness of the jersey as I turned her towards me. She was trembling.

I was going to kiss her, to try and put things right, but as I bent towards her she suddenly twisted and turned away. "No, Jess," she whispered, "don't kiss me."

"Why not, Kate?" I said. "We've been happy together."

"No, I'd rather not." Her voice trembled as she spoke.

"Is there someone else, Kate?" I asked, puzzled.

"No, Jess," she whispered, "there's no one else."

"Then what is it?" I felt a little irritated. Something was worrying her but she wouldn't take me into her confidence, and it annoyed me. "Why won't you let me kiss you, Kate?"

"No, Jess," she murmured unhappily. "I'd rather you didn't."

I dropped my hands from her elbows. I knew what the trouble was. She'd been self-dependent too long, and she'd seen that look in my eyes in the boat out beyond St Andrew Head.

"I'm sorry, Kate." I spoke slowly as I moved away. "I felt we'd got on well together."

We parted awkwardly at the gate. I had an idea she distrusted me. Then I got to thinking she was looking for someone who could offer her more than I could, and I began to get angry.

"Good night, Kate," I said coolly. "Be seeing you again sometime."

I knew she was watching me as I walked away. But there was nothing I could do about it. It seemed to be up to her now.

four

The following days dragged past like an old tramp in heavy weather. Even the dinghy beyond St Andrew Light seemed to have lost its attraction. Kate seemed inaccessible. During the day it seemed she was busy and in the evening she'd other interests. I'd been handed my cards...

It was at the end of this period that I ran across Pat Fee again, the same gaudy Pat as before, with the same fleshy face that had just too wide a smile and eyes that were just a little too close together, the same good looks and the same glib tongue. The same old Pat you could trust as far as you could throw a grand piano.

His clothes were flashy and he looked like the prosperous bookmaker he'd become, a long way removed from the shabby lodging-house where the smell of kippers and fish and chips seemed to cling to the damp walls.

" 'Ello, young Jess," he said, waving a cigar between his thick fingers. "Hear you've been seen around with our Kate. You want to be careful of her, brother. She's ice, man, ice. She fair gives me the shivers when she looks at me. Give me a gel with a bit of warmth about her and come-to-bed eyes."

I wasn't wanting company just then, especially company that took pleasure in reminding me of Kate, but he slapped me on the back and grinned into my face. "Oh, come on, young Jess. Keep your hair on. Come and have a drink. Pat Fee's not the bloke to bear a grudge. If I've narked you come and see it off with a pint, man, or a drop of rum if it suits you best."

I followed him into the hotel he chose. I was indifferent for once whether he went or stayed, and hardly heard as he began to tell me how his business was flourishing.

"I'm doing fine, man," he grinned. "You ought to see me on the job. Pat Fee keeps his hands clean these days. Still do a bit of buyin' and sellin' from time to time, mind you. Scrap, y'know. Money in it. Times are good just now." He leaned forward and I noticed he'd acquired the habit of talking behind an outstretched palm – slyly, shiftily. "But it's the betting where I make me cash, Jess, boy. Got on like a house on fire as soon as I set up on me own. Got a good tip, by the way, if you'd like me to put 'alf a quid on for you. No?" He raised his eyebrows at my refusal. "Oh, well, no accounting for tastes. Some people I know'd give their right arm for the chance." His talk was fast, slick and oily, the market-seller's line, the dockside shyster's gab. Suddenly he reminded me of Nanjizel, the little shark I met the night I went to sea, the little rat in the bowler hat who'd got away with my suit-case. Remembering that Pat had had hold of my lapel in one of his more intimate confidences, I instinctively felt for my wallet.

His flow of conversation continued. It was pretty onesided, for I was answering in monosyllables, my mind elsewhere. But it wasn't long before it dawned on me he was only seeking reassurance on something that was troubling him. I expect that was the only reason he'd bothered to speak to me. He was worried about the uneasy state of the Continent and its effect on his business.

" 'Ere, Jess," he said, after beating about the bush for a while, going to Cape Town to get to Glasgow sort of stuff. "You've been about a bit. Hamburg and them places. D'you reckon these Nazzies are wantin' another war?"

"I don't know," I said. I didn't either. "You'd better read the papers. They'll tell you more than I can."

"Oh, come off it, man!" Pat had the landbound man's respect for the traveller. "You musta seen something. All this Heil Hitler lark. Ain't you seen that?"

"I suppose so," I admitted. "But I'm blowed if I know what it's all about."

"*I* reckon there's a war brewin' up," he said gloomily, as though he were disappointed at my inability to reassure him. "Proper gets me down, it does, too. Just when a chap's gettin' a bit of a business together, a dust-up comes along and knocks the bottom out of it. Still" – he brightened up – "chaps'll still want a bit of a flutter even if there's fightin', won't they?"

I grinned. Still the same old Pat. Come the end of the world, he'd be thinking up some catch-penny scheme.

Reckon I'll get a job in the docks if the balloon does go up," he was saying, staring at his fingernails. "They'd find me something to do. There's a few blokes there as owes me money. Might be glad to find me something if I was to square the debt for 'em. I shouldn't be called up if I was on important war work, would I? And I could still run me business in me spare time. Might pick up a customer or two, in fact."

I laughed. "You'd better look slippy," I said. "The Navy might get you first." The sudden startled look on Pat's face was like a tot of rum to me. "You're just about the right age, I said, rubbing salt into the wound. "You'd look a bit of all right in bell-bottoms with those posh hands of yours holding a fender overside for a destroyer to come alongside."

"Oh, well!" Pat feigned indifference he didn't seem to feel. "It's all the same. Wun't mind if they did, really. I've 'ad about enough of this bloody 'ole. It's as dead as mutton. Might even join up without 'em fetching me."

"How about comin' to sea, Pat?" I suggested, feeling for once I'd got the measure of him. "I'd look after you."

"I might at that," he said, though he flashed me a sour look. "After all," he went on, "there's plenty of birds. A wife in every port. I know you blokes." He grinned with a sudden malicious look and made a thrust back at me.

"Been along to Minnie's since you came home?" he asked.

I glanced quickly at him and caught a sly cunning in his eye that made me feel almost certain he knew of the incident of Minnie's kiss before I left for sea.

His words suddenly reminded me of her, and her hot, veiled eyes, and I realised I'd almost forgotten her in spite of the hold she'd had on me once. There'd been a time in my early days at sea when in a flood of sentimentality I'd sent her letters, one at every port we touched, letters she'd never bothered to answer. And parcels. Big ones. Parcels of dress material and knick-knacks from bazaars in ports east of Suez. That had been over and done with for a long time now, but as Pat mentioned her I found my lips had gone hot and dry and I had to swallow before I could speak.

"What's happened to Minnie these days?" I asked carelessly. Too carelessly it must have been, for Pat grinned. I'd suddenly forgotten Kate as Minnie appeared in my mind, sharp and clear as if I'd seen her only the day before yesterday, full-bodied and warm-lipped, her eyes making promises she never kept. "Yes," I said slowly, "what's happened to Minnie?"

Pat picked up his glass suddenly and buried his nose in it.

"Minnie?" he said, and his words were hollow inside it. "Oh, she gets me down."

As he spoke I saw his glance flicker backwards in a shifty look, and I went hot with rage as I realised there was still something between Pat and Minnie, as there always had been and probably always would be.

"What's she doing now?" I repeated, and my voice sounded harder.

"Minnie?" Pat was fiddling with a cigarette packet now. "Lookin' after the Steam Packet, of course. What you expect? Gawd, I don't know," he said fiercely. "Ain't seen 'er for weeks. Her Ma got the dropsy, you know, and Minnie's runnin' the pub."

"How is she?" I asked, suddenly desperate for news of her.

"Same as always," Pat said.

"What's she look like?"

"What's she look like? Same as before. Pretty as a picture, of course. Always did like them buxom women, me."

I clenched my fists. These suggestions of illicit love-making that Pat was so fond of always made me want to knock his teeth down his throat.

"Tell me some more," I asked, forcing the thought away for the sake of news of Minnie.

"Some more? Christ, do you want me to draw you a picture?" Pat stared. "What's up? Fancy yer chances? Listen, chum," he went on. "You go along an' see 'er. Minnie ain't no angel, you take it from me. You go and try your 'and."

I was just going to tell him what I thought of him and his dirty little confidences but at that moment the door opened and another customer walked in towards the bar, a flashy-looking chap with padded shoulders and yellow shoes.

" 'Ello, Pat." He was smiling, but there was no friendliness or humour in the gesture. "Been lookin' all over town for you, I 'ave. Where you been?"

"Oh, knockin' about," Pat said warily.

"Knockin' about, eh? 'Avin' a drink or two, I suppose?" The man's words were soft but his voice was dry and hard with anger.

"One or two," Pat agreed.

"An' a little flutter 'ere and there?"

"Yes, I suppose so."

"Then if you can bloody well amuse yerself boozing an' gambling you can at least leave my missis alone," the newcomer said, suddenly ugly.

"Your missis?" Pat's face was a mask of innocence, as though butter wouldn't melt in his mouth. "What you talkin' about? I don't know your missis. Never met 'er." His eyes flickered beyond the newcomer and he put his hand on the man's lapel. " 'Alf a mo' mate. Just got to go to the Gentlemen. If you're still here when I come back I'll buy you a drink – if that's all you want."

Before he could be stopped he'd slid away with the ease of a professional boxer escaping a clinch and was half-way through the door in a moment.

The man whirled. "No, you don't!" he shouted. "I know you, Pat Fee!" And he was out of the door after Pat, and I was left alone almost before the scene had registered on my mind.

"A proper card, that Fee," the barman pointed out casually as he wiped the sloppy counter. "I dare bet you half a dollar you'll not see 'im in 'ere for a week or two."

I finished my drink thoughtfully, my mind busy, and went to the door. There was no sign of Pat or his pal.

I shrugged. I was still thinking about Minnie. I'd forgotten Kate suddenly in remembering Minnie, and I felt better. I lit a cigarette and, putting on a roll to let everyone know I was just home from sea, I ran down the steps.

I was so busy cutting a dash with myself I never saw the woman I crashed into until it was too late.

"Now look what you've done," she said, her voice shrill with indignation. "If only people would be more careful, there'd be fewer accidents." She pushed her hat straight, jerked her skirt and jacket into their proper places and began to smooth herself down.

"People who don't look where they're goin' shouldn't be allowed on the streets," she went on loudly as she bent to pick up the parcels she'd dropped. "Well?" She turned and looked up over her shoulder at me. "Don't think of helping people, do you? An' who're *you* staring at? What you think I am? A tart, or something?"

I couldn't say anything at first. I was gaping at her, delight in my eyes, my mouth in a wide smile.

"Minnie," I managed to get out at last.

"Who do you think you're Minnie-ing?" she said indignantly. "My, you're a fast worker, aren't you? You'll be askin' me out next."

Then, as she saw me staring in obvious admiration, her temper softened and she thrust at her hair with plump white fingers, flattered and embarrassed.

I was still gaping, startled that she should appear so unexpectedly. All the anger I'd felt at Pat's comments on her disappeared as I grinned at her.

She was no different from the Minnie I remembered. Just a little more mature. Just a little fuller and rounder. Her bosom was deeper and softer, and there were lines at the corners of her eyes. But otherwise she'd not altered a scrap. She was the same Minnie who'd kissed me to make me wet my britches and then had laughed at my embarrassment. But I'd forgotten all that now. To me, fresh home from sea and soft as any sailor over a girl – soft as a brush, I was – this was no bawdy Minnie, lusty and sensual. This was the Minnie I'd dreamed about in the night watches, the Minnie I'd sentimentally pictured as I chipped rusty ironwork and slapped on paint in the steaming heat of the tropics. This was the Minnie whose figure and face and soft body had come to my mind on torrid nights on the Equator, and given me sleepless, tossing hours, until the distance and the passage of years had finally made her image faint.

"Minnie," I grinned, "don't you remember me?"

She stared, then her full, red lips opened in a broad smile that showed strong white teeth, as sturdy and animal as herself.

"Well, if it isn't young Jess!" She stared at me in genuine pleasure. "My Gawd, you're a bit of a one, aren't you? A proper card, you are."

"Remember that kiss you gave me, Minnie?" I asked. "Before I went off to sea?"

"Went off to sea, did you?" Her eyes widened. "My word! You're a caution. Of course I remember it. Let's give you another for coming home." She flung her arms round my neck in a full-blooded hearty gesture and planted a noisy wet kiss smack on my lips.

I suddenly remembered what Pat had told me.

"Heard your Ma was sick," I said awkwardly. "Sorry about it, Minnie."

"Sorry? So am I." She suddenly looked downcast and bent to pick up her parcels. "Hospital. That's where she is, and me runnin' the pub on me own."

"Looking after that place on your own?" I asked. "Aren't you frightened?"

"Frightened? What, of them old bums as come in there? Not me." She looked capable of dealing with anyone or anything as she spoke. Then she was suddenly drooping and miserable again. "But I get sick of it, Jess. 'Tisn't the work that's hurting me. I'm strong as a horse. But I get scared in case Ma dies."

"You'll be all right, Minnie," I clumsily tried to reassure her. "You've always got the business."

"That's just the trouble," she snapped. "I haven't. If Ma pops off, what happens to me? The licensing bench'll have the licence off me right sharp, and no messing."

"Licence?" I gaped, uncomprehending.

"Yes, stupid. The pub! They won't let an unmarried woman keep a pub. Didn't you know that?"

"Oh! Won't they?" I hadn't been aware of the intricacies of the licensing laws.

"Think I'll not conduct the place properly," she said savagely. "Ma's all right, being a widow. But I'm not a fit and proper person, not being married. Reckon I need a man about the place, they do. Off their onions, they are. Lot of old grannies. Queen Victoria stuff, that is. A man!" She made a gesture that was very much like a spit. "Man! I can manage that lot as comes in the Steam Packet with one hand tied behind me back. Still" – she gave me a sidelong glance and her eyes were veiled suddenly – "perhaps I *could* do with a man about the place sometimes, come to think of it. Come on home with me, Jess, and have a drink. I get a bit lonely at times. We can catch a bus along the road."

"Never mind the bus," I said enthusiastically, gallant as you please. "Let's have a taxi."

"A taxi? My word." Minnie laughed. "I haven't been in a taxi since I went to Pa's funeral. You in the money, or something?"

"Six months' pay!"

"Six months' pay! My!" Minnie took my hand in her hot, moist palm. "At sea all that time? Well, come and have a cup of tea with me and I'll give you a meal such as you haven't had since you left home, I'll bet. I'm on me own. It'll be cosy, just the two of us."

I smiled down at her, conscious of a pulse in my temple that had started to throb.

"Just me and you," Minnie said. "Won't that be nice?"

five

From the moment that Minnie took me home I was a dead duck. I never left her alone in the days that followed. Sailors are simple people really, and I was no match for her slick sophistication, and for wits that had been sharpened by contact with men every day of her life. She had me trussed and hog-tied in twenty-four hours. Within two days there was room for no one but her in my brain.

Neglecting Dig, I began to hang around the Steam Packet, waiting for a chance to see her, smoking too many cigarettes, drinking too much ale and getting too little fresh air. I'd been admitted freely into the untidy back kitchen to do my drinking and Minnie would come with her glass of gin and talk to me while the rest of the Steam Packet struggled along with only an elderly barman to keep them company. It was there, even, with a cat pawing at one leg, that I had my suppers, prepared by Minnie's own hands.

She was a clever woman, crafty even, and I never knew what she was thinking, or what was going on behind those veiled eyes of hers. She wasn't in love with me. I knew that. She liked Pat Fee's type best, the sort who could buy her things, but she seemed to snatch at my company just then as if I was the only eligible chap in the town. I suppose, if the truth were known, the reason for her mateyness was that Pat Fee's interests were elsewhere just then. Several times in the past he'd had his eye on the Steam Packet, but he'd made the mistake of taking his embraces to other quarters just at the

147

time Minnie's Ma had gone to hospital. When I came home they were passing through one of the not infrequent periods when they weren't on speaking terms.

As for me, I was being a fool, I knew, but I couldn't do anything to stop it. There was something about Minnie that took the spine out of my resolution. She was a lusty animal who needed a man's arms round her and his lips on hers. She returned my embraces with gusto and enjoyment, and with twice the enthusiasm because she needed me to keep the licence. The Steam Packet was as much to Minnie as her life. It had been the source of income to her family for two or three generations, and I expect she couldn't imagine herself living anywhere else.

Kate Fee might have saved me from my own foolishness, but there was a coolness between us that Minnie didn't help to disperse. Had Kate only known it, I needed her tenderness and serenity after the tumult of life at sea. I needed her gentleness after the rough vulgarity of forecastle conversation that was centred around women, booze and ships – in that order. There'd been other girls in other ports but they'd been merely milestones in a sailor's life, and in the warmth of Kate – like the warmth of a happy house – there was something that had been missing all my life. In the shabby, threadbare house in Atlantic Street there was precious little affection to spare for anyone with Ma as she was, and less still for me – the unwanted child.

Old Boxer and Yorky were still in town but keeping out of my way as Old Boxer had promised. Their money must have been running low, though, because I knew they'd begun to borrow on the wages of the next voyage. I saw them occasionally, bleary-eyed and stale-looking, often unshaven, their clothes rumpled through being slept in, Yorky with the inevitable parcel under his arm, bursting through its brown paper like a fat man's stomach through his waistcoat. They were still living at Pat Fee's lodging-house, feeding on sandwiches and buns and fish and chips.

When I met them they were diffident and cautious, as though the two of them, one vast and ramshackle, like some crumbling wreck, the other small and plump and white, rough and ready and Yorkshire as Ilkley Moor, had plotted to let me spend my leave in my own fashion, away for once from the sort of haunts we'd been in the habit of frequenting ashore.

It was "Having a good time, Jess?" or "Ready for going back yet, Jess?"

My replies were always non-committal. I was too deep in my affair with Minnie to know exactly what was happening to me. She affected people like that, so they didn't know whether they were coming or going. All I knew was that I was unsure of myself and my future. But I'd long ago made up my mind on *one* count.

"I'm not going to take my ticket this trip," I said. "It can wait a bit longer. I've decided to enjoy myself instead."

"Don't be a damned fool!" Old Boxer snapped immediately. His look was sour with a fortnight's drinking.

"There's plenty of time," I pointed out. "All the time in the world."

"There's never plenty of time. *I* thought there was plenty of time and look where I've ended up."

"But you was so keen, mate." Yorky shoved his concertina from one arm to the other with an asthmatic wheeze as he spoke. "You can't go off like that. We was looking forward to the party when you got your ticket, me and 'Orace. Jeeze, we'll push the boat out that night!"

"You can't go anywhere without a mate's ticket, you young fool," Old Boxer said irritably. "You don't want to live in the forecastle with a bunch of old shellbacks like us for the rest of your life, do you?"

I hesitated. "Might even take a shore job," I murmured. The idea had occurred to me some time before, but I was ashamed and half afraid of it, and I'd tried to forget it.

"What!" Yorky's sudden start set the concertina squawking. "A born sailor like you?"

"Shore job! Tchah!" Old Boxer spluttered his disgust. "You talk like a Sunday-school teacher all of a sudden. What's come over you? What is it, Jess?" he asked more gently. "When a man like you talks like that it's either a ship or a girl."

"It isn't a ship," I said. "I'm in no hurry. That's all."

"Dammit, you're right, too," he agreed. "Then it's a girl."

I shrugged and nodded.

"Yes," I said. "Suppose it is."

Yorky had moved in front of me and was staring up at me excitedly. "Well, by gum," he said. "Is it that dark young lady I saw you wi'?"

Old Boxer was silent. "Thinking of marriage, Jess?" he queried after a pause.

"Might be," I admitted.

He scratched at his two-day-old beard, his fingernail making a rasping sound on the stubble.

"Be careful, lad," he said earnestly. "Be careful, for God's sake."

"Careful?" I stared. "What for?"

"Sailors are notoriously sentimental creatures, lad, especially where women are concerned. If only because they go for long periods without their company. Sure you aren't seeing her through rose-tinted glass?"

" 'Course I'm not," I growled.

"Well, what the devil is it?" He stared at me with suddenly bright eyes. "Are you ashamed of her?"

I looked up sharply at him but his expression told me nothing of the thoughts that were going on inside his head. His words had caught me unawares, though, and for a moment I didn't know how to answer. In the end I decided I couldn't explain and I said nothing.

The Steam Packet was only a small place, but it had stood in Gibraltar Lane near to the river since before Trafalgar. It was a square, box-like little building of grey stone. Its interior was old-fashioned and had an air of faded gentility about it that hadn't improved under the management of Minnie's Ma with her slap-dash, untidy, gin-drinking habits. The steam packet it took its name from had long since disappeared and given place to the oil-tankers that used the docks to discharge their cargoes. But the aspidistras and the old-fashioned pictures on the walls that were popular while it still plied remained, an odd, dusty background to the brighter chintzes and cheap prints that Minnie had introduced. The place had a suggestion of having lived beyond its time. Its ceilings were cracked, its planks feeble and its doors ill-fitting so that the whole structure seemed to groan when anyone crossed the floor.

Occasionally, when I was hanging about the bar there in the glow of Minnie's smile, I saw Old Boxer and Yorky, eyeing me resentfully from the tap-room. They were looking for a sign that the affair was coming to an end, I reckon. They were waiting for me, putting off ship after ship in the hope I'd join them. As a result they were short of cash and often on the cadge, after free drinks, with Yorky offering a tune on his concertina in exchange.

"What d'yer fancy, miss," he'd say to Minnie. " 'Down at the Old Bull and Bush' or 'Tararaboomdeay'?"

His repertoire was limited, but Minnie always asked for something he could play. She was sharp enough to realise his goodwill was worth cultivating.

As for me, I was indifferent to anyone's opinion by that time. There was only one thing in my consciousness. And that was Minnie. The desire to be near her, which had been a murmur in me ever since I was a boy, had grown to a shout now and I couldn't deny it any longer.

And I was wanting more than merely Minnie's conversation. God knows, it was threadbare enough. I was wanting Minnie herself. I was wanting to possess her, and the thought of being married to her stood out in my brain as big as the *Queen Mary*. Deep down inside me, I knew I was making a fool of myself, but some trick of fate had made us so that I could never quite throw her out of my mind.

Her disagreements with the elderly barman she employed became more frequent and violent – I didn't know then they were cunningly engineered by Minnie's diamond-sharp little brain – and they reached their climax one night in a crescendo of strong words and high voices that left me and Minnie alone in the Steam Packet at closing time.

Minnie was sniffing loudly as she wiped a glass in a corner.

"Dunno what I'm going to do now," she mumbled. "People never seem to behave like you expect 'em."

"We'll manage all right, Minnie," I said awkwardly. "Don't worry. We'll be all right."

"It's a good job it's closing time."

"And tomorrow we'll sign on somebody else. Somebody who'll do as he's told."

"Don't know what I'm going to do about that licence if Ma pops off," she complained. "Them magistrates'll think I can't run a pub if I can't keep a barman. People take advantage of me proper because I'm only a girl." She sniffed loudly. "Don't dash off, Jess. Stay and have a bit of supper with me and a drink. I'm feeling a bit low."

There was a huge fire in the back kitchen when we went there after we'd locked the doors and hung the glass-clothes over the pumps to dry.

"Cold outside," Minnie said, putting more coal on the fire. "We might as well be cosy."

"People are a worry to me," she said as she sat back on the settee beside me. "You seem to be the only person I can trust, Jess. Give us a kiss."

As I released her she stretched luxuriously and pushed the cat to the floor.

"Hop it, you," she said. "There isn't room for three of us on here." She turned and eyed me sleepily. "Get us another gin, Jess, love."

She leaned against me as she sipped the drink, then slid an arm round my neck. "Give us another kiss, Jess," she said in her hearty manner. "A real one, this time."

My embrace was fierce and passionate, and Minnie eventually pushed me away, laughing.

"You are a one, aren't you!" she giggled. "Gawd, it's gone warm in here all of a sudden. It's you, Jess, making a girl's blood boil." She looked sideways at me and began to fiddle with her beads.

"I'm goin' to undo me frock a bit," she said archly. "That's the worst of being fleshy like me. I get so hot."

She unbuttoned her dress at the throat and leaned back languorously on the sofa, eyeing me under veiled lids.

" 'Smatter, Jess?" she asked innocently. "You findin' it hot, too?"

All I could see was a white throat and the curve of white, swelling breasts, and a suggestion of satin that only partly hid the shadow between them.

"Minnie," I said, leaning towards her. My lips were suddenly stiff.

She put her arms round me and drew me towards her, strongly, passionately, and kissed me with a warm, moist mouth. Then she pushed me away again, abruptly, roughly, almost as though she'd no time for me.

"It's no good, Jess," she said. "I'll have to have these damn' corsets off."

She rose and moved towards the stairs. As the door closed behind her I heard a bump and a cry, and, darting after her, I found her holding her ankle.

153

"Oh, blast it!" she wailed. "Everything's going wrong. I've twisted me ankle now, Jess. Help me upstairs. You're broadminded. You won't mind being in a lady's bedroom."

My arm round her, we began to stumble up the stairs and I sensed I was being caught by the oldest trick in the world. But my common sense was fogged by the desire in me.

She turned to me, managing a pathetic smile, though her brain must have been ice-cold and clear. I was a nice enough lad, she was thinking, I'll bet, and she might even grow to like me. Not as exciting as Pat Fee. He'd that look in his eyes that made a girl feel he was undressing her. I'd seen it often, and Minnie liked that kind of look.

"You go and sit down, Jess," she said. "It's not as bad as I thought." But she leaned a little more heavily on me, so that her breast pressed softly on the back of my hand as I held her elbow.

"I'll see you upstairs safely first," I said. I was suddenly aware of a thunderous pulse in my temple and a dryness in my throat.

In the middle of the bedroom was an old-fashioned wooden bed, square and ungainly, and there was a comfortlessness about the room I hadn't expected. Minnie pushed me away and sat down on the bed, fiddling with her dress.

"Gawd, that room," she said.

She lay back on the pillows, smiling up at me, her eyes suddenly bright, her lips parted, her teeth showing. There seemed to be more satin showing at her breast now and more blue-veined white skin and soft round flesh.

I suddenly noticed a picture on the table by the bed, and I saw Minnie frown as I stared at it. Pat Fee's heavy, handsome face gazed out at me from the silver frame, starting a whole host of uneasy thoughts at the intimacy it suggested.

Then Minnie's hand snatched the picture away from under my eyes and slammed it face downwards on the floor by the side of the bed.

"It's an old one, Jess," she said. "It is, honest,"

I wasn't convinced, and there must have been a stubborn look in my eyes, for Minnie turned her face sideways into the pillow.

"Jess," she murmured, "I thought you loved me. Be nice to me. I'm frightened of this old place on my own."

I leaned over and took her in my arms. She twisted on to her back and flung her arms round my neck, warm and soft and fiercely passionate, and her fingers were in my hair. Her mouth was by my ear, whispering urgently, her breath hot on my skin.

"Jess," she begged, "don't leave me tonight. Stay here with me."

Desire like a sweeping wave surged over me, and I kissed her white throat and down to the soft flesh that was no longer hidden by satin.

Minnie was staring at the ceiling when I awoke, her eyes bright and alert. She turned as she saw me move and slipped silently into my arms.

In the grey light of the morning the room seemed smaller and shabbier and more untidy. I became aware of clothes crumpled and shapeless on the chairs and a pair of curling shoes under an old-fashioned wash-hand stand.

Minnie's voice was by my ear, meek and ashamed.

"Jess, we oughtn't to have done it. It wasn't right."

"Don't be soft, Minnie," I said. "You can't help things like that. After all, you're a grown woman and I'm a man."

"But, Jess, what will people say?" She suddenly put a hand to her mouth and began to moan. "What if I have a baby? I'd have to leave the Steam Packet if Ma was taken. Oh, Gawd!"

She began to sniff and seemed to shrink in my arms.

"They'll find out!" she wailed. "They'll not stand for this, them magistrates. Me! An unmarried woman!"

"You won't be unmarried long, Minnie," I said softly.

She raised her eyes to mine and, God help me, I failed to see the bright, eager light in them.

"Do you mean that? Do you mean you want to marry me?"

I hadn't really meant that at all, but, suddenly, it was said, and I felt as though I'd put another milestone in my life behind me. Minnie kissed me fiercely – though, fortunately for my peace of mind, I didn't realise then just what in-stigated her passionate enthusiasm.

"Oh, Jess," she said, hugging me happily. "Now I shall never have to leave the Steam Packet."

And, in spite of the warmth and softness of her and her fierce embraces, I suddenly felt there was an anti-climax, and the room seemed bleak.

six

Minnie and I were married with a haste that opened a few eyes and set the tongues wagging round the neighbourhood.

Dig expressed an unhappy, fumbling disapproval but it was ineffectual and indefinite, and useless as an opinion. "It's your affair," he said shyly. "It's nothing to do with me. You're old enough to know your own business, but are you sure you're doing what's right?"

"Why shouldn't I be?" I was touchy and resentful of criticism.

He shrugged and flapped his hands awkwardly, then picked up a magazine and appeared to immerse himself in it.

"That's for you to decide," he said into the book. "If you've thought it over, there's no need for me to say anything."

Ma's comment was terse and to the point. "I married beneath me," she said. "Why shouldn't you?"

The days before the wedding were a bit of a trial for everybody. Even Old Boxer disapproved and showed his disapproval strongly.

"She's a wrong 'un, Jess," he snapped. "I know she's a wrong 'un. God knows what she's up to, for she's not your type any more than you're hers."

"Don't he damn' silly," I said. "Why should she be up to anything? Why should she want to marry me, apart from love? I've got nothing. I'm only a sailor."

"You *were* a sailor, Jess," he said, and there was a contempt in his voice that made me squirm inside. "You smell stale now with too much drinking."

He drew his hand across his face hurriedly.

"God!" he said. "Listen to me! 'Too much drinking,' and me boozing myself bow-legged every night. I'm a sanctimonious old devil. My God, I am!" He looked earnestly at me. "Take no notice of me, lad." He hesitated, then, as though the words were wrenched from him, he burst out: "But you're too good for this bitch of a woman! You're wasting yourself on her!"

He watched my face and seemed to shrink into himself. "I'm sorry, Jess," he mumbled. "I shouldn't have said that about her. It was wrong. It'll do no good at all."

"I'm blowed if I know what you've got against her," I said.

"I'm blowed if I know myself," he sighed. "But she's a wrong 'un, Jess. Doesn't anyone's opinion mean anything to you?" He seemed to be trying to tell me something without using all the words, but I was in no mood just then to understand anyone. I could hardly understand myself.

"It doesn't mean as much as Minnie," I said coldly.

The concentrated disapproval of everyone around me seemed to make me all the more determined. It was almost as if the issue had ceased to be whether I loved Minnie or not, but whether I was going to triumph over the opposition to the marriage.

"And, anyway," I asked, "why is she a wrong 'un? Just tell me that. How do you know?"

"How does anyone know?" Old Boxer queried wearily. "But I've known too many. God knows I have."

"I don't know what's wrong with her, Jess," he went on, as though he were making a tremendous effort to be lucid. "But there's something about her I don't like – something that never sees daylight – "

"You're a damned old hypocrite!" I shouted in a sudden fury. "Go back to your bloody booze and leave me to sort out my own affairs!"

A look of torment crossed his face, almost as if I'd struck him, and he turned away.

"I'm sorry, Jess," he said quietly. "You're quite right. It's nothing to do with me. I shall come to your wedding, of course, if I may."

"Though at first you might like to be best man," I mumbled. I felt as unhappy as he did. In actual fact, I hadn't expected seeing him at the wedding, decrepit, sick at heart and shabby, enough to take the pleasure out of anything, but I had to say something to cheer him up.

He turned a bleak look on me, as though his heart were being torn out of him.

"I'd be glad to, Jess," he said. "I'd be glad to."

Neither Dig nor Ma were at the wedding. Dig sent his excuses, saying he couldn't get away from work, and even stayed late at the office – much to Ma's annoyance – in case I should call to enquire. But his subterfuge was easy to penetrate, as he must have known it was.

Kate Fee's invitation had been answered with a brief note that showed none of her emotions and left me feeling depressed. I thought of her several times before I left for the wedding. She'd been to blame at first for the coldness between us, but I'd done nothing to help her overcome her fears. In fact, dashing after Minnie the way I had and whipping her off to church as though I couldn't wait to get her into bed must have made her more than ever convinced she was right in her opinion of me...

Although he was far from sober, Old Boxer performed his duties as best man with a curious old-world dignity, gravely polite to Minnie's relations in a way that was instinctive rather than studied. But afterwards, back at the Steam

Packet, without saying a word to anyone, without even congratulating me and Minnie, he proceeded to drink himself stupid. He sagged speechlessly in a corner, oblivious to the other guests and the noise around him, still drinking long after he was drunk. He stood swaying on his feet, spilling the whisky from his glass on to the guests near him while he gave the conventional toast, which was the only thing he said all afternoon.

Only Minnie, brazenly in white and chirpy as a cricket beside me, cheered me up as she dragged me away to introduce me to her relations.

A dreary bunch they were, too, all of them with faces as long as fiddles because Minnie's Ma was still in hospital.

"Thought you might 'ave waited till she was better," one of them even pointed out acidly.

"I'd wait till I was dead before Ma came out," Minnie said coolly. "She'll never come out till she comes out feet first."

I was aware of their shocked faces as she spoke. They were all determined to make it more of an occasion for mourning Minnie's Ma than a celebration for her daughter's wedding.

As I turned away I found myself face to face with Pat Fee. He was smarter than anyone else there, in a pearl-grey suit with a carnation in his buttonhole. His black hair was sleeked down with oil and the inevitable cigar was between his thick fingers.

" 'Lo, Jess." He grinned, showing white teeth beneath his black moustache. "Congratulations to the happy bridegroom. You're all right now, eh?" He winked and I'd have liked to have closed the other eye with my fist.

I hadn't wanted him to be present at all, but Minnie had insisted.

"But what's *he* got to be at the reception for?" I'd asked.

Minnie's anger at the question had startled me, for her eyes had blazed suddenly. "I'll show him," she grated in a fury. "He's made me mad more than once. I'll show *him* what it feels like."

I'd felt an uneasy jealousy.

"Minnie," I said, "there isn't something between you and Pat Fee, is there? You aren't wanting to marry me just to get your own back on him, are you?"

Her reply was fierce, but oddly unconvincing. "Between me and Pat Fee? A dirty bookie? Me?"

Her laugh was harsh and bitter. I'd only consented to Pat's presence because I hoped that Kate might come, too. Now, as I stared at his sardonically smiling face, I realised that Minnie's strenuous denial hadn't been a denial at all. And if Minnie had hoped to annoy Pat she failed dismally for he seemed to be enjoying himself immensely. He even went so far as to flirt with Minnie's cousin, a bouncing, fat girl with a shriek for a laugh.

"Enjoyin' yourself, Mister Fee, aren't you?" Minnie said bitterly as she passed round the sandwiches, all the liveliness gone from her suddenly.

"Always do," Pat grinned back. "Like my birds on the well-built side, Minnie, as you know."

Seething rage was in my throat as he spoke, but Minnie snatched at my arm and dragged me away.

"What did you have to invite him for?" I whispered furiously to her. "I'd like to knock his teeth down his throat."

"Wish I hadn't, now," Minnie admitted savagely. "It's sickening to see him hanging round that soft bitch. Likes 'em well-built indeed! She's *fat*. And she's over thirty if she's a day." She allowed herself a last glare at Pat, who returned it with a knowing wink and a smile that spoke worlds.

"The dirty rat!" she hissed viperishly. "And them teeth of his are only china ones, I bet."

It wasn't a happy reception. There were odd, strained silences and uncomfortable pauses when everyone stared at each other, searching for conversation. Yorky, very tipsy in a borrowed blue suit that nowhere near fitted his dumpy frame, tried to help by singing a comic song.

"There was Brown – " he yelled in a breathy tenor that set your teeth on edge

" *– upside down,*
Mopping up the whisky off the floor.
'Booze, booze!' the firemen cried,
As they came knocking at the door…"

And worst of all, there was Old Boxer in a corner, dazed and fuddled but still drinking with a fierce determination, his eyes always on me or Minnie.

Finally, long after I was sick of the whole shooting match and wanting to get away somewhere on my own in the fresh air and have a bit of peace, Minnie's Uncle Fred made a speech. I only remember its length and bad taste.

"There's one thing about this old carry-on," he said as it drew to a close. "There's one thing we can be 'appy about, anyway, even if we 'ave to be sorry for Minnie's poor old Ma in 'ospital. At least we know that if anything 'appens to 'er, we shall still be able to keep the Steam Packet in the family now that Minnie's got 'erself a 'usband."

I saw Old Boxer's head jerk up as Uncle Fred finished, and for a moment intelligence showed in his dull eyes.

"Ha!" he snorted, and all eyes in the room whipped round to him. "Ha! Now we have it! Now the cat's out of the bloody bag!"

Minnie had never liked Old Boxer. He'd always treated her with grave courtesy – for my sake, I reckon – but with a contempt he made no attempt to disguise. Everything he'd ever said to her seemed to have a veiling of sarcasm over it, and there was a sneer in his eyes whenever he looked at her.

He had the gift of making her feel embarrassed and uncomfortable, which, with Minnie, was something of a feat, and made her detest him all the more.

We were having no honeymoon – there was no one to look after the pub – and on the morning after the reception, when Minnie went downstairs, her eyes bleary with the wedding-day gin she'd drunk and her hair frizzy from the perm she'd had to get married in, she found him asleep on the seat in the taproom where he must have been all night. She came bounding back upstairs to me, her eyes glowing with fury.

"That blasted old fool's here!" she said fiercely. She was still wearing the blowsy remains of her finery, though her wedding-day bloom seemed a little faded even to me. "Your pal! Boxer!"

"He's doing no harm, is he?" I queried.

"I don't care whether he is or not. Get him out! He's no pal of mine an' he looks at me as if I was dirt. Get him out!" Her voice rose hysterically. "He's tryin' to get you away from me, Jess."

"Don't be soft," I said soothingly, startled by her anger. "There's no harm in him."

"Well, I'm not having him. Get him out. I married you. Not both of you."

"He'll go," I said angrily. "He's got enough sense not to stay longer than he's wanted. There's no need to throw him out."

"If you don't, I shall!" Minnie screamed.

"Shut up, Minnie!" I snapped. "Don't be daft. I shan't throw him out."

That started our first argument. It was an undignified affair, with us shouting at each other in the untidy bedroom, among Minnie's rumpled wedding clothes. Then, suddenly aware of what was happening. I listened to Minnie's voice in silence. Something had disappeared from my marriage already. Within a few hours of leaving church, something decent had been lost.

Minnie was a different person from the clinging, hot-eyed girl of a week ago, different even from the brazen lover. This was a new Minnie, harsh-voiced, hard-faced and independent. Or rather, this was the old Minnie, the real Minnie; and the Minnie I'd known during the last few days was the new one.

I pushed the idea aside as soon as it was born. I was determined nothing was going to spoil things. God, I'd only been married twenty-four hours!

Old Boxer was already on his feet when I arrived downstairs. He appeared to be quite sober and was trying weakly to smooth his suit. But his hands were trembling and clumsy.

"You can just get your hat and coat," Minnie was saying in a high-pitched angry voice, "an' be off. We've no time for old bums like you, Jess and me. He's a married man now and he doesn't want to be bothered with the likes of you any more."

"Damn you, shut up, Minnie!" I interrupted.

Old Boxer's eyes wavered to my face, and he gestured with his hand. "Don't worry, Jess," he said. "I'm going. I'm going home."

"You're going back to sea?"

"Only home I have."

"Let him go!" Minnie snapped. "And good riddance!"

"Shut up!" I turned furiously on her, and she backed away.

Old Boxer stared at me. "To be quite honest, Jess," he said, "I feel the need of clean sea winds and spray on me face." He looked at Minnie as he spoke and her mouth tightened. She thrust his hat at him.

"Come on, let's have you!" she hissed.

Old Boxer turned slowly towards her. Ponderously and heavily.

"My dear Messalina," he said mildly, "you're too late. I'm going. I've got to go. I couldn't stay here and watch you ruin Jess' life."

"What do you mean?" Minnie demanded loudly. "Who's ruining anybody's life? People like you want to mind what they're sayin'."

"I know now why you married him," he said. "God forgive you, I only hope he's strong enough to rid himself of you before he's sunk as low as you have."

He turned away, taking his hat out of Minnie's nerveless fingers as he moved. Then he placed a heavy hand on my shoulder for a second and walked out of the door.

seven

I hadn't been married long before I began to suspect that Minnie had made a fool of me. This Minnie I was living with was as far removed from the woman I'd dreamed of at sea thousands of miles away as I was from the kid I'd been when I first fell for her. She was even different from the lusty, hearty, loving Minnie who'd infatuated me during my leave.

This Minnie – and I realised with a shock I was supposed to live with her for the rest of my life – was a person I'd never known. She was a slattern who liked her gin, and her habits around the Steam Packet startled me.

It was useless trying to coax any order into her affairs, a waste of time trying to get things shipshape. Having made the effort to capture me she didn't seem able to produce any more interest or energy to continue it.

"It was all right for me before I married you," she complained. "It was all right for Ma. And you weren't so bothered about it before the wedding. All you wanted then was to get your hands on me."

It was a queer situation. Physically, we were perfectly matched. I was able to satisfy Minnie's desires, and she mine, and it forged strong links that prevented us from drifting apart. She was a healthy animal, full-bodied and lustful, and – though the thought was a torment to my brain – was experienced in the art of love-making. There were occasions, too, when our quarrels dissolved into merriment, for Minnie had a bawdy humour and left me shouting with laughter more than once in the middle of hot words. But these were only few and life began to have an unrestful drabness such as I'd known only in Atlantic Street before I went to sea.

It was full of deadly routine, but without any of the things that should have come from routine – comfort, cleanliness and good food. To Minnie food was a nuisance right up to the time it was eaten. She'd have starved without the frying-pan and the jam-pot.

And I suddenly began to realise with a shock that even my conversation had never roused a great deal of enthusiasm in her, in spite of the absorption she'd shown for it before we were married. Java and Bali and the Far East were of no interest to Minnie and never had been. She probably thought they were suburbs of London or somewhere like Blackpool, with a pleasure beach and roundabouts.

"I think you only married me to keep the pub," I said bitterly. And as Minnie's wide violet eyes stared up at me and she accepted the accusation without comment, I realised how right I was.

I'd had no intention when I married of forsaking the sea. I was a sailor and will be to my dying day. But Minnie seemed to have taken it for granted that I would, and she wasn't easy to argue with.

"Not much good to me at the other side of the world, are you?" she said, blunt and forthright. "Use a bit of common. I married you to keep me warm in bed, and a fat lot of good you'd be for that if you were in New York."

There seemed to be no answer to that.

There were other things, too, that didn't work out the way I'd expected. The Steam Packet, for instance. It was only when I lived in one and watched the weeks roll by that I found I'd no taste for life inside a pub. Pubs were places I'd known only for celebrations on reaching land, where matelots spent their wages in one great joyous blow-out after being kept away from drink and women and bright lights for weeks at a time. But to live in, they could soon assume the proportions of a prison.

I began to feel suffocated and as though I wanted to stretch in great muscle-cracking heaves that would shove the walls down and let the air into these stale little rooms.

Once, and only once, like a breath of sea breeze, came an unexpected letter from Old Boxer, written in a hand that was obviously unsteady. It came from Singapore, and the postmark made my heart jump awkwardly.

"*I'm in the steamer* Eastern Star," he wrote, and his bitterness showed even in the grubby, thumbed pages and the handwriting that was educated and well-formed in spite of the trembling fingers that had written it. "*She's an ill-designed, meanly-found, cock-eyed vessel built by a set of profit-making ship owners who consider cargo space before the souls of the men who have to sail in her. But still, God be praised and no thanks to them, she's heading at a rate of knots for the rising sun with the wind and tide on her stern...*"

As I stood in the beer-cellar with the sheet of paper which had been torn from an exercise book in my hand, I felt a hard lump in my throat at all that the words conjured up: the cramped forecastle, with its grumbling men and its profanity and abuse. The smell of hot engine oil, steam, straw and wet steel. The sun, brassy in the heavens and hitting upwards in hammer-blows from the iron decks. Or a soft night with the wide-eyed moon like a yellow orange on the horizon, and the Southern Cross and the glowing phosphorescence of the wake; and the cry of the watch on the forecastle head, "Two bells and all's well!"

I could just imagine Old Boxer folding the paper and putting away a borrowed stub of pencil as the watch was called out, heaving his great bulk from the comfortless forecastle bench. I could almost see him on the deck, rolling to the swing of the ship that sent the mastheads reeling round the stars, dignified by his size and the remains of breeding that still clung to him.

It was then that I suddenly realised I missed him...

I shoved the letter angrily into my pocket and poured myself a drink. I knew I was drinking too much, but it was always so easy with so much of it around. I mounted the steps from the cellar and stared through the back doorway across the river. There, near the back of the Steam Packet, it had none of the romance and bustle of the dock area or the broad freedom of the sea. There it was the receptacle for rusty tin cans and old buckets and cast-off hats and shoes.

A fine change it was, I thought bitterly, from a fresh sea breeze or a hot wind that blew from the desert. A fine change from white beaches shining in the sun, and coral gleaming in the surf. A fine change from palms and the hot red of frangipani and the glint of flying-fish.

I tossed aside my half-smoked cigarette irritably and went to the bar in an ugly temper.

Pat Fee was there, leaning on the counter, whispering to Minnie. Their heads were close together, and as I pushed open the door Pat caught sight of me out of the corner of his eye and laughed as he drew away.

"Bet you never heard that one before," he said, his voice changing.

Minnie caught the warning signal and she laughed in his face, a harsh laugh, just a bit too loud to be mirthful.

"That's a good one," she said. "Where you hear it?"

I scowled, well aware that Pat's whispering had been no smutty joke. It was the first time he'd been in the Steam Packet since Minnie's marriage, but their quarrel was obviously patched up. Minnie and Pat would always be like this, one minute not on speaking terms, the next whispering in corners in low undertones that seemed to expose all sorts of lewdness, all sorts of sordidness and cunning and distrust that made marriage into a cheap jeer.

"What do *you* want?" I demanded, glaring at Pat. I knew his presence would be the prelude to one of the stormy periods which had become a part of my life with Minnie.

Pat waved a ringed hand and leaned comfortably on the bar.

"Only come in for a drink," he said easily, chewing at his cigar. "That's what this place's for, ain't it?"

"Give him his drink, Minnie," I said shortly. "Then let him drink it up and get out."

Pat stared as he put the money on the counter.

"That's a fine welcome, I don't think," he said. "That's a proper way to get customers."

"I can just see him hurryin' in here again," Minnie added bitterly, "after you've spoke to him like that."

Pat sipped his drink and studied me coolly.

"Seen our Kate lately?" he asked suddenly.

"No," I replied shortly, hoping there was no change in my expression, for Kate's name and all the gentleness and kindness and decency it suggested gave an odd tug at my heart.

Pat shrugged, unmoved by my shortness, and continued to lean on the bar. Minnie was obviously waiting for me to go, but I stood with my hands in my pockets staring at Pat.

Eventually, even Pat – brassy as he was – began to grow restless as I stared at him, and be swallowed his drink and hurried out.

"Well, so long," he said – and he was speaking to Minnie, not to me. "I'll be seein' you."

Minnie rounded furiously on me as he left, her hands on her plump hips.

"You're a fine one," she snapped. "You're not right in your head – driving customers out. Anybody'd think we were rollin' in dough."

"Pat Fee's not the sort of customer we want here," I said.

"Even if other people don't like him" – Minnie was indignant – "he might be a friend of mine."

"It isn't so long since you'd have cut his throat," I reminded her.

"That was different. Just a little quarrel. All over now."

I looked at her, bold-eyed and full-bosomed, and I felt suddenly cold and angry.

"Just what is there between you and Pat Fee, Minnie?" I asked.

"Between me and Pat Fee?" Minnie seemed to be caught off her guard for once. "Nothing. What should there be?"

"I don't know." I turned away. "Knowing Pat Fee – and knowing you, too, I suppose – there might be anything."

"What are you accusing me of?" Minnie demanded shrilly. "Me. Your own wife. The woman you promised for better for worse, for richer for poorer, in sickness in health."

"To love and cherish till death us do part," I ended for her. "Remember that as well, Minnie."

"Why should *I* remember it so special?" Minnie stared at me for a second, then her eyes blazed suddenly, and she screamed at me. "And for God's sake stop walkin' up and down!"

I stopped dead. I'd been pacing backwards and forwards with the old habit of the deck, a habit I'd never get out of.

"Up and down. Up and down. Like a yo-yo. For God's sake, stop it!" Minnie screamed. "You drive a woman daft. You aren't on your blasted ship now."

"I sometimes wish I was."

"That's a fine thing to say," Minnie shrilled. "In front of your own wife."

"Oh, for God's sake, Minnie, shut up!" I begged. "Leave me alone for a bit."

"When I married you I thought I might get a bit of help about the place, but all I've ever had is complaints. I seen you," she said. "I seen you looking at pictures. I seen you by the river. Ships. Ships. Ships. You look at 'em like you never look at me. Why didn't you marry one? Go on. Tell me. Why didn't you marry one?"

Life became an erratic, untranquil thing. Temper was never very far after laughter, and angry words chased hot-blooded passion. It was an unpredictable, unstable affair that was still paradoxically monotonous. At times, Minnie would melt and become the loving, clinging Minnie who'd first attracted me, or a hot-eyed, voluptuous, sensual Minnie full of urgent whisperings; then the next day, all the pleasure of knowing her would he swept aside by her shrewish tempers and her slovenliness.

The tragic unevenness of our life wasn't entirely Minnie's fault. I couldn't lay *all* the blame on her. Partly it was the Steam Packet's and partly it was mine. I'd seen too much. I'd lived too fully and tasted too much of life to settle easily into the narrow confines of the town. The smell of the sea was always in my nostrils, the sound of it always in my ears.

I remembered something Yorky had once said to me: "It's easy to get to sea, son, but it's flamin' 'ard to be shot of it."

Yorky was more right than he ever suspected. I ached to see that cold, grey expanse of water and hear the hiss as it lashed across the deck and round the stanchions. I itched to feel the pulse of a vessel; to hear the creak and beat of it; to feel the rails trembling under my hand and the shrouds drumming in the wind; to feel the heaving of the forecastle and the crash as the waves hit at its steel sides. For all its lack of comfort, its burgoo and man-eating bugs, for all the calendars scarred with pencil-marks to tick off the days, for all the swearing and the dirty packs of cards that whiled away the time, there was something about it all that drew at me with a pull that was almost a physical pain.

I needed a Western Ocean blow just then to shift the cobwebs from me – one of those shut-down screaming gales that lifted the spray parallel with the iron-grey sea and clawed the foam in long white streaks down the valleys of the waves; one of those howling blasts that made a ship groan in torment and set her doing everything except stand on her head.

Gradually, almost without realising it – almost without being aware of it even – I began to find my way to Wiggins' boat-yard again. It was the only place I knew where I could get the feel of a ship again and know that it had a soul and a life as real as my own.

Dig was busy those days. Since the Munich crisis the yard was building naval launches, which had forced them to expand. The wall that had separated Wiggins' from the dilapidated wreck that had once been Old Boxer's property had been pulled down. The rubbish had been cleared and the hones of the ancient vessel that had propped up the wharf had been taken apart and given a decent resting-place. New slips had been laid where she'd rotted, and the thump of carpenters' adzes and the scream of mechanical saws were being heard again by the old wharf. Already the ribs and framework of the first of the new launches were in place.

Dig was always careful to avoid mention of Minnie when I saw him. For all his unworldliness, it hadn't taken him long to realise that something was wrong.

"Take the dinghy out, Jess," he said. "Take her beyond St Andrew. I'll fix it with the boss. It'll do you good. You're looking fidgety these days."

So, occasionally, I began to escape from Minnie in the afternoons, taking the dinghy along the shimmering water of the river to where the evening light fell, trailing a mackerel line, drawing great gulps of fresh air as though I'd been cheated of it for years. I helped them at the yard, too, when they were shorthanded, moving launches up-river or over to St Clewes even, once or twice, down the coast. I was glad of the trips, glad of the fresh breeze and the feel of a living vessel under my feet.

There was little feeling of security abroad those days, mind you. The papers were full of war scares. Every time Hitler gave a speech we all felt there was something evil darkening the sunshine. People sought their enjoyment nervously, hurriedly, anxious to make sure of it before it was snatched away from them. Gaiety became important – a sort of last port of call between peace and the disaster we all knew was on the way.

Several times I'd turned these things over in my mind as an excuse to get back to sea. Obviously my life at the Steam Packet was becoming a farce. I was nothing more than wet-nurse to a pub.

I drove the dinghy hard that summer. I must have terrified Dig with the hours I spent out of sight of the river mouth. However, I weathered the sudden squalls that blew up the Channel and returned drenched and cold and hungry. But with a strange feeling of exultation in me, as though I'd snatched something from the sea – just one breath of clean wind, just one touch of damp breeze.

Unknown to me, Kate Fee watched me go often. We exchanged only a few brief words when we met, but our early happiness together was a subject we daren't discuss.

Kate never said much, and went on watching me, those great dark eyes of hers sad, as though she was blaming herself for something that was really more my fault than hers.

"You look as though you'd lost a shilling and found tuppence," she said to me once as I came ashore.

"I reckon I did just that very thing," I replied, and I was thinking of her as I spoke.

Kate kept her eyes on the water. The wharf was deserted and she took the gear from me as I handed it to her from the boat.

"Aren't you happy, Jess?" she said suddenly, as though the words had burst out of her control.

"Not very." It was no good trying to lie to her. "I get a bit fed up sometimes."

Kate pretended to be busy with the gear she was putting aside, but I knew she was only avoiding looking at me.

"I'm sorry, Jess," she murmured.

"I'm sorry, too," I said.

I put on my jacket over the old blue jersey I wore and Kate stared at me mutely, as though she didn't know what to reply to this sudden rush of confidence. I climbed out of the boat and touched her hand. I couldn't help comparing her with Minnie. She was paler, thinner, her clothes cheaper but somehow neater, and she had an honest look in her eyes that Minnie couldn't have managed if she'd tried till she was black in the face.

"Kate," I said quietly, "you and me are a couple of fools, and the worst of it is we both know it now."

High summer was on us almost before we were aware of it. It was a rich summer, full of brittle laughter that echoed hollowly on the breezes that were blowing across the Channel.

I was nervous, restless and edgy. Angry words came quickly and laughter was rare in the resentment Minnie and I felt for each other. We'd reached the stage when we just didn't get along. We weren't at open loggerheads or not on speaking terms. We spoke, laughed sometimes, made love to each other – but there was always something missing, and it took the spice out of life and made it a flat, uninteresting thing.

There could be only one ending to it all. It was as inevitable as tomorrow. There was only one answer to the urge inside me to get back to sea, and to the hatred that had been growing on me for the Steam Packet.

The papers were full of requests for men to give a little extra to the country, as Territorials, with the Air Force, in the Navy reserve. Snatching the breath that Hitler had given them time for at Munich, the Government was doing what it should have done years before, and was building up its defences. Everybody was talking ARP and Civil Defence. People were giving themselves the wind-up trying on gas-masks. Bomb shelters had begun to appear. Peace-time conscription arrived in England for the first time in history. Slowly, desperately slowly, they did it, always trying to avoid alarm yet pathetic in their appeals for patriotism.

It was these appeals that gave me the loophole I needed. I've never particularly been one for patriotism, but I snatched at it then as the best excuse I could think of.

Minnie didn't take kindly to my decision, but, then, I'd never expected she would, and I was in no mood to argue. Yorky had been seen in the town again, and I'd heard the *Eastern Star* was in port. There was a sudden clamouring inside me to be aboard, with shipmates I knew. If I hurried I knew I'd catch her before she left. I'd made a point of finding out how long she was staying. She'd been in collision, I'd heard, and the dock workers were aboard her. I'd just got time to do one thing I wanted.

Minnie watched me with cold, unfriendly eyes as I packed my bags. "Well," she commented, "so you're leaving me, eh? Running away? Back to that carry-on."

"Listen, Minnie," I explained. "I'm going to do my job. I'm a sailor, and no sailor can do his job ashore."

"The Steam Packet needs you more'n any ship," Minnie said. "For all you care, I could starve."

"See here, Minnie." I was uncomfortable. She made me feel I was deserting her. "You managed before I came along, and you'll manage just as well now I'm going. You always said you could run this place with one hand tied behind your back."

She stared at me, angry and silent.

"I'm going up to London first to sit for my mate's ticket," I went on. "I've been jogging my memory lately, doing some swotting on the quiet. I wrote 'em weeks ago, and they've given me the 'Go-ahead'. And when I've got that in my pocket you'll be a captain's lady in no time, who's never short of cash."

"I don't want cash," she said sulkily, "I want you."

"Besides," I said, "there's trouble coming, and England needs sailors just now. That's why I've got to go."

Even as I spoke I knew the words had a shifty, dishonest sound about them.

Minnie was aware of it also, apparently, for she laughed. "Sharp, aren't you?" she said. "Straight out of the knife-box. Got all your excuses handy. England!" she sneered. "That's a fine way to talk! You know damn' fine it isn't that what's sending you off. Sailor! A fine thing I did marrying a sailor. I oughta known. I seen plenty of 'em. If I'd had any sense I'd have married Pat Fee."

I rounded on her angrily. "I sometimes wish to God you had!" I snapped.

"What's the matter with Pat Fee?" Minnie demanded. "If Kate Fee's good enough for you, Pat's good enough for me."

"Shut up, Minnie!" I shouted, suddenly furious. "Shut up!"

"Ha! Hark at him! It's different now, isn't it?" Minnie yelled, realising she'd touched me where it hurt. "Now that *her* name's come into it, it's very different."

I stepped forward and Minnie backed away. "Shut up, Minnie!" I breathed. "Or, by God, I'll fetch you one!"

She was silent, watching me with furious eyes as I picked up my bags.

"All right," she grated at last, "you can go. But you needn't be in such a hurry to come back."

eight

There was an evening mist hanging over the water when I walked along the dockside towards the *Eastern Star*. Out in midstream a tug boomed and away in the distance the St Andrew Light winked sharply. You could just see its flash on the bend of the river.

The *Eastern Star,* just as Old Boxer had described it, was an ill-designed, crank, wry-necked vessel with a bow that was just too high. She had a tall, cigarette-shaped funnel and rusty goalpost derricks. Welders were at work on her, bending over their crackling bright-blue flames. The decks were covered with loops of heavy mooring-ropes and agonised coils of wire that ended round the winches. The familiar smell of engine oil and steam and straw was in the air. It was always the first thing that hit me when I set foot aboard a ship.

As I stepped on the deck I felt the old thrill come over me – the same old thrill I'd always felt after a spell ashore. And then I knew I'd never leave the sea as long as I drew breath.

Minnie could have offered me the biggest pub in the world, with gold-plated bars and diamond-studded beer-engines, but it would never appeal to me half as much as one whiff of that scent I'd caught as I approached the *Eastern Star*. I was lost for ever to the sea the first day I ever set foot aboard a ship.

Those grey, heaving wastes I'd travelled in the last few years had put a spell on me. I was bewitched by them. There were times when I detested them – what sailor doesn't when the living's hard? – but when I was ashore the merest whiff of them was enough to make me heart-sick for their motion. Many a time at the Steam Packet I'd dived into the cupboard in the back bedroom and fished out my sea-bag and my knife, and the sea-boots with the coating of mildew and salt on them, on the pretext of using them to do some job. But I'd only toyed with them, not knowing whether to be glad because the sea was behind me or miserable. Mostly I was miserable without really knowing why.

I'd often thought I was smart to pack it up before I was old and salt-caked, and with the stamp of bunk-springs on my behind. But I wasn't. If I'd been smart I'd have been aboard months before. When the sea gets you as it had got me, you only starve yourself of light and air and happiness when you turn your back on it...

The forecastle seemed to be empty when I dropped my kit-bag, but as I lit a cigarette I became aware of an unshaven, bleary face staring at me over the top of a pile of ruffled blankets.

"Yorky!"

A pair of white arms appeared, and I saw a podgy body wearing nothing but the remains of a torn shirt.

"Jess, me old flower! You've come back to us?"

Yorky heaved himself from his bunk and hurried across to me to clutch my hand, his fat bare legs white and hairless, the colour of dough.

"Gawd, mate, it's proper nice to see you!" he suddenly frowned and held his forehead for a moment, then he tottered back to his bunk and crawled into it again.

"Pardon me, Jess. I look like a queeny in this rig. 'Aving a bit of a kip I was, see? There's seaweed round me funnel, kid. I'm under way but only just. I need a little liver pill or summat."

"What was it, Yorky?" I grinned. "A heavy night?"

"Not 'alf. Party. Posh do it was. Nearly floated outa the door on the booze. Young ladies, too." He frowned at his headache. "That's why I'm aboard of 'er now. No money left. Subbed off the Skipper till 'e won't cough up no more. P'r'aps it's as well, though. The Dock Police swore they'd run me in if they seen me ashore again this trip. Brought me 'ome last night."

He groaned at the memory and cadged a cigarette. "A spit an a drag'll put me right."

"Got one of me own somewhere," he said dismally, fishing under his pillow.

Out came the inevitable brown-paper parcel, which he started to unwrap.

"Keep sayin' I'll make meself a kit-bag," he observed gloomily, half to himself. "But I don't seem to get around to it."

He drew on his cigarette for a while as I sat on the forecastle bench and waited for him to come round a bit. The dingy little space was chilly with the dampness and the mist. But there was a whiff of the sea in it that cheered me up in spite of its comfortlessness.

"You're only just in time, lad," Yorky said. "Sailing tomorrer."

I stared at my cigarette-end for a moment, then I looked up suddenly at him.

"Chain Locker," he said without waiting for my question. "First boozer outside the dock gates. He never gets beyond the first one these days, kid."

I nodded and rose.

"You'll see a bit of a change in 'im," Yorky went on drearily, as though he were making a confession. " 'E's beginnin' to look like somethin' the cat drug outa the knacker's yard. I've tried, but 'e's stubborn, mate."

He sat up suddenly, and the blankets slid to the deck.

"Tried to put 'is name down for that list of Navy reserve of officers you'll 'ave 'eard about, Jess, see? Wouldn't 'ave 'im. An' 'e took it a bit to 'eart. Gawd knows why 'e thought the Navy'd want *'im*, though. 'E's obviously rotten with booze and looks it. You could put a wreck marker over 'im just now and write 'im off as a dead loss. They don't want blokes like that. They want youngsters like you, Jess, wot's got a bit o' red blood left in 'em. Christ, 'e's a fair caution these days." He stared at me with red-rimmed eyes. " 'E's drinkin' in a way what frightens me. I seen some boozin' in me time, but 'e's drinkin' now like somethin's chasin' 'im.' "

"Something is," I said.

"Reelly? No kid? What?"

'His own thoughts. They've been chasing him for twenty years."

The Chain Locker was a derelict little dump and its proprietor matched it for desolation. I almost expected him to smell as if he'd just been dragged out of an attic corner.

"In there," he said in answer to my question, and he indicated the room opposite the bar. "You come to take 'im away?"

Old Boxer was alone, his flabby bulk sagging in a corner of a wooden settle, as though he were a part of the decrepit whole that was the pub.

He stared up at me, and it seemed ages before he spoke.

"God," he said at last, "I do believe …" He struggled to speak, and I saw there were tears in his eyes. "Jess," he croaked, "why didn't you say you were comin'? Catching a chap like this with a list on him. It's like callin' for a woman while she's still got her hair unpinned."

He heaved himself ponderously to his feet and stood swaying. He was hanging on to the mantelpiece, and I saw his fingers were trembling as they clutched at it.

"I'm more keel than funnel at the moment," he said, "and my brain seems knotted like an old woman's entrails. Steer me back to the *Eastern Star,* lad. You wouldn't see a shipmate stranded, would you?"

"Come on, you old donkey, you," I said gently.

"Are you with us again, Jess?" he queried as I manoeuvred him carefully through the door.

"Yes, I'm with you. I've slipped me cable and got myself signed on the *Eastern Star.*"

"Praise be to God," he said fervently, and he began to sing in a wobbly cracked voice that was pathetic in its wretchedness:

> "Farewell and adieu to you, Spanish ladies,
> Farewell and adieu, ladies of Spain."

He stumbled a little on the uneven cobbles.

"Bit of an awkward cross-swell here," he said. "No, I'm mink. That's what it is. I'm a copper-bottomed old fool with a rum bottle for a nose. What shall we do with the drunken sailor? What shall we do with the drunken sailor...?"

His voice trailed off into a monotonous chant, and he shuffled after me, a stale-smelling old wreck of a man.

"She's a starvation bastard, the *Eastern Star,* with cockroaches big as tomcats," he went on. "You can make her loaves into fenders. You can caulk seams with her duff. And her salt pork you can use to frighten the gulls away." Leaning heavily on me and on legs that buckled under him, he babbled on as we made our way to the docks. "Her skipper couldn't navigate driftwood round a duckpond, and she's designed by a corkscrew maker, but she's home lad, to me."

"Cheer up, man," I said, depressed by the windy rigmarole of misery. "Pull yourself together."

"Never pull myself together again, lad. They don't want me. The Navy's no time for me. God, and they're crying out for men, too. Better if I'd gone down with my ship 'stead of living to see them throw me out – and throw me out again."

I got another grip on him as he began to bend a little at the knees.

"Too old, they said! Too old. Didn't ask about my record. Don't suppose they're bothered, anyway. Just took one look at me and said, 'Too old.' Just like that. And they wrinkled their noses as if they'd picked something up on their boots."

"Were you sober?"

"Sober as a judge, Jess. Just come from sea." His words tumbled over themselves in his eagerness to convince. "Had to be sober. First call soon as I set foot ashore. Just had one or two to bolster me up. That's all. Shaky with nerves, man. But only one or two. No more. Only an eyeful. Just one or two to keep me going. They ask so many questions, Jess. They get you dizzy. Didn't know whether I was coming or going. But I was sober, Jess. Honest I was."

I could well imagine the interview. Old Boxer would be remembering his disgrace all the time. The grey ghosts of the past would be haunting him. He'd be guiltily aware he was hiding a bad record, sensing all the time they'd never have him. He'd be nervous at the start, awed a little by the smart uniforms, ashamed of his own untidiness, and more than likely dazed with rum, more than likely with a chip on his shoulder.

His voice broke in on my thoughts. "Too old," he said, and it seemed as though the years were jostling him unwillingly along. "God, it's awful to get to my age, Jess. Should have gone down with the ship. I know I should."

"Oh, shut up, man!" I said irritably, growing angry at his self-pity.

"Only old age and a shabby lodging-house. That's what I've got coming to me." He seemed to be staring into the eyes of idiot reality. "Pauper's grave. Parson at the workhouse. That's all."

Something seemed to have gone from him. Once there'd been a ponderous grandeur about his drunkenness. Now he was just a stupid, drivelling, glassy-eyed old fool. The spine had gone out of him and he'd lost his grip on hope.

nine

Even as the *Eastern Star* slipped her moorings and headed across the Bay of Biscay and into the Mediterranean sunshine, the lights were beginning to go out in Europe. Those speeches of Hitler's had come to a head at last.

A wireless message told us to hurry, and we set off for Gibraltar like the clappers of hell. They got the engines knocking up revs she'd not produced in twenty years or more and set the old ship rattling from stem to stern, all the ladder stagings buzzing with the vibration and the bolts rattling in the plates; and all the mugs and knives and forks in the mess-deck playing a tune as they danced up and down the table.

We'd reached Gibraltar when the news of the Polish invasion came through, and we huddled on the foredeck between watches to hear the wireless in the officers' saloon, eager for news.

"The bastards," I heard Yorky murmuring. "The bastards. Them bleeden politicians 'as let us in for it again."

The old hands among the crew were silent, remembering their experiences in the last war, and Old Boxer was the most taciturn of the lot.

The declaration of war came at last, and a typewritten notice from the Captain's cabin was stuck up in the forecastle, a bleak little message that was repeated by the signalling lamp of a sleek, grey destroyer as she hurried past us, heading for Malta: "War has broken out with Germany. Do not put into any German port."

"Well," someone said, "I hope that old blighter with the umbrella's happy now.

The forecastle was full of buzzes immediately. It was blacked out the first night after we got the news and the dropped deadlights created the atmosphere of an oven in the Red Sea evenings. New watches had to be fitted in and gallons of grey paint had to be slapped on to the white deck-work to reduce it to a drab, wartime camouflage. Rumours, half of them imaginary, went round the ship, of vessels sunk in the Indian Ocean by a German pocket battleship which was reported to be just ahead of us, and of collisions in convoys as ships strayed from their positions in the dark through lack of experience.

That trip of the *Eastern Star* wasn't a happy one for me. Those high hopes I'd had, those sea fevers that had given me restless nights, seemed to have come to nothing. The trip was a dreadful anti-climax that was symbolised by Old Boxer's attitude.

We both tried hard to behave normally towards each other, but I was married, and that link there'd been between us was broken by the existence of Minnie. We never got on with each other in quite the same way, from the minute the winches began to bang and rattle as we coiled mooring-ropes until the anchor chain roared through the hawse-hole in Mombasa harbour.

I wasn't sorry when the voyage was over and we were tied up within sight of St Andrew Head again.

I walked away from the *Eastern Star* slowly. I could hear the sound of "Shendandoah" played on Yorky's concertina. It was a bit uneven because Yorky had had one or two already – when he went to buy the usual railway ticket to Hull I knew he'd never use. The yearning melody seemed a fitting accompaniment to my thoughts. There was something oppressive in the air I couldn't put my finger on, in spite of the brand-new mate's ticket I'd been told was waiting for me when I wanted to collect it. I'd wanted the sea – badly – but Old Boxer's strangeness had left me with a bitter taste of disappointment.

I stopped dead suddenly in the dusty street that was littered with bus tickets and fragments of newspaper and orange peel.

"Blast him!" I said aloud. "Damn and blast the silly old fool! Why should I worry whether he's upset or not?"

I thrust my hands deep into my pockets and hurried away, my coat flapping in the wind that was getting up and stirring the rubbish in the gutter.

England was like a foreign country with its sandbags and uniforms, and all the daft little cardboard boxes everyone carried for gas-masks. But the nervous look in people's eyes was gone. In its place was gravity, but there was a certain amount of relief, too, and I more than once heard: "Well, thank God, it's here. We do know where we stand now."

There was a warmth that I hadn't expected in Minnie's greeting when I reached home. Just one quick flicker of her eyes towards the door that seemed to shout out loud she'd been unfaithful, then she'd flung her arms round my neck and was kissing me hungrily. And, though I knew she was a wanton, the warmth of her and the lusty animal way she greeted me drew me to her just the same as before, smothering the resentment and the distrust, jostling aside the knowledge that it wouldn't last.

The Steam Packet was the same untidy, slovenly place behind the scenes it always had been. The brasses on the front door and on the beer-engine were polished bright, but the kitchen with its roaring fire had its usual drunken, slip-shod appearance, like a shifty old man caught with his collar off. The same pair of shoes seemed to be under the sink. The same rumpled frock was on the sofa. The same used gin-glass was on the sideboard. The same cat was asleep in the same place in the hearth, almost as though it had been there ever since I walked out.

But it was a happier home-coming than I'd expected, with Minnie flushed and excited by the presence of a man in the house again, nibbling at my ear and whispering to me as I held her in my arms. I noticed she seemed plumper than before, and there was a smell of gin in her breath although it was hardly past midday. Then I suddenly realised that in ten years' time she'd probably be a fat, lazy good-for-nothing, and it jolted me a little. But I forgot it again as I felt her arms tighten round my neck once more.

In her way she was more than glad to see me. She was a passionate creature who needed a man. Her nature shouted out loud for a man's attention, her body for a man's love-making, her foolish little mind for a man's flattery.

Then, suddenly, she noticed I'd only one small bag with me, and her face fell.

"Where's all your kit?" she demanded harshly.

"Aboard ship," I said. "I left it."

"You going back?" Her arms fell to her sides, and there was a hostile look in her eyes. All the affection was gone immediately.

"Yes" I said. "There's a war on now, you know, but I shan't be away long. I wasn't this time, was I?"

"You're no good to me when you're at sea, I tell you," she accused bitterly.

There seemed to be no arguing with her. "What are you worrying for?" I said. "I'm home for weeks. We're having a boiler-clean."

"I wish the blasted old cow would sink," Minnie fumed.

"Don't let's go over all that again," I said, suddenly weary. "Not when I've only just come home."

"I need a man about the house!"

I turned silently on my heel. This seemed to be a stupid ending to what had been an unhappy voyage. I mounted the stairs with my bag and Minnie followed, still complaining.

"I wish the blasted boilers would blow up," she said tempestuously. "I wish the masts would all fall down. I wish the bottom would drop out. I wish all your pals would get drowned."

"Shut up!" I shouted, turning in the doorway of the bedroom.

"I wish they'd all sink to the bottom of the sea – miles down – and get ett by fishes!" she screamed. There was a note of hysteria in her voice.

"Blast you, shut up!" I slapped her face and her shouts stopped abruptly. She gazed at me angrily, her eyes wide and furious, a red weal on her cheek where my fingers had struck her.

I stared at her, panting a little, then turned abruptly to the chest of drawers where I kept my shore-side clothes. Even as I opened it, however, Minnie jumped forward and snatched something from under my hand. I caught only a glimpse of what she held, but it was enough to make me grab at her wrist.

"Give me that!" I said.

"No!" Minnie screamed. "Blast you and your stinking ships! I hope they all go to the bottom!"

"Give me that!" I said again, twisting her wrist as she began to strike at me with her free hand.

Eventually I pushed her back over the bed and forced her hand open. She held a crumpled cigar, broken with the clutch of her fingers. I stared at it, then pushed her hand away savagely, and the cigar fell to the floor. Minnie kicked it under the bed with her heel.

"There you are, Clever," she sneered. "It's only an old cigar. If you'd keep 'em in your pocket they wouldn't litter up your drawers. Now it's all broke up."

She glared at me, her eyes angry. Her hair was awry and she was dowdy and untidy and vulgar, yet with the flush on her cheeks she was still desirable.

I was staring at the bits of the cigar on the floor. "You know I never smoked a cigar in my life," I said.

Minnie looked at me silently. Her expression showed she was thinking fast. She suddenly stretched out a hand to mine and the fire went out of her eyes. She smiled and tried to pull me to her.

"Oh, it must be an old one of Pa's, then," she said, and her voice was velvety. "Must have been there years. Jess, come closer to me. Forget that old thing."

"If it was only your father's, why did you snatch it away?"

"Thought you wouldn't want it in your drawer," she said with a sly little smile. "That's all. Honest. Gospel. But you will go and get me wrong and lose your temper."

"Pat Fee smokes cigars like that," I said quietly.

Minnie looked at me under a lock of hair. There was a suggestion of defiance in her attitude.

"Well, what about it?" she said.

"What's Pat Fee's cigar doing in this bedroom?" I snapped.

"Oh, my Gawd!" Minnie said. "Some people haven't half got suspicious natures. You'll be the death of me."

"What's it doing here?" I almost shouted, furious that this old monster about Pat Fee should keep frightening me. I knew the meaning now of Minnie's scared glance when I'd arrived. Suddenly the room in the dim light that came through the half-pulled curtains seemed sordid and full of an unpleasant staleness that suffocated me.

"Oh, shut up, Jess," Minnie said. "If you must know, it *is* Pat Fee's. He left it on the bar one night. I put it away for safety till he asked for it. He's not been in since. That's all."

I said nothing. Minnie suddenly seemed no better than a dockside drab.

"I don't know why you're goin' on about Pat Fee," she said, as though she were reading my thoughts. "He never comes in here these days. He's too busy."

"Busy? Where is he?"

"In the docks. Got a job there the week before the war broke out, the cowardly swine. Only out to dodge being called up. I think he likes night work, too, with them women they've taken on."

I sensed the bitterness in her voice. It was nothing more nor less than the fury of a woman scorned. And though I had no proof, had never had any proof, of anything between Minnie and Pat Fee, I was certain that Pat had slept in this same bed with her, and had finally thrown her on one side as someone else absorbed his attention.

"The docks, eh?" I said slowly, hoping she'd say more. "So he scuttled for safety, after all."

"The blasted scrim-shankin' no-good scrounger!" Minnie spoke slowly. There was a chilly fury in her tones, and at that moment there was hatred in her heart for Pat Fee.

But I knew perfectly well it wouldn't last long, and that odd trick of their sexes that bound her to Pat would inevitably tug her towards him again, unable to be indifferent to him for long.

"What you thinkin' about?" Minnie asked suddenly. "Starin' like that."

She was lounging on the bed where I'd thrown her, voluptuous, her eyes half veiled, a lock of hair over her shoulder.

"So Pat's slipped his cable again, eh?" I said. "No wonder you were glad to have *me* home."

"What do you mean?" she said harshly. "Pat Fee's nothing to me. He never has been. I hate the sight of him." There was so much desire to convince in her voice that it seemed to condemn her.

I laughed. "You're a bad little bitch, Minnie," I said, and I didn't feel angry, curiously enough. "And I ought to give you a hiding. But I'm not going to. You're lucky."

She stared at me unwinkingly for a second, then she sat up suddenly, her hand to her throat.

"Oh, my word!" she said with a sudden deep intake of breath. "It's gone hot in here all of a sudden, Jess."

Her fingers unbuttoned her frock at her throat. I grinned at her. The same old trick. Minnie was trying to capture me again, now she felt the crisis was past.

I tilted her head until she gazed upwards at me. That odd attraction she had for me made me flush like a schoolboy. Her arms tightened round my neck.

"Come closer, Jess," she breathed urgently. "Come and have a bit of a lie-down with me."

She fluttered her lashes and tried to kiss me, but I thrust her aside, breaking her grip. She stared at me, the hot light in her eyes changing to a startled stare as I put her hands away from me.

"No, Minnie," I said. "You're not half good enough at acting. You'd have to do much better than that this time."

She sat up, suddenly cold and unsmiling. She savagely did up the buttons of her dress as I began to unpack, and swing her feet to the floor.

"OK, Mr Clever," she said, more to herself than to me, her voice harsh with temper. "OK." She stood up and stared furiously at herself in the mirror as she combed her hair.

"OK," she said again. "Well, you asked for it proper and you're going to get it. Just wait till you go back."

t e n

That leave was about the longest I ever spent. Neither Minnie nor I made any effort to patch up the quarrel. Neither of us particularly wanted to. We moved about the Steam Packet outwardly indifferent to each other, but both coldly hostile, seething with words we'd have liked to have said and didn't. Our life together had always been difficult and erratic, but there'd been a curious hotchpotch of brittle laughter and bad temper. But now even that was gone, leaving only cold, unspeaking fury. Minnie was always busy in the bar, but I was sick of the damned place and its smell of stale beer. I went out early and only returned to sleep.

Minnie watched me angrily. She was jealous of the life I lived at sea, away from her and out of sight. She was indifferent to the women I met in foreign ports, I think, but was envious of the sea itself for its hold on me. Hers was a demanding nature, wanting all of a man for herself, wanting him body and soul, but greedy enough to want someone else while he was away.

Dig sought me out occasionally but I found myself avoiding him. After my life at sea, Dig's way of living seemed unbelievably narrow. Even the town seemed only a hamlet that could be crossed with a couple of giant's strides from the seven-league boots a sailor wears after his wandering. Besides, though I knew I'd eventually die within the echoes of its church bells, the place was an ugly reminder of Pat Fee and that soiled, tawdry question mark of his relationship with Minnie.

Long before I was due back aboard the *Eastern Star* I was itching to be away, itching to smell the clean air of the sea and feel its damp saltiness in my hands.

My last evening home arrived eventually and long before dark I'd dumped my kit aboard, in the tiny white cabin to which the mate's ticket now in my pocket entitled me. It was a curious feeling being in a cabin to myself – as though I was a stranger in the familiar old ship. Every creak and every groan of her had become like a living breath to me, but I was feeling as new to it all as a snotty-nosed deck-boy on his first trip.

Ashore again, I debated what to do. I could indulge in a procession round the pubs and bump into Yorky and Old Boxer somewhere en route, or I could go and sit with Dig, stifled in the tiny house in Atlantic Street. Neither appealed to me and in the end, seeing the lights still on at Wiggins', I went there, trying to persuade myself it was to say goodbye to Dig, but knowing perfectly well that it was in the hope of seeing Katie Fee.

She was just leaving as I arrived and she halted on the corner by the gate to talk to me. She looked tired in the last of the daylight, but she smiled.

"Hello, Jess," she said. "Will you walk home with me?"

"I was hoping you'd say that, Kate," I admitted.

We moved away in silence towards the High Street.

"I'm off back to sea tomorrow," I said after a while.

"Are you, Jess?" Kate stopped and faced me. "Oh, I do hope – I..." She hesitated, then she ended simply: "Good luck, Jess. The best of luck."

She watched me for a second, then she asked, "Has it been a miserable leave, Jess?"

I laughed shortly. "I know where I stand now, anyway," I said.

"It's a funny feeling," I went on, "knowing your wife's indifferent to you and you're indifferent to her, that you just don't give a damn any more what happens."

Kate stood close to me, close enough to kiss her if I'd wanted. "Oh, Jess!" Her words were limping and awkward. "It seems so tragic."

We were silent for a while, then Kate went on, "It's Pat, of course, isn't it?"

I stared at her. "Yes," I said. "How did you know?"

"I always knew, I think. There was always something between them. Do you hate him dreadfully?"

"Pat?" I laughed. "No, Kate. Sailor's lot, I suppose. In any case, it's six of one and half a dozen of the other. Minnie's as bad as he is."

She looked up at me and I saw her eyes were suddenly frightened. "Jess," she said, "will you do something for me?"

"What is it, Kate?"

She unclasped something from round her neck. "Wear this, Jess. It's a St Christopher medallion. I suppose everyone's giving them to soldiers and sailors and airmen these days. I know they don't mean anything, really, but – well – I'll feel you're just a little safer."

I took it from her gravely. "We've made a rare mess of our lives, Kate, haven't we?" I said.

She nodded mutely. "Perhaps it'll all come straight in the end, Jess," she said hopelessly.

"Will you write to me sometimes, Kate?" I asked.

"If you want me to, Jess," she said, but there was no enthusiasm in her voice. She knew as well as I did how unwise we'd be. Letters to each other could only make our unhappiness darker.

From the moment she left her berth I had a feeling the *Eastern Star* would never reach home again. Almost as she moved down the river, with Old Boxer still unconscious in his bunk and stale with liquor, I could tell things weren't going to go right. Salt water got into her tanks and made her drinking-water foul, and we sank a fishing-boat off the Newfoundland coast. In New York harbour a docker was killed by a swinging boom that also put one of the crew in hospital.

It was while we were in New York that the news of Norway came through. The Germans were showing their hand at last and the war of stagnation was over. There was a suddenness about the news that shocked us. But there were more shocks coming. Before we'd properly absorbed that lot, Norway had fallen, then Holland; and the Allied armies were being split by a German drive across France to the coast.

We were aghast as we heard the news. The crew came crowding silently on to the foredeck near the officers' saloon to hear the six o'clock news over the wireless. The whole of the tortured Continent seemed a sheet of flame. We were bewildered by the savagery of it, and thankful for that narrow stretch of water which was all that could prevent the Germans sweeping on to London. Desperately we clung to the hope that the French would rally and fling them back. But we knew all the time there was no rally left in them. There wasn't even the spirit for defence.

As the *Eastern Star* limped home on creaking engines that had long been due for the scrapyard, faces were worried and more than one of the crew was taut with apprehension.

"I've got a lad with the Gunners," I heard. "I hope to God he's all right."

"He'll be OK, mate. Our boys are heading for the coast."

"Not half they aren't! Christ, and the war not twelve months old yet!"

"The bastards are machine-gunning women and kids," Yorky breathed. The ruthlessness of this new form of warfare seemed to bewilder him. "And parachute blokes dressed like parsons and women. Jeeze," he said savagely. "I know there's a war on but you can't go off like that."

Old Boxer never had his ears far from the wireless those first days of the battles in France, a stark look in his watery old eyes, a drawn expression about his mouth. His tongue was full of bitter comments on the War Office authorities, but I knew his bitterness was only a defence against sour thoughts on a system that had twice rejected him...

Then the wind rose and the ship began to stagger a little. One of her engines ceased its revolutions altogether. and we left the wireless and its grim news and turned our attention to the more immediate emergency of getting the ship home. Like all sailors, we felt our calling was above the pettiness of nations. Our only enemy was the sea.

But I wasn't the only one, I'll bet, who felt uneasy when the skipper had to indicate our inability to keep up with the rest of the convoy, and we received the return signal from the guardian destroyers to continue alone.

"Well, mates," I heard Yorky say down on the foredeck, as we watched the other ships disappear hull down over the horizon, the last of the sunshine on them, "you can start off singing 'Nearer, My God, to Thee'."

It was two hours before daylight, with the night at its darkest, when the submarine got us. The clanging, screaming crash of the explosion brought the ship to a shuddering halt and left her wallowing in the dark valleys of the waves. The tremendous blackness of the night was lit suddenly by a vast sheet of flame that sent flickering points of light racing along the wavetops.

The watches were just changing and Old Boxer and I were together near the bridge when the crash brought us to our knees.

"God Almighty!" Old Boxer muttered fearfully. "He's got us!"

The flash had disappeared, leaving us again in utter blackness, our eyes blinded by the glare. He didn't put another into us. He probably knew one would be enough for the old *Eastern Star.* The sound of the engines had stopped and there was only the slap and swish of the waves against the hull as the ship began to swing beam-on to the sea.

Number One, who was officer-of-the-watch, came tumbling down the bridge companionway. Torches were visible in the forecastle alley silhouetting running figures of men. Aft, I could see a flicker of flame – only a lick still, but already clawing its way across the deck.

"Jump to it!" I heard the skipper shouting in the darkness. "Get these boats away!"

I stumbled away to my boat-station, my feet clumsy on decks that were already sloping, then the ship lurched and I heard another crash. As I reached my boat I realised Old Boxer had disappeared.

Around me was the frantic hurrying of men clutching all manner of private possessions, treasured things, poor things mostly, all they could snatch up and carry with them. A damp breeze was blowing into my face, and I remember enjoying it even in that moment of excitement, with the ship sinking underneath my feet.

But there wasn't time to stand about, thinking what a lovely night it was. By the light of flashing torches I was aware of half-dressed figures stumbling past me, bulky with lifebelts, and carrying overcoats and jerseys. Some of them had been in the lifeboats before and knew how cold it could be.

The Bosun was swinging a hammer at a refractory bolt that had been jammed by the explosion and wouldn't move, and the clanging added to the din. He was swearing all the time as he worked, not in panic, but in desperate, furious anger.

"The bloody thing's never stuck before," he was saying. "Every bloody boat drill it came out. And now it has to bloody well stick when the old cow's sinking under us."

He stopped to let one of the engine-room crew past, stumbling under the weight of another figure – it looked like the donkeyman. The newcomer bundled his load into the boat without ceremony and climbed in after him.

"Fell down the ladder, the clod," he said. "Nearly brained me. Knocked 'isself out on the 'andrail."

I could just make out in the beam of my torch steel stanchions twisted into knots by the explosion and steel plates torn like paper round a gaping hole in her side just abaft the funnel. Then someone bumped into me in the darkness and I turned to curse him for his clumsiness.

It was Yorky. I recognised him by his short figure and his vest, which had a flat-iron mark on the front where he'd burned it. As he clambered towards a boat I saw he had his concertina under his arm.

"Where's 'Orace?" he shouted.

"God knows," I said. "Are you all right?"

"Just got out the engine-room in time. The other poor devils must 'ave copped it. The 'ole bloody lot come down on top of 'em, ladder-staging and boilders and Gawd knows what. Where's 'Orace, Jess?" His voice was cracked and sharp with apprehension.

"Never mind him," I said. "He'll turn up. He's alive. I've seen him. Get into that boat. You're holding up the traffic."

"OK, Mister Mate." He grinned and tumbled into the lifeboat with the others.

Someone was calling a roll on the starboard side of the ship. "Axsen."

"Here, sir."

"Abrahams."

"Aye, aye."

"Garnett."

" 'E's 'ere, sir. Only 'e's got a lump on 'is 'ead like a bleeden egg. 'E's all right, though."

"Right. Young."

Suddenly someone jostled my elbow and I turned angrily to face old Boxer. "Where've you been?" I demanded angrily. Someone else was having to do his job.

"Sorry," he said. "Had to get something."

"Well, you're wanted on those falls. Lay on that rope."

As the boat descended with the shrieking of pulleys we could hear the gurgle of water in the scuppers aft where the deck was awash. The mainmast was lying over the side in a tangle of rigging, and the deck was buckled in a great bulge like a blister. The alleyways were only gloomy caverns, hollow shells that were no longer part of a living ship, tombs in which our voices and the sound of escaping steam echoed. Already boxes were floating about the decks, with smashed hatch covers and broken doors, and we could hear them bumping against the stanchions.

Even as we shoved the boat away from the ship's side the *Eastern Star* lurched again in the oily water, and through an open port above the slapping of the waves I heard a crash as a cupboard burst open and knives and forks and plates were slung across the decks after the forms and the clothes and the grey sea-water that had begun to seep into the cabins.

"Come on, heave away!" I shouted from the stern of the boat. "This is no time for sight-seeing! Lay on those oars!"

When daylight rose the *Eastern Star* had settled lower in the water in a great patch of shining oil, but she was still in sight, her bows high in the air, groaning with the stress on her plates as though she were alive. Of the submarine that had destroyed her there was no sign. For a while, without waiting for the order, the oars stopped their movement and everyone looked back at her, useless, reeling from the sloshing of the waves under a lowering sky, lopsided and ugly, like a drab old vulture with a broken wing, her sides split open and the cargo and the oil spilling out of her.

"Well," Yorky said, "now we *are* up the bleeden pole, we are. Proper. There goes our little grey 'ome in the west, complete with the roses round the door."

Her bows rose higher as we watched until the keel was clear and red and rusty above the water.

"She's going," I said.

Almost without a gurgle she slipped away beneath the water like a great drowning animal, with only bubbles of air to mark her grave, and the spreading patch of oil on the water dotted with floating objects.

We watched her disappear, our eyes red-rimmed with weariness, our faces haggard with the cold. One of the men in the bottom of the boat was whimpering slightly with the pain of a broken arm. The muttering grew silent for a moment as we became aware of the vastness of the sea and our own puny smallness on its great plains.

"Keep your eyes skinned," I said as briskly as I could manage, trying to keep their spirits up. "There's bound to be a destroyer come back for us."

My voice sounded happier than I felt. Seeing all that water and the size of our boat on it started that damned lonely feeling again. It shut down on me like a fog in the Channel, chill and depressing and damp.

We huddled down out of the wind to wait, our stiff faces coated with the salt rime that blew over the bow of the lifeboat as she lifted out of the valleys in the grey-green waves. The lonely feeling grew stronger on me as I swayed to the movement of her. I held the tiller, steadying her when she corkscrewed through the swell and, oddly enough, just then I thought of Minnie and my unfortunate marriage. I felt I'd been too near to death for us to carry on as we had been doing. I felt I had to make some effort when I got home to sort out our affairs. Surely, I thought, something could be salvaged from the wreck. War was no time for domestic misery.

I glanced across at Yorky, wondering what he was thinking. From one swinging hand trailed the concertina. His face was devoid of expression. Old Boxer was next to him, leaning across the gunwale, staring forward, grey wisps of sparse hair blown across his eyes, his face gaunt and bleak as the weather. His throat was bare and lean, and there were flecks of white whiskers on his face.

"I'm a flying-fish sailor just 'ome from 'Ong Kong!" Yorky suddenly started to sing and the words were blown aft to me. There was no light-heartedness in the song, though, only a futile determination to be cheerful.

When the destroyer came in sight we raised a cheer, but it died quickly. Yorky watched her shrewdly as she swung broadside on to the waves to make a lee of calm water for us to pull alongside.

"Looks a bit smarter nor the *Eastern Star*," he commented. " 'Ow'd you fancy serving in 'er, 'Orace? That's the job for a matelot. Nice clean quarters. None of the old straw mattress to sleep on. None of the old donkey's breakfast in the Navy, eh, I'll bet."

Old Boxer suddenly turned his back on the battleship as we headed towards her. His eyes were glittering pin-points and I noticed he was nursing the only thing he'd bothered to save from the *Eastern Star*, the thing he'd gone back to the forecastle to salvage. His fingers were blue with cold as they clutched the shabby naval sword and scabbard that was the symbol of Boxer tradition, its silver facings tarnished and green with salt rime.

BOOK THREE

one

When I reached home the first thing I saw as I came out of the station was the crowd round Wiggins' boat-yard and my interest was roused immediately. All the same, I never intended crossing the road to see what was going on, but so obviously there was something in the air it drew me towards it. At first I imagined there'd been an accident, and I thought immediately of Kate Fee and Dig. Then I saw it wasn't that kind of crowd. There seemed to be hardly any staring and not much comment. It mostly consisted of men – though it's true there were a few women there – and they were waiting, not watching.

I must have looked a bit of a sight as I stepped out of the station. My clothes were filthy with salt water and oil. My chief concern in the train from Liverpool, where we'd landed after crossing over from Ireland, was to get some money and a clean shirt, because when the Navy dumped us in Londonderry none of us had anything but what he stood up in. But in spite of my scarecrow appearance, not one of the people outside Wiggins' looked twice at me.

I'd decided on the way home I was going to enjoy myself for a week or two. I was tired and dirty and had no ship to worry about. I felt that for a few days, until they sent for me, I could quietly forget the war. I'd plenty to keep me busy for a while.

I watched Old Boxer and Yorky hurrying away from the train to the pubs with a couple of quid they'd borrowed, one carrying the shabby naval sword, the other a parcel and the battered concertina. I let them go. For once I felt I wanted to be alone. I wanted to get home to Minnie and sort things out with her. I wanted peace and affection at that moment. Not a pub crawl.

But peace wasn't heading in my direction just then. My cards hadn't been marked that way. The crowd at Wiggins' gate drew me like a magnet...

It was clearly not just an ordinary crowd, but it wasn't until I'd left the station entrance that I realised that the people in the road were only the overflow from inside. Then I saw there was a policeman on duty to keep the sightseers away and a petrol lorry was standing in the roadway. Inside the yard another lorry was discharging its cargo into the storage tanks. Obviously there was something in the wind.

As I picked my way through the crowd towards the offices I saw fishermen, trawlermen and merchant seamen around me, a few civilians in jerseys, and even a clergyman still wearing his clerical collar. Men were sitting on bedrolls and hammocks and planks. They were lounging on the piles of canvas and even squatting on the stacked wash-basins. A group of naval one- and two-ringers were chatting by the office door with a few ratings, complete with kit-bags and oilskins. I caught the word "Dunkirk" over and over again as I pushed past.

Beyond the wharf, I noticed the biggest collection of small boats I'd ever seen. There were yachts, motor-launches, small fishing-vessels, boats that normally plied out to the Light and back from the beaches round the headland, and the *Skylarks* and the *Daisybells* that did the trip up the river with holiday-makers aboard. They were moored haphazardly alongside, one to another, their masts and rigging a spider's web across the sky. And at the stern of them, bobbing and curtseying to the movement of the water, there seemed to be every rowing-boat and whaler that the river had ever floated. The creeks and loading-steps must have been scraped bare. They weaved and danced in the wash of passing vessels; old and new; red, white, yellow, green and blue; the bright and the varnished rubbing shoulders with the paintless and the worm-eaten. Then I remembered an item of news I'd heard on the wireless, days before the *Eastern Star* was torpedoed, and I knew just what they were waiting for.

The Admiralty had asked the owners of all self-propelled pleasure craft to send in their particulars. As I'd heard it I'd wondered what it was all about. Now I suddenly knew. The War Office was preparing to evacuate the Continent.

The Londonderry newspapers we'd bought, to catch up with the news when we landed from the destroyer, had been full of strong black headlines, dark and foreboding as mourning clothes, as sombre as that speech of old Churchill's we'd heard on the hotel wireless where they billeted us. His words had a heaviness that didn't hide the fact that something had gone wrong. There'd been a disaster to British arms and the retreating BEF was streaming into Dunkirk.

And now boats were needed to save them. Small boats, big ships, anything that would float, and the staff officers had come to the river requisitioning whatever they required, everything that was available. They were doing the same, had we only known it, at Teddington, Kingston, Hampton Wick, Ranelagh, Chiswick, right up to the Wash and west to Weymouth and the border of Cornwall. Huge tows of pulling boats had already left for Dover and the evacuation had begun.

All day, while the windows in Dover and Ramsgate shook and rattled to the roll of gunfire across the narrow stretch of water, the stream of vessels had gone out and returned, bringing back the first of the grimy men from Dunkirk harbour, their faces drawn with weariness, their clothes coated with dust and stained with oil and water. They were pouring into Dover, rank after rank of them, cramming every available space on every available vessel that could carry them, English and French together; wounded helping the wounded, streaming from the ships across the docks into the waiting trains; gulping gratefully at clear air and snatching hungrily at the cigarettes and cups of tea the girls held out to them. They were already appearing in back areas in the country, dog-tired, asleep on their feet, flooding into town halls and church rooms, and flinging themselves down and snoring.

We didn't know all this then, though, for there was only a hint of it in the papers still. But as fast as boats came back to Dover, more went out. The SOS had gone across England like the beacons that had warned of the Armada – to the rivers and harbours half-way round the country. They'd decided to lift men direct from the beaches.

Wiggins', as the biggest boat-builders in the town, had been instructed to act as agents for the Admiralty, and every boat in the river that would move under its own power was being collected at their wharf. All day naval ratings had been fitting what guns they had to whatever boats could carry them, and there'd been a constant procession of men into the office where Katie Fee was struggling with documents and satisfying the demands of those who were wanting papers, compasses, charts, rations, fuel and water. A policeman outside the door was directing the volunteers. There were holiday-makers – the early ones – in blazers, alongside dock labourers and merchant seamen from ships laying up for repairs, some sober and some none too sober.

Kate had been dragged from her bed in the early hours of the morning by an urgent message that had sent her to the taxi waiting outside the door and down to the boat-yard by the weak light of dawn, just as the first of the boats and the first of the men had begun to arrive. She'd been at it ever since. Her meals had been brought in on trays, and the bobby at the door had brought her cups of coffee from a café across the road.

She'd had her eyes on the papers that littered her desk all day, hardly raising them to eat and drink, and when I walked in she was looking pretty done in. She glanced up quickly as I closed the door, however, almost as though she knew it was me, and I saw the exhaustion cross her face and the tears flood into her eyes.

She threw down her pen and came round the table to me. "Oh, Jess," was all she said as she leaned against me, light-headed with fatigue. Then she lifted her head and sighed.

"We've been at it all day. We've scoured the town for charts and compasses."

"What's it all about?" I asked. "I was on my way home from the station when I saw the crowd. Is it what we've been expecting? Are they going to fetch the Army out?"

Kate nodded. "I think so, Jess." She drew a deep, shuddering breath. "Oh, Jess, it'll be so dreadful if they have to do it all with these small boats."

"We can do it, Kate," I grinned. I'd no idea then just what was proposed, but I was trying to cheer her up. "Come on, give us a smile."

She raised her eyes and gave me a weak smile then she brushed the hair out of her eyes and sat down.

"Where's Dig?" I asked.

"In the manager's office. He must be worn out. He's been on that telephone all day, taking it in turns with the manager. First it's the Senior Naval Officer. Then it's the police. Then it's the harbourmaster."

Dig was alone when I found him, talking into the mouthpiece of the telephone, polite, quiet, dusty and dried-up as ever, but suddenly alive. He looked up as I entered, and his eyes smiled, though he went on talking. Eventually he put the instrument down and I saw the tired, prematurely old look had gone from him. He looked excited and alert.

He didn't waste his breath welcoming me. "This is a dreadful thing, Jess," was all he said.

I didn't reply. Words seemed suddenly inadequate. "Can I help?" I asked.

"It's almost all done now, Jess."

He wiped his brow with the back of his hand and seemed to droop with weariness. "I'm ever so pleased you came, Jess," he said. "I'm glad I've seen you before I go."

"Go?" I stared. "Are *you* going?"

"Yes." Dig replied. "They're our boats, a lot of them."

I stared again. "But you don't know one end of a boat from the other."

"Rubbish!" Dig's voice was unexpectedly firm. "You can't work in a boat-yard all your life and learn nothing about boats. Besides, the manager's going. Old Wiggins has gone already and he's seventy if he's a day. Surely *I* can help? Everyone's needed." He was poking at papers on the desk, his eyes down and hidden as usual. "P'r'aps they can even manage better here without me."

"You'll be sick," I said, and suddenly felt how stupid the words were.

"I know." Dig smiled shyly, looking up for a moment. "I always am. Still, I 'spect other people will be, too."

Suddenly a feeling of affection for him swept over me. He was drooping and dusty and thin and far from strong. His sense of duty to Ma had dulled his appetite for happiness. But he was risking his little share, offering himself with the meanest of them, the roughest of them, taking a chance on the sea he hated and feared.

I thought of Minnie. I'd been breaking my neck to get home to her and sort things out, but I decided this was a bigger thing. This couldn't wait. Minnie could.

"I'm coming with you," I said abruptly. "Could you use another hand?"

Dig was silent for a moment, fiddling with a pencil, then he looked up. "Not half, Jess. We could – especially people with experience." He paused. "But, Jess, didn't you ought to go down to the docks? There's big ships down there going over. They're wanting officers to relieve 'em."

"No," I said. "I'm here now. I'll stay here. I can handle a boat as well as a ship – probably better."

We stared at each other for a moment, both of us embarrassed by our own emotions, and I caught a glimpse of moisture sparkling at the corner of his eyes. Then, while we were still waiting for words to come, the telephone rang again, harsh and sharp and nervous in the silent room.

Dig gulped suddenly. "Give your name to Kate, Jess," he said.

He paused and reached for the telephone, halting with his hand on it while it continued to ring in jarring tones.

"It's fitters we're short of, Jess. We've got to get to Dover and these engines haven't been run all winter."

"Yorky's in town," I said, thinking of him immediately. "He's only across the road. He'll go."

Dig spoke over the shriek of the telephone. "Ask him, Jess," he said. "Let him know what it's all about, though. It wouldn't be fair, else."

"Listen here" – I spoke slowly – "can't you stay behind?" He looked at me gravely. "No, Jess! I'm going. Wiggins' have no right to let people go on this business – whatever it is – without us offering to go ourselves. 'Sides, suppose something happens? It's best it should be me 'stead o' someone younger and hopeful and happy."

The overflow of the crowd outside the boat-yard had drifted into the pub across the road, a shabby little place that had something of a station bar-room's cheerlessness about it. A stone-topped counter it had, I remember, and cast-iron table legs. The only things that didn't seem out of keeping with the

211

silent-faced men in oilskins and jerseys were the lurid pictures of windjammers in Cape storms that hung in vast frames on the walls.

Dance music was blaring from an unvarnished loudspeaker on the black marble mantelpiece alongside the bar. By the way no one was listening, I reckon it must have been bawling out music all day long, carelessly, as though this were just another summer. But the grave-voiced announcer, who interrupted with the news even as I entered, was the real reason for its volume.

There wasn't much happiness in the bar, only a bleakness, like the chill of funerals. Everyone there seemed to be aware now of what was going on across the road and across the Channel. The news was brief but enough to set everyone's mind racing and take the pleasure out of drinking.

Only Yorky was an oasis of happiness in the room. He and Old Boxer were not drunk but they were obviously well on the way. Yorky had reached the state when he was insisting on entertaining everybody.

"What's it to be?" he was saying as he gave his concertina a few preliminary squeezes. " 'Down at the Old Bull and Bush'? 'All the Nice Girls Love a Sailor'? Or 'ow about the old ballad, 'Throw Out the Lifeline, Mother, Someone is Sinking Tonight'."

Without giving anyone the chance to reply he plunged into his old favourite, the only thing he could play properly, the nostalgic "Shenandoah", his rasping voice croaking in time to the tune.

Old Boxer was in a corner, as usual, like a man with his back to the wall defying anyone to deny him drink, a group of empty glasses in front of him. He looked up as I arrived, and hurriedly emptied the glass he held.

"Yorky," I said, "they want you at Wiggins'."

"Shenandoah" whined to a stop. "Me? What for? What the 'ell's goin' off? What's everybody muckin' about at?"

"There's something big in the wind," I said. "They want all the small craft they can lay their hands on. Wiggins' are running the show here. They want to know if you'll go."

Yorky stared at me in silence for a while, then he took a hurried swig at his drink. "I thought summat was up," he said. He closed the concertina methodically and finished his drink. Then, "Is it dangerous, love?" he asked calmly.

"Probably," I said. "Is it a go?"

"Is it for our lads on t'other side o' t'Channel?" He looked up over his shoulder. I nodded and he dragged his cap straight on his round head and unhooked his feet from his stool.

"OK," he said. "I'll 'ave a 'ap'orth, kid."

He paused and glanced at Old Boxer sitting huddled in his corner. "They want deck-'ands, too?" he queried.

Old Boxer glared up at him, taking the hint. "They didn't want me before," he snapped. "Now they're shouting out for me."

"There's no shouting being done," I said.

Old Boxer seemed to shake himself free of the inertia that had been on him for days, ever since the destroyer had landed us in Ireland. "I'll go," he said dully.

" 'Ere, Jess." Yorky jabbed me with his concertina.

"What about a bit o' gear, though? A bloke can't go to sea like this 'ere." He dragged at the waistcoat they'd given him in Londonderry, a tight blue affair that forced his stomach out between the buttons. "Can't say I fancy muckin' about underneath a engine with a weskit on."

"I've got a kit-bag full of stuff at Ernie the Weasel's place," Old Boxer said wearily. "That god-damned Fee took it to pay me rent last time I was home."

"I'll get it for you," I said. "I pass the place on my way to the Steam Packet. We can share it."

We hurried outside and split up, Yorky bustling across the road towards the boat-yard, his concertina under one arm, his parcel under the other. Old Boxer hesitated on the step for a moment as I moved away.

"I'll just nip back," he said, "and get a bottle of something to keep us warm. Might need it if we're out all night."

"Then for God's sake bloody well stay sober!" Yorky bawled almost from the other side of the road. "You'll be no good to them lads over there if you're drunk."

t w o

As I pushed through the crowd to the dark street I felt the desire to get home to Minnie growing more urgent. The idea that we should try and put our affairs in order had been getting stronger for days – all the way home – and the nearness of this desperate thing I was undertaking made it all the more important that I should leave with her blessing if not her love. Perhaps I was being melodramatic with myself, but it occurred to me I might not come back, and that if I didn't get things straightened out now I might never get the chance. And I hated the idea of leaving the world without attempting it.

I wasn't afraid. I don't think I was being morbid. It was just a feeling that I wanted to see my affairs in order. Just as a chap might write a letter home before going into action or something like that. Minnie and I had been indifferent to each other too long. There was still plenty we could save from the wreck. There'd been happiness – even if its stay had been brief – and war, with death never very far off, wasn't the time for domestic upheavals.

There were still a few people about when I eventually halted in the blackout under the point of light that indicated the entrance to Pat Fee's lodging-house. Inside, I looked about me impatiently, anxious to be with Minnie. There was so little time before I must leave her again. There was so much to explain and, God knows, she wasn't a good listener.

A little man with a long moustache and a stringy neck, who was playing patience in a room off the hall, jumped up as I entered, and whirled round almost as though he expected to be assaulted and robbed. There seemed to be something familiar about his stooped back, even about the fistful of cards he held in his hand.

"What's this caper?" he was demanding. "Can't a bloke 'ave a game of patience without chaps bustin' in? Don't know what this world's comin' to. Next thing, I'll 'ave to lock meself in the closet for a bit o' peace. 'Ere I was just settin' 'avin' a quiet game – "

"I've come to collect a kit-bag," I said, interrupting. "Belonging to Horatio Boxer."

" 'Orace Boxer!" he almost spat. "That drunken old swine. Time 'e paid 'is rent. Owes me five bob 'e borrowed for booze. Time 'e came back. Where's 'is money? If 'e thinks 'e's goin' to get anythink without payin' 'is rent 'e's got another think comin' – "

"It'll be paid." I said. "*I'll* pay you."

"Ho, will you?" he said aggressively. "Well, you won't pay me. 'Cos I ain't got his bloomin' bag. See? I don't keep them things 'ere. Use yer loaf. Just the way to get beat up an' 'ave 'em all pinched back. The boss keeps 'em. 'E's bigger'n me. 'E can use 'is fists a bit, too. 'E takes charge of all unclaimed kit."

"Where's he live?" I demanded.

"You've 'ad yer time, mate. Can't tell you." He was picking his teeth with a match, half his dirty fist inside his mouth, and the words came out in a mumble. "Ain't allowed to. 'E 'as other affairs not connected with this place. 'E don't want dirty great matelots worryin' 'im. 'E's a gentleman."

"Where's he live?" I snapped, grabbing him by the arm and swinging him round. "This is urgent, you damn' fool!" I was growing impatient, desperate to get home to Minnie, feeling almost as though fate was playing the dirty on me and keeping me away from her now that I'd made up my mind to settle our differences.

"Not so much of yer carry-on," the little man was grumbling. "I ain't allowed to tell you, I say. My boss is a gent an' 'e likes to entertain young ladies now and then. 'E don't want worryin' with you. This ain't the Waldorf, y'know, with a resident manager an' a maid to scrub yer back in the bath."

"Blast you!" I almost shouted. "If you don't shut your rattle and come across with it I'll screw your dirty little neck round!"

I hoisted him to the toes of his shabby shoes by the bunched coat in my fist.

"OK, OK. Let go me coat. You're creasing it something cruel." He struggled feebly inside his clothes, for all the world like a hooked fish, and held up a hand that still clutched a fistful of greasy cards. " 'Ere you are. 'Ere you are. I've got it. 'Ere's 'is address. I've found it. You can see 'im in the mornin'. "

Something in his gesture as he brought a slip of pasteboard from his waistcoat pocket nudged my memory and swung me back across the years. I glanced round hurriedly. Sure enough there was a bowler hat hanging on the back of the door.

"Ernest Nanjizel!" I almost shouted. "Ernest Nanjizel! So you're Ernie the Weasel! By God, I've caught up with you at last!"

Released from my grasp, he brushed down his shabby coat with a genteel air. "Ernest Nanjizel's the name," he agreed. "Never mind this Weasel stuff. I don't like it, see? I don't go much on it. Ernest Nanjizel's the name. Always willing to oblige anyone. Used to be in business meself."

"Not half you didn't," I grinned. I grabbed his arm again. "It consisted of pinching my suitcase about ten years ago, you little shyster."

He'd obviously forgotten me, for there was bewilderment mixed with startled amazement in his eyes.

"I ain't pinched nothing," he said. "Don't come the old acid 'ere, mate. I ain't got no suitcase belonging to you or anyone else neither. You let a chap go."

"I might have known I'd find you mixed up with Pat Fee," I said. "What dirty games do you do for him besides swindling drunken matelots here?"

"Do a bit of runnin' for him," he admitted shiftily, a little subdued now. "Street-corner bettin' and that." He glanced at me suspiciously and asked, "You a cop, mister?"

"No." I released him and glanced at the pasteboard in my hand, then I whirled as I saw him creeping to the door. I bounded after him and the two of us stumbled and fell against a rickety chair which promptly collapsed. "You little rat!" I snapped, still on my knees, "This isn't his address. It's his office in the town."

"Oh, Gawd!" Nanjizel was lying among the wreckage of the chair, his arms flapping feebly, heedless of my urgent tones. "Oh, Christ!" he was moaning. "You've broke me back!"

"I'll break your neck if you don't give me his address," I said. "This is urgent, you stupid little fool!"

I was good and mad by this time. If he hadn't been Ernest Nanjizel I might have forgotten all about the address, and knocked up some shopkeeper for a jersey or borrowed some oilskins. But I was suddenly determined he wasn't going to trick me again.

"OK, OK." Nanjizel shuffled sideways out of my reach – with a clatter as the wreckage of the chair round his legs moved after him. "I'll tell you." He babbled the name of a street and I scrambled to my feet.

"If it isn't right," I said, "I'll come back and hand you over to the police. Or I'll break your dirty little neck myself and enjoy it."

"It's right, it's right," he moaned. "You go away and leave me to die. You've broke me back."

The address Nanjizel had given me was in one of the better-class districts of the town, and I decided to call there before going on to the Steam Packet in case Pat Fee was in bed. It was getting late by this time.

My thoughts were sour as I remembered little Nanjizel and his slyness. I was far from surprised to have found him in Pat Fee's seedy lodging-house and grudged the time I'd wasted arguing with him. The Steam Packet was still a long way from me, and there was still a lot to do and precious little time to do it in.

"Blast Old Boxer," I thought to myself, cursing him for the trouble he was causing.

I turned in at the block of flats where Pat Fee lived and rang the bell of the basement apartment. Pat seemed to have flourished and done well for himself, I decided, as I stared round the polished oak panelling. These were the places that had been occupied by the yachtsmen from St Clewes across the river before the war; the types with fancy caps and badges and not a single callus on their hands; the types who were careful to say "starn" for stern and had their photos taken holding the wheel well out to sea, but had a bloke to do all the pulling and heaving, and take over the steering when they wanted to come alongside.

The click of the door-handle interrupted my thoughts and Pat appeared. He was in his shirt-sleeves and braces and he seemed startled to see me. "Oh, Jesus!" he said, and he tried to slam the door to, but I shoved my foot in the opening.

"I haven't got it," he said hurriedly in answer to my demand, still trying to shut the door in my face. "It's not here. Go on. Scarper!"

Something in his eyes made me suspicious, and I put my shoulder against the door. "Come on, Pat," I said, "hand it over."

"I tell you I ain't got it," Pat was saying, endeavouring to push me out. "It isn't here. It's – it's at me office."

I knew he was lying and it antagonised me. It seemed as though his whole organisation was trying to place obstacles in my way, from its top to its shabby bottom.

"Listen, Pat," I said, just about ready to land him one. "I know you've got that gear, see, and I know it's here, and I'm goings to get it if I have to fetch a cop. This is urgent, man."

Pat appeared to be thinking quickly. "Oh, Christ, come on, then," he said, and his voice sounded harsh and angry. "Let's get it over with."

Inside the flat he moved swiftly across to one of the doors that led off the main lounge and, as he spoke, he was turning the key in the lock. Then he moved towards a desk and fished in a drawer.

"Here," he said, "that's his wallet." He tossed the leather case on to the table. "Nothing in it. Never is with these old bums. Only photographs and bills."

He dived a hand in his pocket and withdrew a bunch of keys. "Here." He threw them on to the table after the wallet. "Help yourself. It's in the garage somewhere. You'll have to find it yourself. I'm busy. Now clear off."

He came to the door with me – all the time between me and the rest of the flat, I noticed, and I guessed he had a woman in there with him. In the hall were two or three suit-cases.

"You going away, Pat?" I queried.

Pat gave me a sidelong glance as though I were joking, then he laughed shortly. "Just for a bit," he said. "That's all. You know – naughty weekend." He winked and nudged me. "How's Minnie, Jess? Is she OK?"

His eyes were sly as he spoke, and I had a feeling, as I always did when listening to Pat's conversation, that dirty paws were turning over my private possessions. Then the night air touched me as Pat opened the door for me and I was grateful for its cleanness.

"Business ain't been paying lately," he said. "These 'ere war savings campaigns is putting me out of business. I'm going up to Blackpool to see what's cooking. Plenty of money up there since all the London firms shifted their offices."

"Hadn't thought of joining up?" I grinned.

He flashed me a sour look. "Not me, mister," he said. "I got a business up in Blackpool to take over when I can arrange things. I'll be all right. They'll not get me. This place won't see Pat Fee again once I'm good and ready to go."

He half pushed me through the door as he spoke. "Shove the keys through the letter-box," he said. "I'm going to bed."

The door had half closed behind me when I heard a handle rattle in the flat. It belonged to the door Pat had locked and it rattled again, sharply, noisily, demanding attention. Pat gave me a quick flickering look, then a woman's voice from beyond the locked door yelped, "Hey, Pat Fee, what's the idea locking people up in bedrooms?"

Pat glanced sharply at me, then suddenly he put his weight behind the door he was holding. But I half turned and gave it a violent shove so that it hit him in the face and sent him reeling backwards, clutching at his nose. Then I bounded past him across to the bedroom where the door-handle was still rattling.

"Open this blasted door, Pat Fee!" the woman beyond was yelling as I turned the key in the lock.

The door was violently wrenched open from inside as the lock slipped back and she burst out straight into my arms. She was dressed in a blowsy-looking kimono and apparently nothing else.

"What's the big idea?" she was demanding. "What's – ?"

Her gaze absorbed my unfamiliar clothes, then her eyes travelled upwards to my face.

"By God, you've got a nerve, Pat!" I breathed, half admiring him despite myself.

She'd stopped dead, her mouth open, then she wrenched herself free and clutched the kimono to her.

"I got wet, Jess," she babbled. "It rained and it's a long way to the Steam Packet. And a girl's got to dry her clothes."

three

The three of us stared at each other for a moment, then Pat picked himself up from the corner where my shove had sent him.

"See here, Jess," he said, licking the blood from his lips. "Don't go jumping to conclusions."

I took no notice and went on looking down at Minnie.

"I thought you was dead, Jess," she said desperately. "People kept saying you was dead. Gospel, they did."

I ignored her obvious groping for an excuse and locked the hall door and pushed the key into my pocket.

"My God," I said slowly, "you've got a nerve, Pat! 'How's Minnie? Is she OK?' I'll say she is."

"Listen, Jess," Pat said, his voice harsh and frightened. "Don't start getting ideas into your head!"

Ideas into my head! I almost laughed aloud. But inside me there was no humour, only a cold, bitter desire to knock that ingratiating look off Pat's face. I'd been right all the time, through all those months of my marriage. Minnie and Pat were lovers, and if the truth were known, had been ever since they were old enough to understand the meaning of sex.

They were both addressing me now, talking wildly, their words falling over themselves.

"Listen, Jess," Minnie was saying. "I keep telling you I thought you was dead. They said your ship had gone down and you'd been drownded. And there's nothing to stop a girl

223

going off with other people when she thinks her husband's dead, is there?"

"Did you think I was dead the last time, too?" There seemed to be no anger in me, only that cold, horrible loneliness again. "I was going home, Minnie," I went on. "I was itching to go home – to you. I was about busting my boilers to get home and straighten things out."

"Was you, Jess?" Minnie said, and there was a foolish expression of affected interest on her face, an expression that had an idiot quality as she clutched the kimono in front of her. "My, you're early, though, aren't you? We – I didn't expect you."

"I can see that."

Minnie came towards me and tried to put her arms round my neck. There seemed to be no coherence in anything she did or said – as though finding me there had shocked her into stupidity. "Jess," she said. "I'd never – if I'd only known. I never knew. They said you was dead," she said again in a foolish repetition.

There was a smell of stale perfume about her, a musty, feminine odour that revolted me. I unlocked her hands from behind my head as she tried to kiss me in an eager, fawning effort to be loving that sickened me. Then I pushed her away angrily and she stumbled over the suitcases in the doorway and sat down heavily, her plump white legs in the air.

"Jess," she said despairingly, her voice cracked and breaking, "they told me you was dead." Even then I reckon she was thinking more about the licence of the Steam Packet than about me.

I turned from her to Pat and he edged away hurriedly.

"Now then, Jess Ferigo," he said, his back against a table. In his voice there was a quality of bluster that showed how frightened he was. "Open that door. Let's have no larks or I'll call a bobby."

"By God," I said through my teeth, "just you try!"

Pat was silent for a second, then he grinned sheepishly. "Now, there's no harm done," he insisted. "Nothing that can't be put right by a little chinwag and a few quid. Don't you go and be 'asty, Jess."

"Pat," I interrupted, "I'm going to give you the biggest walloping of your dirty life. I tried once before, but I didn't quite manage it. This time I'm going to knock the smell of the bedroom off you, and all those filthy stinking ideas out of your head."

"See here, Jess." Pat's eyes were flickering round the room. "You're talking soft. You've got a screw loose, man."

"I've been talking soft for years now." My words came slowly and they felt as chilly as ice. "I should have done this years ago."

Minnie was grovelling beside me on her knees, pulling at my arm, either to reconcile me to her or to attract my attention from Pat. I don't know which.

"Jess," she was saying desperately. "Just let me get me things together and we'll go right home. Everything'll be all right. Just me and you."

I shook her off. "Get away from me!" I almost shouted. "Get away from me, you dirty little bitch! You got what you wanted. Don't come whining back again."

I turned to Pat, calm once more.

"Pat," I said, "you'd better know why I'm going to give you this walloping. It isn't because you've taken Minnie. You can have her, and I hope she does you as little good as she's done me. No, it's not that. It's because of all those things that happened in the past. All those dirty things you said, and all those shabby ideas in that grubby little mind of yours. All those filthy tricks you've played on me, all those little swindles you've practised. They've been waiting a long time, Pat, but they've caught up with you at last."

As I was speaking Pat was edging away from me, nearer to the fireplace. "Me and you's got a bit of settling up to do," I went on. "A few accounts that want clearing."

Pat had put a cigarette to his lips with shaking fingers, and tearing a strip from the newspaper he twisted it into a spill and bent with it as though to switch on the electric fire in the hearth. His back was to me for a moment and he grabbed for the poker and whirled round again.

"No, Pat, for God's sake!" Minnie's scream split the tension. "You'll kill him!"

I leapt aside as Pat's arm came down and the poker struck me across the shoulder with a sickening blow that numbed it. Then I snatched the weapon and flung it clattering across the room with one hand as I brought the other round in a great scything blow. Pat went sprawling into the fireplace, all arms and legs, his feet sending the electric fire flying. He scrambled up again, his face livid, and the two of us wrestled together in the middle of the room, turning chairs over, while Minnie stood in the corner, still half-naked, yelling for the police in a hard, dry scream that seemed to rasp in her throat.

As we crashed against it the table teetered and fell on its side, sending a bowl of fruit flying across the room, apples and oranges rolling under the settee. Pat had lost none of his old skill, but he was soon panting heavily. He was far from fit, with too many cigarettes and women and too much booze to blame for it, I reckon, and the cold fury I felt made me heedless of his blows. We hadn't been at it long before he shoved me away to get his wind. He was bleeding from a cut lip and he spat out a tooth as he leaned for a second on a chair, trying to catch the breath that whistled into his lungs through his heaving chest.

"You bloody bully!" Minnie was screaming, trying to snatch at my arm. "Leave him be!" I flung her aside again as Pat made another rush at me and I brought him up sharp with a smack in the face that split my knuckles. But I felt a savage delight in the pain as the blow jarred home and Pat's head clicked back. He staggered against a standard lamp that crashed to the floor with the pop of an exploding bulb, recovered himself with an effort, and stumbled forward on buckling knees. I sent him reeling away again to the wall. A flying elbow – mine or Pat's, I don't know whose – swept the clock from the mantelpiece, then desperately, with a swing of his arm that was more a shove than a blow, Pat brought me to my knees and fell on top of me.

I heaved myself up and dragged Pat's heavy body after me. One-handed it was, in a great muscle-cracking heave. With an effort that gave me a bitter pleasure I slammed him back into the fireplace again.

The room was wrecked by this time, and Pat was beginning to look the worse for wear. He fought for breath in great wrenching gasps, his mouth hanging open, saliva mixed with the blood that was smeared across his cut lips. One eye was closed and his nose was bleeding badly.

Minnie was still dancing on the edge of the fight, her kimono torn in the struggle, and she turned again on me. Her hair was round her shoulders, her breasts bare, and there was an almost savage light in her eyes. She had the look of a witch about her as her lips mouthed obscenities and her fingernails clawed at my cheeks.

Pat came at me again and, exulting, a vast orchestra pounding out a brassy song of triumph inside me, I drove my fist savagely into his battered face. He staggered back, tottering, and I went after him, fiercely, joyously driving him backwards again until, at last, his knees gave way and he toppled forward on to his face, writhing, the blood and saliva bubbling through his lips.

"I've 'ad enough!" he moaned. "Take 'er away! Take the bitch out of me sight!"

I brushed the hair from my eyes and wiped the perspiration from my face. I stared down at Pat, all the meanness of

227

the past wiped away, all the unhappiness gone in one tremendous demand on my strength; then I bent among the wreckage, seeking the belongings which had fallen out of my pockets in the struggle. I stuffed Old Boxer's wallet away first and stooped to retrieve its spilled contents.

Minnie was kneeling in the hearth by Pat, hugging his half-unconscious head to her breast, kissing him frantically, turning to curse at me, naked and unashamedly rotten, common and cheap and vulgar, and impudently faithless.

"You bloody bully!" she was sobbing. "You dirty swine! He hadn't hurt you. God, you dirty dog, if I'd known I'd never have married you! I only married you to make sure the pub was safe, anyway. I always wanted Pat, you bloody rat! I never wanted you. I was Pat's – I always was – before I married you and ever since."

I went on stuffing things into my pockets – keys, papers, photographs, money – hardly noticing the stream of obscenities and filth that were wrenched from Minnie's writhing mouth. I picked up a bunch of photographs and stood staring at them, dazed and dizzy, still struggling for my breath.

"You dirty dog!" Minnie was moaning. "You've half killed him, you swine!"

I wrenched my torn jacket straight with my free hand, still staring at the photographs in my hand. Minnie was swearing quietly at me, like a cat, spitting and mouthing, hissing the words venomously; then Pat shuffled to his knees and shoved her away from him.

"Get away from me!" he said. "You've fetched me into a nice old mess, you have!"

"Pat!" Minnie's word was a scream, and she'd forgotten me immediately. "Don't say that! Don't say that, Pat! You can't leave me now!"

"Can't I, though?" Pat was swaying on his feet. "Can't I? I've 'ad enough trouble with you, missis. I'll get meself a bird without a husband next time. Go on! Scram!"

"Pat, you swine!" Minnie leapt at him, her fingers clawing at his face. "I was good enough in bed for you and now you're yellow!"

Pat grabbed her wrists and, thrusting her aside, stumbled towards the bathroom. Minnie was on her knees grovelling after him, trying to kiss his feet, pleading with him.

"Pat! Patty darling! You can't leave me now! Where are you going?"

"I'm going to wash meself," Pat said. "And then I'm going to scarper."

He placed his foot on her shoulder and gave her a shove so that she rolled over and lay sprawling. Then he slipped into the bathroom and closed the door. Even as Minnie scrambled after him, still on all fours, I heard the bolt click on the inside.

"Oh God, Pat!" she wailed. "You can't leave me now! You rat, you can't go without me!" Her moans turned into a fierce spit of hatred, then back again into a wail. "Pat, Pat! Oh, Pat, answer me!"

There was only the sound of a tap running on the inside.

Minnie scrambled to her feet, clutching the torn remains of her kimono about her; then she whirled, looking for me, her eyes sharp and bright and plotting again.

"Jess," she said, then she stopped dead.

I was just leaving, and the door of the flat was gaping open. Even as she stared at me I saw the hall porter and his wife come up behind me.

"Oh, my God!" Minnie squealed and dived for the bedroom.

four

Midnight had chimed from the Town Hall clock when the little ships cast off from Wiggins' wharf and headed for the Eastern Channel. There was no excitement and very little comment. Just a few shouted "Let go's" and a deeper note in the drum of the idling engines, then one by one the bows began to swing out and head into the river. I remember seeing Dig, who was standing by the forepeak, silhouetted against the silvery grey of the river as the sharp nose of our boat swung out into midstream. Then, with a naval launch to lead us, we left the harbour in groups of two, each group following the stern lights of the boats ahead, downstream, round St Andrew Head and east-nor'-east.

My face felt tense and set in the darkness as we hit the seas beyond the point and the boat began to bump. Suddenly she became alive with a chorus of protesting creaks and groans. I could see the bow rising and falling, its black silhouette circling the bright dot of light ahead that was a stern light. I felt better with the breeze on my face. It was like a sedative to me and soothed my raw spirit, and I thanked God for the pleasure I could get from the smell of the sea and the stars above my head.

I could hear no talking, though "Shenandoah" came filtering through the steady drumming of the engines and the swish of the water around me. The wake was churning the sea into a phosphorescent road that trailed away behind us, writhing and tumbled, like some silvery ribbon to the west.

Though we knew nothing of it then, all round the country convoys like ours were butting their way out of rivers into the open sea, most of them manned by crews like ours.

I held the wheel of a big passenger-carrying motor-launch, built like a Brixham trawler. Broad in the beam as a cart-horse, she was, sturdy and reliable, with a high wheelhouse. She was clumsy, though, and I was glad I'd handled boats at Wiggins' often.

Dig crouched stiffly behind a hatch cover, half invisible in the darkness. Yorky was in the engine-room, sitting between the thundering engines, oblivious to the noise. Now and again he wiped them with loving care, leaning heavily on the slow-moving rag as he worked. In the cabin, stretched on one of the cushioned seats, Old Boxer was fast asleep and snoring – drunk.

"Gawd!" Yorky had said when I arrived back at the boat-yard. "I telled him! You know I telled 'im! But when I come aboard 'e was flaked out 'ere already, see?" He grabbed at the old man's shoulder and shook it. "You drunken old bastard, you! Boozed up! Stinking! Rotten ripe!" he yelled in his high-pitched voice. "What bloody good are you to us like this?"

Dig was worried for a while by Old Boxer's state, but I reassured him.

"He hasn't been to sea sober yet," I said. "When he comes round he'll be all right."

My voice as I spoke felt flat and emotionless. The shock of finding Minnie in Pat's flat had knocked all the stuffing out of me. I'd walked slowly back to the boat-yard, still unable to hate Pat Fee and Minnie, all the time saying to myself: "I told you so. I told you so."

I wasn't the first sailor to come home and find his wife playing cuckoo in someone else's bed. It was among the

231

chances a sailor took when he went to sea, and had been ever since Columbus sailed for America.

I ought to have known long before that Minnie was no more trustworthy than Pat. They were grown in the same garden.

I'd felt old as I turned into the boat-yard and as I climbed over the crowded decks towards the launch they'd given me I realised I'd been walking for hours.

When I arrived Dig was on the foredeck sorting out the mass of equipment he'd unearthed – an old duffel coat, sou'-westers, oilskins, jerseys, binoculars even, and a sextant.

"I thought you might need it, Jess," he explained shyly.

"We'll need no sextant," Yorky said bluntly. "It'll be guesswork, a bleeden lot o' luck and Gawd 'elp 'im 'oo 'elps 'isself where *we're* goin'."

I made my way into the forecastle, a little closet of a cabin where sea-sick passengers had been in the habit of lying down on the boat's trips round the lighthouse. It was lit by a couple of tiny bulbs in the deck-head, and in the forrard corner, half in shadow, Old Boxer sprawled, stinking of rum, his mouth open and snoring.

Half under his great flabby body was the naval sword that was all he had left of a career. Some drunken whim had persuaded him to buckle the tarnished belt round his sagging waist, either because it was easier to carry that way or because his twisted mind saw in it a parody of gallantry. Perhaps he saw himself in some private joke – drunken and old and unwanted as he headed for glory stinking of booze. He lay with its shabby scabbard protruding from beneath him, a mockery of courage and high tradition.

I sat down wearily, my brain numb with too much think-ing, and glanced at the old man huddled in his corner, his head crooked to that impossible angle only a drunk can manage. There was a lot we had to talk about when he was sober again, but for the moment, in my mind, there was only that ugly knowledge that Minnie had been playing me dirty all our married life and even before. And with it came that unhappy, unwanted feeling of loneliness – just as I'd felt when I found out about my parentage, a feeling that seemed to have been recurring throughout my whole life.

I sat in silence for what seemed hours, then Dig called me to go to the office for briefing.

"Last-minute instructions, Jess, boy," he said. He must have been aware that something had happened to me. So must Yorky. My eye was bruised, and my lips were split. But Dig said nothing. "The Navy people want to go over it again with the cox'ns," was his only remark.

I only dimly heard the lieutenant-commander who told us what we had to do. My mind was still busy elsewhere, and I wasn't completely conscious of the scene in the little room, and the tense, taut faces that were greyish in the high, yellow light in the ceiling. The voice of the calm, confident officer, apparently undisturbed by the magnitude of the task we were undertaking, grated on my raw nerves yet still only skimmed the surface of my consciousness, so that I knew what I had to do without really absorbing it.

I can remember what he said now better than I could then: "We don't know how long we've got. I've no signals and no notes. I've even no plans. Events are moving too fast for 'em. They're out of date before they're put into operation. We can't help you with maintenance or supplies. All I know is that we've got to throw in everything we have."

"Which way do we go?" somebody asked.

"They'll tell you that at Dover – if you're going," the commander said. "The normal route's impassable because of shore batteries. I expect it'll be from the North Goodwin Light direct."

"Blimey, that'll be nearly a hundred miles!" the chap next to me burst out. "It's only thirty straight across."

"It's either that or be blown out of the water," the commander pointed out, his alert, handsome face calm. "The Pongos are on the beaches of Malo-les-bains and we've got to fetch 'em off."

"Where's Malo-les-bains?" someone asked.

"You'll find it all right. Don't worry."

"And what about the shoals off Dunkirk, mister?" The old boy who spoke this time sounded like a retired master mariner, and he seemed to be addressing his first mate.

"There'll be charts. The printing presses at Dover'll be red-hot by now."

"What about pensions if we stop one? What about our kids? *We* ain't in the Navy, y'know." It was a little bloke in an outsize oilskin who asked the question.

The commander's face was flushed for the first time as he replied: "I don't know about pensions. I don't know about anything like that. I only know the Pongos are waiting to be taken off and we've got to do it. If you don't like the idea no one's forcing you to go."

Nobody else asked any questions.

We made our way back to the boats, mostly in silence. There was a long journey ahead of us, a journey that several of us would never complete, and beyond that there was only a big question mark.

I stopped as I saw Kate Fee standing near the edge of the wharf. She smiled wryly, no happiness in the gesture.

"Well, Jess," she said in that soft voice of hers that was still steady in spite of the hysteria and emotion and excitement of the day. "This is it. Goodbye and God bless you. I'll be here when you come back."

I smiled without speaking and kissed her gently. Her lips were cold but her fingers gripped my arms tightly. Then I turned away, aware that she was still on the wharf, motionless and silent, huddled inside an overcoat borrowed from a bobby. I felt a soothing glow of comfort for the first time that night, like the warmth that comes from rum in a cold body, a consciousness of affection and an odd feeling that I wasn't entirely unwanted.

Yorky met me as I climbed aboard. " 'Ow long we got, love?" he demanded soberly. "Are we off straightaway?"

I nodded.

"Everything's ready, Jess," Dig was saying. "Everything you're likely to need."

I nodded my thanks, and we arranged watches, with Old Boxer taking the last trick at the wheel to give him time to sober up.

A naval tug in the river was signalling by lamp to the launch that was to lead us, then Yorky arrived and took my attention with a chatter that jarred on my tired nerves.

"She's OK, kid," he said. "Off we go. Sixpence round the bleeden light'ouse. 'Er engines is lovely. She'll cruise from 'ere to Singapore so long as you take 'er nice and easy. I'll give you a 'and at castin' off, then I'll nip below and mash a cup of char afore I get me 'ead down. P'r'aps it'll bring Old 'Orace round. Silly old fool," he muttered as he moved towards the stern rope. "All 'e does is go to bloody sleep..."

The hours passed slowly. They were long and weary and marked by mugs of scalding tea that were accompanied by the north-country twang of a man in love with life. To Yorky everything was exciting and important and interesting, as it always had been to him, whether it was a gleaming engine or merely a dockside carousal.

I killed the time by forcing my mind to stay away from that picture of Minnie I still had in my eyes, naked and mean and sly, holding Pat Fee's head to her breast, passionately defiant, a stream of filthy, obscene abuse coming from her mouth, a Minnie I'd never imagined even in my wildest moments. I'd been aware for a long time she wasn't all I'd expected when I married her, but the shabbiness of her sly little mind had been hidden by her laughter and her passionate nature. Now I'd seen her stripped of the few pleasant things in her character, raw and ugly and mean.

I stood at the wheel almost until dawn broke, then Dig took over from me, cautiously, nervous of the job. He seemed to regard me as if I were a stranger to him.

"Will we get there today, Jess?" he asked.

"Doubt it," I said, my mind only half on what he said. "Might stay the night somewhere. Let the engines cool and give everybody a sleep. Probably make Dover tomorrow or the day after."

"I see." Dig paused and I hesitated for a moment before going below, for he obviously wanted to talk to me.

"I'll manage all right now, Jess," he said, indicating the wheel. He seemed to be trying to pluck up courage to say something. "I'm glad I had a bit of a go at this job, Jess," he suddenly burst out. "I feel it's the first man-sized thing I've done."

I said nothing and Dig went on, shyly, not looking at me, but for once with no book to hide his eyes: "I'm proper glad, Jess. I'm not frightened now, and I wasn't very sick during the night. You see, Jess," he said quietly, "I'm a bit old and daft and a bit dusty. It'll do nobody any harm if I don't come back."

I looked quickly at him, and he went on. Not as though he was tormenting himself with the idea of death, but with a complete calm, as though he'd spent the night in deliberate thought.

"I've been a bit of a failure, really, Jess," he said. "I made a mess of marriage, and I reckon I've been no great value to the boat-yard neither." He sighed. "Your Ma'll be well provided for in case I don't come back," he said. "I've always tried to do me best for her, though she's been a bit of a trial at times."

He paused, then he said, as though in conclusion, "I hope I'll not be too much in the way, Jess boy."

I put a hand on his skinny shoulder and squeezed it. "You're doing fine," I said, and went below.

I was stumbling with weariness when I reached the cabin, where Yorky was just rising from one of the seats.

"Been 'avin' a nap, Jess, for ten minutes," he said as he ascended the ladder. "Old 'Orace 'as sobered up now. 'E'll be able to take a trick at the wheel soon."

Old Boxer was sitting up squinting in the early sunshine that fell on his haggard face through the porthole. He was huddled in a corner, a mug of tea on the deck between his feet. The old overcoat he wore was screwed round his body so that he looked like an untidily wrapped parcel. The shabby naval sword, its tarnished silver almost black, lay discarded on the leather cushions by his side.

He gave me a sidelong glance as I sat down at the opposite side of the forecastle, and there was silence for a while except for the creaking of timbers and the slap of water outside. The engines were nothing more than a pulsing vibration here in the forrard part of the vessel.

"How do you feel?" I asked, lighting a cigarette.

"All right now." His voice was dry and harsh. "Fit as a fiddle. Sorry. Don't know how it happened. Only had one or two while I was waiting."

His face was grey, and he looked older than ever and frail despite his bulk.

I said nothing but drew his wallet out of my pocket and tossed it across to him.

"I didn't get your gear," I said as he pocketed it. "I had a bit of bother with Pat Fee and came away without it. You can borrow some, though. There'll be plenty to spare where we're going."

He nodded dully, and I fished again in my pocket and withdrew a photograph. I tossed it across and it fell alongside his hand. He picked it up idly and glanced at it, then he looked sharply at me.

"Where did you get this?" he asked.

"It was in your wallet," I said. "It fell out and I picked it up."

There was a long silence, then I spoke again. "It's my Ma," I said, and Old Boxer's trembling fingers became still as he held the photograph half in and half out of the wallet. "There's one exactly like it at home."

He said nothing, and I went on, "Dig kept it there because it was a photograph of her when she was young and pretty."

Old Boxer suddenly began to stuff the picture away in the wallet with clumsy fingers.

"God, the booze's got me proper," he said.

I watched as he lit a cigarette and stuffed the wallet awkwardly into his pocket again; then I said, "You're my father, aren't you?"

I felt no emotion as I spoke, only an emptiness inside me, a sudden returning of that chilly loneliness.

Old Boxer pushed the wallet into his hip pocket in silence. Then he took a deep puff at his cigarette and blew out the smoke before answering.

"Yes," he said. "I am."

We were silent for a long time, staring at each other; then I went on, "Go on, it's about your turn now."

Old Boxer drew on his cigarette and for a moment his face was in shadow. He appeared to be thinking. On deck I could hear Dig and Yorky conversing in low tones and the click of the chain as the helm moved.

Old Boxer seemed to be searching his mind not only for words but for comprehensive thought. I expect it was still fuddled with drink and the shock of what I'd said had fogged it even more. He appeared to be groping into it, calling into it for advice. But it was re-echoing like an empty hall to him, deserted and cobwebbed. He looked as though a trick had been played on him – as though something he'd been trying to forget for years was now in front of him, as vast and lifelike and frightening as if it had happened the day before, as if a long-forgotten nightmare had suddenly been repeated.

He looked across at me. I was still waiting for a reply.

"Give me a moment, Jess," he said. "My mind's limping along like a flat foot just now."

He drew a deep breath. "I knew you were my son, Jess," he said, and the words seemed to drag heavy-footed one after the other. "I always knew. I thought I'd manage to forget, but I didn't. It's not as easy as that. You're the spittin' image of me when I was young. I saw myself often in you, the way I'd hoped to be and knew I never would be." He seemed to be speaking to himself.

"I suppose I'm not what you expected as a father," he went on, and he appeared to be asking a question. "But after they threw me out of the Navy I couldn't go home and it was easier to drink than remember. Do you see? God, Jess," he said suddenly, as though trying to excuse himself – and excuse himself to himself rather than to me, it seemed – "it's awful when you know there's no one who gives a damn about what happens to you."

"There was no one to give a damn about what happened to me, either," I said, and I was bitter as I recalled my own loneliness.

I suddenly felt angry at him sitting there, whining about having no one to care for him. I'd spent all my life with no one to give me any affection, in a loneliness that was caused even before I was born.

His humiliation infuriated me. He'd been full of bounce all his life and, now he was having a dose of what I'd known all through my childhood, he was complaining.

Then his next words took away all the malice in me and made me realise what he must have gone through.

"All the time," he said, "I had to watch you growing up, trying to do my best to cultivate the spirit in you that I knew was there. And yet all the time I was scared stiff you'd realise who I was."

"If I'd found out twenty years ago," I said slowly, "we might both have enjoyed ourselves a bit more."

He was silent for a moment. "It sounds easy now, Jess," he admitted, "but it never seemed easy to me."

"Reckon you've been running away from a shadow all your life," I said. "Other people have illegitimate kids and still manage to get over it."

"But some of us are weak, Jess," he pleaded, lighting another cigarette from the stub of the old one. "You're not. Thank God you've got more backbone than I ever had.

"Besides," he went on, throwing the fag-end away and grinding it flat with his boot, "there was nothing I could do. I couldn't accept responsibility for you. I could only sit back and thank God you were growing up as I'd hoped you would. Don't you understand, lad? I'd no right to anything else. I'd nothing to give you. I've still nothing to give you. I'll never have anything to give you."

I listened, watching the smoke of my cigarette as it moved, oddly and jerkily when the boat bumped in the waves. I wasn't shocked, either by my discovery or by the humiliation of Old Boxer and his grovelling desire to explain himself. There was so little to admire in this father of mine and I had a sudden mental picture of him as I'd seen him so often: debauched, stale, and smelling of booze, with people laughing at him or dodging out of his way as he stumbled along, wretched and jaded and tormented by his own thoughts.

"What are we going to do about it, Jess?" he said.

"Do?" I tossed my fag-end out of the open porthole behind me. "Nothing, I suppose. Just now we've got a bit of a job to do. We'll think about this lot later on."

I lifted my legs on to the cushions and pulled a blanket over me. My eyelids drooped with weariness and I felt too tired to care much one way or the other what we did.

"You're on watch next," I said. "You've got about ten minutes. Drink your tea."

I noticed the roughness had gone out of my voice.

I lay back, my head on a life-jacket. Old Boxer must have thought I was asleep, but I could see him through half-closed eyes. He picked up his mug of tea, long since cold, and seemed to shrink within himself.

"Thank God, thank God," he was murmuring to himself in a desperate repetition. "Thank God." I don't know what was going through his mind but I suspect he was grateful that it was all over at last and the bogey he'd been dodging for years had been brought out into the daylight. I watched him as he fumbled with his cigarette. I could have been so proud of him if I'd only had the chance, but there wasn't much about Old Boxer to admire.

He sat still for a moment and his clumsy, fuddled thoughts seemed to be trudging past like shuffling, grey old men, his tormented eyes showing the agony in his mind.

"God damn the booze!" he said aloud, and he fished in his overcoat pocket. He drew out a bottle of rum and took a swig at it. Something ugly was trying to get through to the surface, something cold and mean and dark, and it showed in his face. I saw him thrust it away out of his mind as plainly as if he'd actually warded it off.

He shuddered suddenly, and I realised he was afraid of the job in front of us and the bloodiness of the question mark that lay just over the horizon. Like a dying man clinging to life, he was shrinking at the thought of death and pain. He was afraid, I knew, afraid so that his inside was queasy at the thought of it, so afraid he'd had to drink himself silly to get aboard at all. It was the booze that had unmanned him and he knew it as well as I did. Once he'd been strong, but now he was rotten with a moral as well as a physical fear. And I knew then that behind his boastfulness and strength and size there'd always been this weakness.

It had destroyed his ship and his career and his whole life. It had prevented him from marrying Ma and destroyed her, too, furious and bitter that Old Boxer – a glittering, magnificent figure he must have been in those days – had not stood by her. No wonder he hated Dig. Inside Dig's slight figure and behind his shy nature there was solid, slogging courage. There must have been, the way he'd looked after Ma across the years and never complained.

Old Boxer drew in his breath sharply and seemed to gather himself, as though he were trying to forget his fear. He'd forgotten it before, he was telling himself furiously, forgotten all manner of things, forgotten bitterness, dislike, tenderness, everything, even his own son, taking refuge in booze.

His hand strayed again to the bottle in his pocket but stopped half-way as Yorky's voice at the hatch cover called him.

"Come on, 'Orace," it said. "Play the bleeden game. We've 'ad our turn. Now it's yourn."

Old Boxer sighed deeply and dragged himself on to his unsteady legs, his face drawn and gaunt, and pulled himself as though he were a heavy load up the companionway to the sunlight.

f i v e

Dover shone brightly in the early morning sunshine when we shut down and lay drifting in the slight swell that was running. The harbour was crowded with craft already. There were tugs, drifters, destroyers, sloops, motor-boats; fishing-boats, eel-boats, Dutch schuits, mudhoppers, dumb barges, and every kind of rowing-boat and pulling-boat imaginable. Outside, in the waters of the Channel, hundreds more small craft were moored alongside the anchored bigger vessels, their holiday paint gay in the sunshine.

We'd halted overnight at Pompey to cool our engines and give the crews some rest, and the boats waiting at Pompey had moved on ahead of us to Dover and Ramsgate. The following morning we'd set off again for the hub of the adventure.

Even as we watched, destroyers whooped their way among the crowded vessels and dashed across the Channel in the direction of the sun, setting the moored boats rolling and bobbing and bouncing against each other in the wash. And, as fast as they went, more vessels were returning – in a stream that had never stopped since the operation had started days before. Out of the sun they came, like tiny dots on the shining surface of the water that glistened in the morning light. There were men aboard them who'd marched hundreds of miles, fighting on the way, and stopped on the beaches of Dunkirk and fought again. They were dusty and dishevelled, their faces black with oil and coal-dust and smoke, their eyes bloodshot with weariness, but they still managed to wave as they moved past us and now and then they even raised a cheer. In great masses they came, crowding the decks of the destroyers and the troopships, seeming almost to swamp the small vessels as they curtseyed in the swell.

I watched them pass in a grim, pathetic, heroic stream. Our own little flotilla, that had set out from Wiggins' wharf, had dwindled already. Some of them were adrift long before Pompey rose out of the horizon. More had broken down the following day. The last of them was just chugging up to us and shutting off its spluttering, overheated engine so that the flotilla was silent and we'd only the lap of the waves against the hulls and the slap of the halyards against the masts for company.

Even as the sound died away, though, the naval launch which had been leading us roared to life again and hurried in a circle round towards us, like an excited terrier with a bone in its teeth.

" 'Ello!" Yorky, scarlet in the face, was resting his elbows on the cover of the engine-room hatch, taking in great gulps of air, his fat bottom jamming up the hatchway through which the fumes of hot oil and petrol seeped. He was idly squeezing a tune out of his concertina, but he squinted keenly at the naval vessel as she approached. " 'E's coming this way," he said. "Now the party's goin' to start."

Old Boxer was lighting a cigarette with trembling hands that were not entirely caused by the chilliness of the morning air or the exhaustion we all felt. As he watched the launch draw closer his eyes were dull with apprehension.

"It's the booze," I could hear him saying fiercely to himself. "It's the booze." And his itching fingers felt for the bottle in his pocket.

The spirit seemed to warm him and took the tremble out of his hands. He watched the launch shut down her engines, her bows sinking into the water as the way went off her.

The lieutenant-commander was bawling at us through a megaphone: "Thanks a lot. Stand by for a naval crew to come aboard. A tender will take you ashore."

"You go chase yourself up a shutter!" Yorky shouted back in a furious explosion of anger that almost lifted him out of the hatchway. "We 'aven't brought this old cow all this way just to let you lot take 'er over. You can't go off like that."

"Sorry," the officer shouted. "Those are the instructions."

"Well, you know what you can do wi' 'em." Yorky's voice was threatening as he flourished his concertina. "Just you let one of them bell-bottomed bastards of yourn put 'is foot aboard of 'ere, an' 'e'll get it straight in the kisser with this 'ere squeeze-box."

The commander had fallen silent and seemed to be thinking fast.

"We're a crew of bloody sailors aboard of 'ere, mate," Yorky was shouting, his face red with indignation. "There's none of yer queenie weekend yachtsmen among us lot. We've sailed big ships and little 'uns, an' we'll make rings round you if you'd like to see us."

The commander was grinning now.

"Who's in command?" he was shouting. "You?"

"No. 'Im." Yorky indicated me with his thumb. " 'E's got 'is mate's ticket so yer needn't bloody worry. An' if you've got a better engineer aboard of that old wash-tub of yourn than me I'd like to see 'im."

The commander was silent for a while, then he shouted back: "All right. I'll report it to the Senior Naval Officer. If he objects you'll still have to go ashore."

" 'E'd better not!" Yorky yelled. "You'll 'ave a job catching us else. These is fast engines, mate, an' they won't break down while I'm in charge of 'em."

The launch crew were grinning now and the officer laughed. "OK," he shouted. "There's a petrol tanker over there…" He flung out a gold-ringed arm. "Fill your tanks and take on rations and water from the ship lying astern of her. They'll give you everything you need. Stay alongside her till you're wanted. You'll be going across under tow – if you're going at all."

"We'll be going, mate!" Yorky shouted. "Don't you worrit!"

The officer waved. "That's all. Understood?"

I waved back, then the launch's engine roared to life again, and her bow rose as she shot ahead to the next boat in the line.

"OK, Yorky," I said. "You got your way. Get below. I'm going to start up."

Yorky grinned. "Don't mind me, Jess. I'm all for the Navy boys, reelly."

I saw Old Boxer flash him a look as he dodged below.

I took the wheel, still watching Old Boxer, who was sitting on a fender forrard. His face was grey and haggard, and his eyes were tormented with something that was more than weariness.

We lay alongside the stern of the supply ship through the hot summer day, lifting on the heave of the pale, oil-slicked sea; smoking and drinking mugs of strong tea brewed by Yorky; from time to time picking up snatches of news from the forecaste wireless of the supply ship.

"Jerry's bombing the hospital ships," they said. "Three destroyers gone in less than an hour. Jerry reckons we'll never get the rest of the boys away."

" 'E's right an' all," Yorky commented dryly. "If we sit on our behinds 'ere all day we'll never get nobody off."

" 'Old yer water, mate," one of the ship's crew said, "your turn'll come."

Yorky muttered something to himself and went on peeling potatoes, assisted by Dig and Old Boxer. I watched the three of them, all older than I, all different: Yorky, aggressively sure of himself and his engines, anxious to get into the turmoil across the narrow strip of water. Dig, quietly confident and unafraid, doing menial tasks with a friendly willingness, certain he'd never see the week out but determined to do his job properly until the end came. Old Boxer, grey-faced and sullen-looking, his hands fumbling and unsteady, uneasy as he heard the news.

I found I still couldn't think of him as my father, and it came as a shock over and over again as I realised this untidy bedraggled old man with the wispy hair and the grey stubble of beard was responsible for my birth, had held Ma in his arms and made love to her. There was little to recommend either of them, I thought: Ma, thwarted and angry and selfish because she was saddled with a child she hadn't wanted and a husband she didn't love; and Old Boxer, defiant always, unsure of himself, aggressive and sardonic, taking refuge in bitterness and drink as he grew older till he'd become just another piece of port flotsam, cared for by nobody, tormented by warring emotions and angry thoughts.

He'd shown a pathetic enthusiasm for the boat at first, touching familiar objects with trembling fingers, remembering his youth, I suppose, when he'd had a boat of his own. But always somewhere in the recesses of his mind there seemed to be an unhappy uncertainty that came from fear, from years of drunkenness that had soured the spirit in him and taken away his courage.

But he was obviously shamed by Dig's quiet confidence and Yorky's tearing desire to get into the thick of it, for he hadn't suggested shirking the adventure, and did his few jobs as we waited with a silent, dull heaviness.

All day we bobbed and bumped alongside the supply vessel, the passing ships bouncing us against its steel sides and setting the mat of small craft that surrounded us weaving and dancing. Overhead, there was the continuous roar of aeroplanes.

And past us, backwards and forwards, all day long, went the poignant procession of little ships.

First went the destroyers and the troopships, then the *Sues* and the *Three Brothers* and the *Two Sisters*, little boats that had registrations that went from the Wash to Poole, their crews the men who'd stood in peace time on the harbour wall shouting: "Any more for the *Skylark*? One shilling round the lighthouse." With them went the huge tows of small craft, yachts and cobles and launches, and the pulling dinghies and whalers. Despite their humble duty they'd a grandeur, a dignity that day that wasn't marred by their scarred paint-work and their unpolished brass. Those little boats were taking part in history.

When they came back – and they came back as fast as others went out – they were crammed to the gunwales with the dun-coloured masses of troops. The destroyers came in fast, heeling over under the numbers they had aboard. Behind them came the lumbering troopships and the schuits and the fishing-vessels and the tugs. And all of them – like the destroyers – hadn't a spare inch of deck space where there wasn't a haggard, red-eyed soldier. Some of them even came in with the swaddies baling with their steel helmets and their hands. But they came and stood by ready to go again.

Some of them were limping badly, their decks splintered by bullets and the dead lying sprawled in corners, their planks leaking from the shock of bombs, their fuel pipes fractured by explosions and engines off their bearers. There wasn't much cheering now and not much excitement.

The sun was shining brilliantly and the scene was like a regatta but for the absence of laughter. There were few signs, apart from the scarred boats and the hurry of the traffic, of the tremendous adventure that was taking place twenty miles away. Occasionally the rumble of cannon and the harsh chatter of the destroyers' anti-aircraft guns hammering away at a too-adventurous German 'plane set the glass rattling in the wheelhouse window.

During the afternoon an RAF launch came alongside us, and we passed over sacks of spuds and tins of bully and helped to refuel her while her exhausted crew dragged at cigarettes and sank mugs of tea.

"It's the dive-bombers are the worst," they said. "Come down at you like bloody banshees, they do. And the din. Gawd!"

"Look out for the stuff in the water when you get across," someone else joined in. "There's floating grass-lines and old rope and wreckage all over the show. Keep one eye aft, or before you know where you are you'll have a couple of fathoms of rope round your props."

Then, swallowing the last of their tea, they cast off and hurried away to pick up naval officers and carry them back to the inferno of Dunkirk.

Even as she left, it seemed, the naval launch arrived and the commander was shouting at us through a megaphone.

"Stand by!" he was yelling.

"We've been bloody well standin' by all the ruddy day," Yorky screamed back. "Soft as a prozzy at a christenin'. My behind's all swole up with sittin' on it."

The commander grinned. "OK. OK," he said. "Your turn's come. An hour or two from now you'll wish you were still standing by."

It was still daylight when we set off, heading eastwards and south to where the fading sunshine fell. We were a hybrid bunch, four miles of us, most of us under tow, with the accompanying destroyers and sloops whooping up and down like yelping dogs. There were Thames barges loaded with ammunition and stores and water for the famished and exhausted troops on the beaches, motor-boats, fishing-boats and tugs, and holiday launches on whose brasses the last of the light winked.

The evening sky had a blue-green glow, I remember, but long before dusk we saw a great pall of smoke in it, hanging over the darkening sea. It was the funeral pyre of dying Dunkirk, and we could hear the mutter of battle now. All the time, passing us in the opposite direction, were boats going home, singly and in groups, at speed or with spluttering engines, all crammed with that brown mass of troops, every inch of deck and cabin space filled with men.

Gradually the pall of smoke on the horizon merged into the night that lifted out of the sea and we could see the glow at its base where the fires burned among the debris of the town. As the sky grew blacker we could hear calls and curses from boats near us, in darkness that was broken only by the glimmer ahead and the shaded stern lights. There was a curious sense of unreality about the whole proceedings and it had been heightened by the donging of a church clock as we left, coming clear and distinct on the wind across the water to us.

As we approached our destination a change came over us. There was a nervous tension in the air and no one talked. Old Boxer was silent and motionless, huddled on a fender aft, struggling with his courage. I left Dig at the wheel to let me know when the signal to cast off the tow came, and went past Old Boxer along the boat for a last check-up.

"You all right?" I asked him sharply.

"Yes," he said, without looking at me. "A bit of sickness. I'll be OK. Just leave me alone, for God's sake."

I moved away. Not since leaving harbour had either of us made any reference to our relationship.

In the engine-room Yorky was sitting on a margarine box between the two engines, picking out a tune on his concertina. His parcel of belongings, burst as usual, was jammed into the top of a tool-box and drips from a leaking oilcan made a greasy smear on the brown paper.

He smiled as I appeared. "Fancy a tune, cock?" he asked. " 'Shenandoah'? Or 'Down at the Old Bull and Bush', or summat?"

I grinned. "Engines all right?" I asked.

"Never been better, love. Shipshape as you like. You needn't worry about them, kid. Only a six-inch shell'll stop 'em once they're started."

"We're going in in the dark," I pointed out.

"I'll be all right, love," he smiled, and there was an affection in his tones that touched me. "You're in good 'ands. And if anythink 'appens I'll be up that there ladder like a rat up a drain."

He paused and frowned, puzzled, as I stood with one foot on the companionway. " 'Orace, Jess? Is 'e all right? The booze's got 'im proper this time. Ain't never seed 'im so bad."

"He's all right," I lied. "Think he's got the wind-up a bit. He'll sort himself out when the time comes."

"Just fancy! Wind-up. Once there wasn't anything could frighten 'im." Yorky's voice was full of wonder. "Just makes you realise what booze can do for you."

Back on deck I glanced towards the shore. There were still fires in the port area of Dunkirk and wrecks lay in the roads and off the beaches. Behind them were the blazing oil-tanks, the cause of that pall of smoke we'd seen. You could feel the heat of them even where we were.

I could see the outline of the town now, a dark huddle of ruined buildings and the stark bones of houses, with a flickering flame here and there; nothing but tragedy and desolation. On my starboard side, by the harbour entrance, were the remains of ships, half submerged, blackened and charred. Still burning some of them were, their masts and upper works still visible. In through the harbour mouth the destroyers were loading against the one serviceable mole, a slender lifeline pitted and broken and repaired with planks, doors and wreckage, and broken and repaired again. Along this, in unbelievable order, plodded long queues of men, shuffling forward, edging along in the darkness towards safety. You could see them when you got close in, silhouetted against the glare in the sky. But there was no shouting, no excitement, only that steady and never-ceasing shuffling stream moving towards the ships.

Outside the entrance the sweepers were at work. Backwards and forwards they went, too and fro, up and down, never stopping, like terriers after a rat.

And all around us on the oily water were the dark, looming bulks of ships and the smaller shadows of boats, their hulls outlined by the glow of the phosphorus their wakes churned up. Away on the bow I could see the wreck of a big vessel, still glowing and white-hot from the flames that clawed away the inside of her and showed through her ports and the shell-holes in her sloping decks. She was settled low in the water, the sea around her a litter of wreckage: smashed lifeboats, lifebelts, ropes, planks, boxes, a mast that trailed over her side.

Ahead, I could see beaches and the lighter line of the surf glowing through the darkness, and beyond it great black masses that sprawled across the sand, stretching from the dunes to the water's edge like dense forests.

Then I suddenly realised these were men. These were the men we'd come to fetch.

There must have been tens of thousands of them on those beaches, hungry and thirsty and probably scared. But they waited silently, huddled into the dark masses that looked like trees, or organised into orderly queues right down to the water and out into the surf itself, ending in a line of bobbing heads. That was the most miraculous thing about Dunkirk. It stuck in my mind afterwards far more than the danger and the din. The orderliness of those men, the incredible patience, and the trust they put in us.

Everything was quiet when we first went inshore. There was no firing, though here and there on the beach I could see flames licking round the dim shape of a lorry or the wreckage of an aircraft.

"OK," they told us "You can get in. Never mind the whalers. Go right in on your engines. We can save the whalers for tomorrow."

We started up engines and cast off the tow, and I remember a feeling of doubt as we found ourselves alone, dependent on our own skill and our own resourcefulness.

"I reckon we'd better get busy," I said. "I don't suppose it'll be as quiet as this when dawn comes."

As I spoke a machine-gun somewhere on shore chattered and a stream of green tracers flew across the dark sky. Then it stopped and the darkness was unbroken again. All around us were other small boats, their engines drumming, their exhaust steam like pale feathers against the black water, moving with us nearer to those masses of men who waited so patiently.

I took the wheel from Dig and swung the bows round at right angles to the shore.

"Steady as she goes, Jess!" Old Boxer's voice came unexpectedly from beside my ear. "Men in the water on the port bow."

His voice seemed suddenly even, as though he'd got a grip on himself at last. "Take it easy, lad, or you'll run 'em down."

I indicated the wheel of the boat. "Take her over," I said, sensing that responsibility would help him to control his courage. "I can p'r'aps be more useful forrard."

He flashed me a glance, his eyes glinting in the glow from the dashboard light, then he took the wheel silently.

I went forrard, just as the bow of the boat nosed up to where the queue of soldiers ended, up to their necks in the dark water, each holding on to the man in front, the current eddying past them in foamy flurries.

"Thank Gawd, mate," a tired voice said. "Thank Gawd you've come. I'm bloody nigh perished. Got a cup o' tea 'andy? Me throat's like sandpaper."

A grimy hand reached up over the gunwale and clung on. I leaned over and grabbed its owner by the seat of his trousers and heaved. Dig joined me and between us we yanked the soldier aboard.

"Thanks, chum," he said. " 'Adn't got the strength to do it meself."

"Get aft," I said, "and sit down."

"OK, chum," he said, and clumped along the deck.

All around us there was the sound of voices, cursing or shouting orders, and the splash of bodies in the water. The sound grew to a crescendo, then, as the hurrying of the ships ceased for a moment, died away again to a murmur.

Dig looked at me in silence, then we reached over and grabbed for the next man in line...

six

All night and all the next day from first light to darkness, and through the night and the day again, we were at it, yanking men aboard as fast as we could grab them, pulling till our arms ached and we had to rest. Then, when we were fully loaded, we ferried them out to the destroyer that waited in the fairway and shoved them aboard, up the boarding nets – dozens of them, load after load of 'em – till we were drenched by the water that dropped back from their saturated clothing.

I'd never have thought we could have carried on so long without rest or food. The time flew past with the hurry of a house on fire. The urgency of the situation and the tremendous task we had to do made us forget the ache in our backs. We stopped only when we couldn't get inshore for the crowd of boats that jostled each other in the surf and made manoeuvring difficult, or to swallow a sandwich of bully-beef from the destroyer and a mug of tea.

When the sun rose we were hard at it again, and when it set we were still there, dog-weary and hungry, our legs buckling under us, asleep on our feet, but still heading backwards and forwards between the beaches and the ships, fisting our fuel aboard in cans.

And all the time, in regular doses, Jerry shelled us from the shore and hammered us from the sky until the noise put the fear of God into us. I wouldn't like to live those two days again. I can't remember much of what went on now, but I'll never forget the racket and the hurry.

There were times when the sky seemed to be falling about our ears and the sea seemed to be heaving upwards in vast, rumbling explosions that flung the water in spray across the decks. When I stopped to think about it I felt like turning the boat round and belting off home at full revs. When I had the time I got the wind-up properly, and it grew worse as the hours went by and I grew more tired. There seemed to be so little protection in those small boats from the stuff they flung at us. Everything but the kitchen stove it was at times. But the Navy had to use little boats like ours because they couldn't get the troopships in in daylight. They'd already lost more destroyers and troopers than they dared think about before we went across. The wrecks of them littered the fairway till it looked like a graveyard and made navigation difficult and dangerous. There was no backing out. I'd have liked to have done so many times, but one look at the beaches stopped all thoughts of hurrying away.

They were white, with grass waving on the dunes behind, just like on the Lincolnshire coast or round the Wash, and it made it all the more unreal that this drama was being acted in what seemed to be so familiar a place.

Those crowded ranks on the sand were still moving with incredible order down to the water's edge where the litter of debris lay. Washed-up equipment mingled with great-coats and every article of clothing imaginable. Smashed and swamped boats were surrounded by boxes and planks and tarpaulins and ropes. The whole beach, vivid in the late sunshine, was dotted from end to end with packs and equipment. Here and there were wrecked vehicles, one or two still smoking, and out in the surf stretched an improvised pier of lorries, shattered into broken heaps by the waves and the bursting shells.

In the shallows, boats were being pulled laboriously out to tugs or launches, sweating sailors, soldiers and civilians handling the heavy oars. As they reached the surf their bows dipped sharply and their crews had to pull fiercely in desperate strokes to give them way to combat the current. Just off shore a destroyer, her funnel dribbling smoke, was moving slowly ahead, boarding nets down, By her side, in her lee, was a huddle of small boats from which men clambered up her steel sides. Ashore, a few of the brighter spirits were playing football and even paddling.

"Look at 'em," Yorky had said in amazement. "Only wants a few winkles to make it like Cleethorpes!"

As the sun began to lose its brassiness we drew off and drifted while we snatched a breather and a hasty meal. Even as we ate, though, we moved about, getting her ready for the next trip in. My legs were like lead by this time and my eyes were smarting for want of sleep.

Yorky, a borrowed steel helmet on the back of his head, was cramming discarded equipment into the forecastle and the after hatch.

"Best tidy up," he said. "Them Nazzies will be back soon and then the balloon'll go up again."

I sat near the bows, numb with weariness. The decks, which had been clean when we started, were now a slushy mess of grey mud. Old Boxer listlessly pulled up a bucket of water on a heaving-line and sloshed it across the deck, too tired to care whether it cleaned the planks or not.

He'd stood at the wheel almost without relief throughout the dark nights. Only the desperate necessity for keeping going had prevented him from succumbing to the fear that had still not left him. The rum in the bottle was low now and I could tell he was afraid of what he'd do when it was gone. I think it was only those swallows of raw, burning spirit that had prevented him from cracking up.

Dig, his eyes bloodshot, was eating a sandwich at the wheel, almost asleep on his feet but exultant at the job he'd proved himself capable of doing. It was only his elation and his sheer dogged guts that had kept his skinny body moving long after it should have stopped.

There was a smell of oil smoke in the air from the great black pall that blew across the town. It mixed with the greasy black clouds from burning buildings and deposited a layer of fine ash and cinders and soot on the deck. The water around us as we drifted was black and greasy with oil, and here and there, patches of shining, iridescent light on its surface marked the grave of a ship or an aircraft.

Suddenly Yorky flung out an arm and my eyes followed the pointing hand that was silhouetted against the sky.

"Here they are, the bastards!" His voice was sharp and cracked with excitement. "Jeeze, if I'd only got a gun I'd learn 'em a thing or two!"

Old Boxer looked up over his shoulder, slowly, as though his weary head wouldn't drag itself round, then he dropped the bucket with a clatter and hurried in a shambling run to the wheelhouse, elbowing Dig from the wheel.

High in the sky, faint and silvery, like midges in the sun, a group of 'planes were heading towards us. The destroyers' guns opened fire with a crash that nearly split my eardrums, the harsh racket of her pom-poms mingling with the crack of the heavier ack-ack.

The 'planes came in low through a sky that was pock-marked with bursting shells and criss-crossed with the lines of tracer. The din was deafening as the screech of projectiles interrupted the peevish crack of cannon.

Old Boxer was looking backwards over his shoulder, I remember, as the first of the 'planes approached. My stomach went sick inside me as I saw the bombs coming down out of a cloudless sky. Then Old Boxer flung all his weight on the wheel and the boat heeled over, turning in her own length.

The kick of the bombs jarred the spokes in his hands and the boat rocked violently, throwing us to our knees.

"Christ!" Yorky yelled. "You'd think the bastards was only after *us!*"

The formations had broken now and the aircraft were coming individually with their machine-guns blazing. Lewis guns from the tugs and smaller craft and the rattle of rifles from the beach joined the general clamour. The sea was flecked with small plumes as the bullets struck its surface and the shell splinters came singing down. Mounting high over our heads were the swirling, monstrous fountains of water the bombs threw up, breaking into spray at their summits, and coloured by the sunshine into rainbow hues.

The destroyer was moving at speed now, the boats cast adrift, twisting and turning, heeling over on her beam ends as she took evasive action. Suddenly she seemed to rear out of the sea as she was straddled by bombs, and as the vast fountains of water crumpled and collapsed upon her she limped slowly away, steam and smoke belching out aft. Beyond her, a tanker was sending up a vast funeral pyre as the flames consumed her.

Dive-bombers were peeling off above us with a howl of motors that added to the havoc and the racket of the bombs. The whole of the sky seemed to be coming down on top of us, pressing us noisily into the sea below the wreckage of boats and rafts and furnishings and planks.

"Get her in!" I shouted. "Get her inshore!"

"Christ!" Yorky popped up out of the engine-room hatch by my side. "It's Sat'day. If I was 'ome I'd be in me ratting suit and out on the ran-tan with a young lady." Then his head vanished as he dropped below again.

We headed stubbornly towards the shore, Old Boxer at the helm flinching with every explosion. He was dreading

every second, I knew, but he was unable to leave the wheel
and obey the urgings of his mind and run terrified for cover.
I was glad then I'd given him the job to do. My eye caught a
pool of blood on the quivering foredeck just in front of me.
It had been there all day, ever since we'd moved the dead
soldier who'd lain there, his staring eyeballs covered with
grit, and no one had thought to wash it off. It was congealing
now, and my weary stomach was queasy as I looked at it. I
knew what Old Boxer was feeling.

"It's the booze," he kept saying to him. "I'll be all right
when it's worked itself off."

Then I saw Yorky running along the deck to the
wheelhouse, his eyes wild. "Switch off, 'Orace!" he was
shouting. "She'll seize up, else. There's a oil-pipe bust. That
last bomb did it."

Then I saw he was drenched with oil that ran black and
greasy and shining in the sunlight over his chest and arms
and down his legs so that his trousers and vest clung to him
in sticky folds.

"You'll 'ave to 'ang on a bit, Jess," he was yelling, "or
she'll run 'erself red-'ot."

"Can you put it right?" I demanded.

"Gimme time an' I can. The planks is sprung, too. It's the
concussion as does it."

"Want any help?" Dig's voice asked quietly and Yorky
nodded.

"Not 'arf," he grinned. "It's a bit of a bloody muck-'eap
down there, though."

Dig laughed with him, and they vanished below while the
boat wallowed and rolled in the wash of moving ships.

The bombing had slackened a little by this time, and Old
Boxer came out of the wheelhouse on trembling legs and sat
down. I stood beside him on the wide deck, staring at the sky,
conscious of our helplessness without the engines that gave
us motion. Every minute while Yorky worked, every silent

second when the engines were useless, I must have sweated blood with anxiety, staring at the sky all the time, jumpy and nervous, miserably aware of being responsible for three men and a useless boat...

The noise had lessened a lot, and you could stand still without wincing at the shock of bombs and speak without shouting. The boat was drifting gently with the current, the wreckage around her thicker than I'd seen it all day. I squinted at the sky and the growing dusk. There were still aircraft about but they were being chased away overhead by a few Spitfires.

I turned, glancing down the hatchway into the engine-room where Dig and Yorky laboured in the hot and dripping oil, their feet slithering on the slimy decks. Old Boxer crouched near me, cowering almost, on the fender where he was huddled, and I saw him lift the rum bottle to his lips.

"How are you?" I asked.

"Tired," he replied. "Shall we have to come back here again tomorrow, Jess?"

"Suppose so." I was non-committal. "Suppose we'll have to stay till we're told to go back."

"Not another day," he said between gritted teeth. "Not mother day like this one." Then he turned away, and I heard that insistent mutter as I'd heard it on and off all day: "It's the booze, you old fool. That's all. You'll be all right when it's worn off." He lifted the bottle and had another mouthful of the rum.

He'd been drinking all the time. There was an empty bottle already in the forecastle. In fact he was so stale with the smell of rum it was hard not to comment on it. But I'd said nothing. He hadn't let us down.

I shrugged wearily and moved aft where I could hear the clang of a hammer through the engine-room hatch and Yorky's tuneless whistling. I was fingering frayed rigging, chafed with rubbing against the steel sides of bigger vessels, touching the scarred and splintered deck with my boot toe. Impatiently I squinted down the engine-room hatch and again at the sky. There were still 'planes about, but the rattle of anti-aircraft fire had died.

I knew I ought to try and take the boat home, but I'd no wish to turn my back yet on the evacuation. I preferred the crowded excitement and desperation of this embarkation to the loneliness I knew I'd feel at home. But the boat was no longer in a fit condition for work, with her oil-pipes severed and patched, her engines missing and her planks leaking.

Then I began to think of Kate and what she'd said to me just before we left Wiggins' wharfside. "God bless you," she'd said. "I'll be here when you come back." And she'd kissed me – for the first time since I'd known her.

As I recalled her pale, tranquil face, calm with the courage in her, I remembered the warmth I'd felt at her words. Suddenly I realised she'd meant what she said, and I knew she'd got over her fear of me, that she'd learned she could trust me.

I stared across the littered sea, my eyes seeing nothing, my mind busy with thoughts of Kate and her calm spirit. If I get out of this lot alive, I thought, I'll make up to her for all those years when she'd been lonely and unhappy. Kate and I had a lot in common, and I'd been a damn' fool over Minnie. A bit of sense on my part at that time and I'd never have let Kate slip out of my fingers.

God knows, though, in spite of Kate I'd been prepared to stick to Minnie if she'd given me half a chance, but she'd been just a bit too damn' clever and she was finished now. Minnie could go to blazes for all I cared. Come hell or high water, I decided, I'd make no mistake a second time. I felt better as I shuffled off Minnie's tawdry coils. In that moment she'd ceased to exist for me. I'd got my perspectives right at last. Just let me get out of this little barney, I thought, and into smooth waters, and Kate would never have to fear again.

The very thought of getting home to her cheered me and I roused myself. I was suddenly impatient for action. We were drifting fast across the beaches and troops still lining the shore, unaware of our difficulties, shouted to us to go closer.

Then I heard Yorky's voice: "OK, Jess. We got the bleeder coughin'," and one of the engines spluttered into a feeble, erratic beat.

But even as the noise became fact, and I felt the boat catch at the current like an animal stirring in its sleep, I became conscious of another sound – the snarl of motors and the chatter of machine-guns.

"Jess! Look out!"

Turning, my glance flung frantically over my shoulder, I had a momentary glimpse of Old Boxer leaping to his feet, the shabby coat flying, his eyes wide and horrified. Then as the sound in my ears snarled into a screaming metallic roar that seemed to envelop the whole boat in quivering sound, he crashed into me, knocking me flying across the deck, and thumped down on top of me with a weight that forced all the breath out of my body. Even as I huddled, dazed, under the shadow of the wheelhouse, Old Boxer sprawling across me, I heard the rattle of guns again and felt the boat shudder as she was hit. The wheelhouse seemed to cry out in protest as splinters flew from it and the windows disintegrated into sharp, flying slivers of glass. Somewhere aft there was an explosion, then the motors above roared away into the general confused murmur of noise.

For a moment I lay collecting my senses, conscious of a ringbolt pressing into my side, and Old Boxer grunting on top of me as though at a blow, then I realised the spluttering marine engine below us had stopped again.

I struggled to my feet still dizzy with shock and wincing from bruised ribs, and saw Old Boxer heaving himself to his knees, holding his side as he dragged himself up by a stanchion.

"Did it get you?" I asked, and he turned a grey, twisted face towards me.

"No, no," he panted, pushing me away fretfully. "Bumped me side. Nothing. Getting old now. That's all."

"Get to the wheel then," I said, "in case he comes back. I'll see if they've got the engine going."

He moved along the deck towards the shattered wheel-house, shuffling and crouching and holding his side with one brown knotted hand, bunching his jersey to his ribs in obvious pain.

I could only spare him a glance, then I hurried to the engine-room. The decks were torn in places to splinters where the bullets had struck and ricocheted off, and there was a gaping hole near the after hatch, a tangle of splintered planks, from which a grey wisp of smoke spiralled upwards. The aircraft had disappeared now, and I realised as I searched the horizon for it that since we'd started drifting dusk had begun to fall, and the ships and wreckage behind us and the smoke over ruined Dunkirk were already hazy with the glow of summer darkness.

As I bent to the engine-room hatch Dig's face appeared, and I saw it was ashen, and that there were splashes of blood among the oil-stains on his coat. There was a look of thunderstruck amazement in his eyes.

"Are you all right?" I grabbed his wrist and yanked him through the hatchway almost off his feet.

"Yes!" He was leaning on the wheelhouse, gasping for breath, brushing the blood off his sleeve with a kind of sick horror. "Didn't touch *me*. It was Yorky." He waved a hand vaguely, then suddenly leaned over the side and vomited violently into the water.

I stared at him for a second, then half jumped into the engine-room.

There was a gaping hole where a cannon-shell had entered through the stem of the boat and exploded in the after hatch.

The bulkheads were scarred and pitted with more holes, and daylight glowed through the jagged rents in the planking. The concertina that had so often wheezed out "Shenandoah" drooped, crumpled and lifeless-looking, over the soap-box where Yorky had sat throughout the interminable day, and his parcel, bursting open inevitably, was still jammed in the top of the tool-box, its brown paper saturated now with the drips from the oilcan.

Yorky was huddled between the starboard engine and the bulkhead, where he'd been working. His grimy body, still shiny and black with oil, was half submerged by the greasy bilge-water that seeped over the floor-boards. His fingers still gripped a severed pipe from which the oil drip-dripped monotonously on to his wrist and down his arm.

seven

Dig appeared to have recovered a little when I reached the deck again, but his thin face was still drained of colour.

"Sorry," he murmured. "It was a bit sudden. One minute he was alive and whistling between his teeth. The next minute..." He drew a deep breath like a sigh and became silent.

I looked round quickly into the growing darkness. We were still drifting, and the beaches were away on the bow now. I could still see the flicker of flames in Dunkirk and where a burning ship sank lower into the water.

Then I remembered the smoke from the after hatch. There was a red glow in it now, sharp and bright against the darkening sea.

"We're on fire," I said. "See if you can put it out. I'll try and get an engine going."

As Dig hurried away I called out to Old Boxer, who was leaning heavily on the wheel.

"Stand by!" I shouted. "There's a lot of wreckage around us. If I get this engine going take her straight out to sea."

I knew he wasn't in a fit state to go below, and I was better without his clumsy fingers dropping things. He was safer where he could do his job well.

He acknowledged the instructions with a wave, and I clattered down the engine-room ladder again.

Below in the dusky greyness I dragged Yorky clear of the engine and, laying him in the narrow alleyway, covered him with a tarpaulin, I remember a feeling of amazement as I looked at him – very little more – at the thought that his vitality had all gone, snuffed out in a second by someone he'd never seen.

As I straightened my back I could see the red glow of flames through the splintered hole aft and could hear Dig's shoes on the deck above my head as he tried to clear the rope and canvas and debris to get at the blaze.

The bilge-water in the engine-room was up to the level of the floor-boards by this time and aft, where the boat had settled a little, they were floating. I climbed round the starboard engine and jammed myself between its warm bulk and the hull, struggling with a pocket torch in water and oil that sloshed backwards and forwards round my ankles to the sluggish movement of the boat. Several times I tried the starters but there was only a dead whirr in response, then I realised the water was flowing in a thick stream through a hole just by my foot. I ripped off my jersey and jammed it into the gashed wood. I reduced the rush of water to a trickle.

The engine-room was in darkness before I knew where I was. The lights had been shattered by the shock of explosions early in the day, and it was lit only by the weak glow of the green summer night in the square of the hatchway and the feeble beam of the ailing torch.

Yorky's body was lapped by the oily black water now, and the forrard floor-boards were floating clear of their rests and bumping gently against the starboard engine. Oil still dripped from a severed pipe into the bilges. I struggled to get the broken ends together, but I knew even as I worked there were further breakages. I could hear a steady drip somewhere in the blackness beyond the port engine.

Suddenly I noticed the engine-room was getting hotter. I reached out and put my hand against the bulkhead, but snatched it away again as it burnt my fingers.

"Dig!" I shouted. "Can't you put it out?"

"No, Jess," I heard him pant. "Can't get at it. There's paraffin in here as well. And oil, I think."

I splashed through the deepening water in the blackness of the engine-room towards the hatchway. Then I bent and lifted Yorky's body, still wrapped in the tarpaulin.

"Leave it," I shouted to Dig, "and give us a hand. We'll have to abandon her. She's leaking like a sieve down here."

Between us we got the sagging little body on deck and rested to get our breath back. I glanced towards the wheel-house, but I could see no sign of Old Boxer.

"Blast the old fool!" I muttered half to myself. "He's down below with that damned bottle again."

The fire was roaring now in the light breeze that had got up, and we could see the redness of the flames through the splintered deck. The boat had settled noticeably by the stern, and she was heeling over a little to starboard.

"I hope somebody sees us," I said. "Keep a sharp lookout and I'll chase Old Boxer out."

I stumbled along the deck and into the wheelhouse, feeling my way with familiar hands, conserving the feeble torch in case we had to use it in the water, for we'd only a life-raft aboard.

"Where are you?" I shouted into the darkness of the wheelhouse. "Come out of there and give a hand!"

My voice re-echoed in a hollow shell. All the life had gone from the boat and she was only a dead thing now, wallowing on the swell. My voice sounded dead with it.

"Come on!" I roared angrily. "What the hell are you doing?"

Then, in the stillness that was broken only by the slapping of water alongside, I heard a heavy breathing near me, and I whirled, expecting to find the old man drunk.

I turned on the torch and in its weak glow I saw his great bulk sagging over the wheel, his eyes staring, his face drawn and twisted into a mask of pain, his hand still clutching at his side.

I leapt to him but he pushed me away feebly.

"Too late, Jess." His voice came weakly and with difficulty through taut lips. "The 'plane got me. Here, in my side."

"Sit down, man!" I lowered him to a sitting position on the deck among the splintered wood and broken glass that crunched under my boots. His side was saturated with blood.

"No good, Jess," he said, and his head lolled back as he spoke. "Too late. It was always too late."

"Don't be a bloody fool!" I said, and I was panicking for the first time. As I stared at the wound in the yellow glow of the torch I knew he was right.

"It was all I had to give you, Jess," he whispered. "Life – that was the only thing I'd got that you could have."

I knelt beside him. I knew already that he was dying.

"It's so cold, Jess," he muttered. "My back's perishing."

"I'll get a coat," I said, half-starting to my feet.

He laid a hand on my arm in the darkness. "No, Jess. Coats are no good. There's a rum bottle in my pocket. Give me a drink. Just a little one."

"That's no good to you," I said.

"It'll help." He smiled feebly.

I fished in the rumpled coat and handed the bottle silently to him.

"Just one, Jess," he said. "Just an eyeful."

As he drank the spirit ran out of the corners of his mouth and down his chin. Then the bottle slipped from his nerveless fingers, and for a second he rolled his head from side to side, his flabby features sharp with pain in the feeble glimmer from the dying torch.

He was silent for a moment, then he whispered something I could hardly catch.

"My sword. In the forecastle. Fetch it, Jess."

I stared at him for a second, then ducked into the fore-castle that was knee-deep in water and found the shabby sword in its tarnished scabbard. Taking it back to him I laid it gently across his sprawling legs.

He shook his head feebly.

"No, Jess," he muttered. "You take it. It's yours by right now.

Dig was peaked and shivering with cold when I got back to the deck.

"What's up?" he said. "Is he drunk?"

"No." I shook my head. "The 'plane got him."

I got a grip on myself with an effort and looked at Dig, who was staring at me, his mouth open. "Anything in sight?" I asked.

"Nothing," Dig said, as though he sensed it wasn't the time to ask questions. "Looks like we're going to spend a cold night."

The boat had settled considerably as we unlashed the life-raft.

"We'll hang on to her as a long as we can," I said. "No sense in swimming before it's necessary."

As I spoke I wondered whether we could lash the bodies to the raft. The bulky heap where Yorky lay huddled under his tarpaulin was hazy in the darkness now. I thought of Old Boxer lolling in the wheelhouse among the rubbish, and the splinters of glass and wood, his old coat still twisted round his great sagging body, his feet flopping from one side to the other, the empty rum bottle rolling backwards and forwards nearby as the boat sagged into the valleys of the swell that set the wheelhouse door banging, and I was aware of sudden stinging tears in my eyes...

The fire aft had died a little when we heard the beat of engines, and we hurried to toss canvas and discarded great-coats and military packs from the cabin into the blaze, making it roar up again so that the flames glowed through the holes in the hull and sparkled on the inky sea around.

The water was little more than a foot or two from the decks now, and had begun to seep through into the wheelhouse and round the body of Old Boxer. The engine-room was only a black cavern where we could hear it slopping over the engines.

"It's a launch of some kind," I said. I cocked my head to listen to the drum of the engines and strained my ears to try and recognise their tone.

"Hope to God they see us," Dig had torn off his jacket and was flapping it above the burning hatchway.

"Hope to God it's one of ours," I said.

Then we saw the white glow of a bow wave, and the beating engines were shut off as the bulk of a boat came gliding towards us out of the darkness. An English voice shouted:

"Hello, there! How many of you are there?"

"Two alive," Dig shouted. The words I was going to speak were stuck in my throat.

"Hang on. We'll take you off."

The engines started up once more, and the launch circled and bumped gently alongside.

"Come on! Look slippy!" The voice came crisp and dis-embodied out of the darkness beyond the glow of the flames. "She won't last long."

It was a naval torpedo-boat, crammed to the gunwales with soldiers and sailors, some of them wounded, some of them saturated and covered with oil, their faces taut in the red glow.

"Christ!" The voice was suddenly sharp and strained. "Don't take all day. There are E-boats out."

"There's two dead." I got the words out at last.

"You'll have to leave 'em," the voice said unemotionally. "Can't take any more. We're top-heavy and dangerous already. You're damn' lucky we saw you."

"There's only two." My voice was cracked with strain.

"Sorry. Not enough room for the living. Come on if you're coming."

I looked silently at Dig, then together we clambered aboard the other boat.

"By Jeeze!" Someone spoke out of the darkness near us as the torpedo-boat moved ahead. "You were lucky, mate. You'd have had to swim for sure in another minute. She's going."

"Full ahead!" The voice from the bridge spoke to the cox'n and the engines roared.

The boat throbbed to life and I clung on among the crowded men round the bridge. Looking back, I saw our own boat heel over as her bows rose, and I had an agonising picture of a great flabby body sliding across the wheelhouse floor with the clattering glass and wood and the rolling bottle, and Yorky huddled underneath his tarpaulin, jammed against the engine-room hatch where we'd left him, then I saw the boat slide out of sight and the flames suddenly died, except for a flicker of burning oil on the surface of the water.

A weary reaction came over me, leaving me weak and numb. So much had happened. So many things had crowded in on me in the last few days. First the torpedoing. Then Minnie. I hurriedly shut her from my mind as I remembered her in Pat's flat, sluttish, wanton and sly, invective streaming from her lips.

Then, when I'd felt there was nothing more could hurt me, I'd found my father, and almost in the same few crowded hours I'd seen him die, smelling of booze – as I'd always known him alive – a rum bottle near his hand, inseparable even in death from Yorky, who'd followed him from one end of the earth to the other. I felt miserable and near to tears suddenly at the thought of him. His had always been a lonely voyage, too, and he'd spent it desperate and solitary, despite the people around him, tormented and afraid. If only he'd had the courage we might both of us have been less lonely.

Dig seemed to sense my thoughts. He couldn't have seen my face in the darkness. He put a hand on my shoulder and there was nothing in him now of the old stumbling inefficiency. He seemed to have grown in stature in the shambles of Dunkirk.

"Funny," he was saying, and his voice had a trace of bewilderment in it. "I thought it'd be me as wouldn't come back."

He'd expected to die. He'd almost hoped he might die, I think, for there was little happiness in his future with Ma. Yet he'd survived to go home and struggle again with the drab remnants of his marriage. Instead, it had been Yorky, with his vast love and his concertina and his everlasting parcel, who'd gone; and Old Boxer, my father, sinking fathoms down into the darkness.

I suddenly realised how he'd always represented the sea to me while Dig had symbolised the land; one restless, shifting and uneasy, never still, never under control, always with a hint of adventure and romance that never quite materialised; the other calm and dusty and solid, unemotional and immovable, as sure as the earth that was his background.

As I thought of Old Boxer, bitter, sardonic and moody, the father I'd lost as soon as I'd found him, I knew there was something predestined in the way everything had worked out. There could never have been a future for us as father and son.

"I was thinking about Yorky and Old Boxer," I said aloud, fingering the shabby scabbard of the old naval sword I clutched in my frozen fingers. "He always said he ought to go down with his ship."

"He's all right, Jess lad. You've no need to be ashamed of him," Dig said, and I realised without looking at him that he'd always known Old Boxer was my father. " 'The sea's a tomb,' Jess," he quoted, " 'that's proper for the brave.' They're in good company."

I nodded. "I reckon so," I said. "But he seemed to have so little in his life."

Dig was silent for a moment. Then I felt him move uneasily. "Perhaps he'd got more than most of us," he ended wistfully.

I nodded again and we huddled among the dark, muttering mass of exhausted men who sheltered in the lee of the bridge from the chilling wind that raced along the decks; staring backwards over the stern of the hurrying, bucketing boat into the blackness that was lit only by the glow from our own tumbling wake.

eight

Kate Fee waited through the days of the evacuation at Wiggins'. The boat-yard was silent and deserted and she sat in the office alone, watching the rats run from underneath the stacked timber into the empty boat-shed. Their hurrying brown bodies seemed to her more a symbol of loneliness and emptiness, she told me afterwards, than anything else in the silent yard; more than the gulls that wheeled in the sky overhead, their cries like the sighs of mourners in the stillness, more than the stolid, inexorable ticking of the office clock.

She stared through the windows with dry eyes, watching the corner where the rats disappeared. She'd been at the yard every day from the time the boats had left, first to arrive in the morning and the last to leave at night.

Sunday arrived, and the drab streets were deserted except for a few children listlessly playing among the orange-peel in the gutter. In the sunshine, away from the bustle of the Narrow Seas, there was nothing to indicate what was happening at the other side of the Channel, nothing beyond an occasional flight of aircraft roaring southwards and eastwards overhead. The papers were full of news, but it was an empty, crowded news that told her nothing beyond what she already knew. Judging by the columns and the staring head lines, most of the excitement was dying now and Britain had done far more than anyone had dared to hope. She'd swept an army from certain destruction and capture.

One of Wiggins' boats had arrived back within twenty-four hours of its departure, limping badly, its engines hot. A second had arrived the previous day, the Saturday, its decks splintered with bullets that had put its steering gear out of action before it had even crossed the Channel. Of the others there'd been no word, no sign, no indication of what was happening to them or to their crews.

Kate had been about the dusty streets in the intervals between waiting at the boat-yard, talking to the dishevelled men in stained and torn uniforms, who'd arrived from the east by train to fall asleep among the abandoned newspapers and tram-tickets in the roadway outside the station as they waited for the lorries to take them away, too tired almost to drink the tea that was offered them and eat the sandwiches they held in their grimy fists.

"There was too many boats, miss," they told her in answer to her questions. "There was too much going on at once."

"Gawd, miss, it was too much of a tea-party to notice anybody in particular."

Outside, beyond the river, the grey, still sea had been like a steel sheet that gave no indication of what was happening beyond the horizon. Occasionally they'd heard rumblings but no more. No more beyond the tramping feet of those tattered men, who'd been housed for the night in the Town Hall and church rooms and schoolrooms, men whose eyes were heavylidded with exhaustion and weariness, men who sometimes had no boots.

Kate had sat all through that morning with every Sunday paper she could lay her hands on, scanning them for even the minutest scrap of information that would cheer her. But there was no rest for her strained nerves in the headlines. She and an elderly foreman had been virtually in charge of the deserted yard. Then, when the foreman went home for his lunch, glad to get away from the silent offices and sheds for a while, Kate was alone with a dry, dusty misery that made her feel sick inside.

Minnie had been to the boat-yard, her face pale and her eyes puffy with weeping. But there was no misery in her heart, I'll bet. Only sorrow for herself, and a cunning little mind that refused to admit defeat. She'd put on her best clothes and was dressed fit to kill. She'd tried to find me at Dig's, I heard, before she went to Wiggins'.

Kate had met Pat in the street as he hurried to the station and, from his incoherent snatches of words as he passed her, she'd gathered something of what had happened. Pat was not trite, not even humble or humiliated with his black eye and bruised face and missing teeth, only anxious to be away before Minnie could catch up with him.

"She can look after 'er bloody self," he'd said as he went. "Got me into enough trouble, she did, the bitch."

Then he'd hurried off in the direction of the station, and Kate had known as he left her that she'd never see him in the town again.

Minnie she greeted coldly when she arrived at the boat-yard, half-defiant and with a simulated humility she didn't wear well.

"When's he coming back?" she'd demanded in reply to Kate's information, feeling foolish and clumsy as she always did, I know, in front of Kate, whose stillness hid a sick heart Minnie couldn't see.

"I don't know." Kate forced her voice to be steady. "Nobody knows."

"Don't know what he'd got to go an' do that for just now." Minnie's tones were aggrieved. "Might have waited till I could see him before he went."

Kate said nothing. There was so obviously nothing to say to this shallow, mean little woman, whose concern was only for herself. Unhappily, she realised Minnie had dressed carefully, with a thin frock over her curves, and scent enough to kill a cat. She'd done it all for me, I reckon. Ready to turn on all her charm.

"Isn't there some way I can get in touch with him?" Minnie asked. "Them boats have wireless and things, don't they? Can't we ring up somebody who'll know when he's comin' back?"

"He may not come back," Kate said, and Minnie's eyes widened, startled and big.

"What? Never? Well, that's a nice thing! That's a bit ripe!"

Then she realised what Kate meant and her jaw dropped. "Oh, Gawd!" she said. "Not killed?"

Kate nodded and Minnie was silent for a moment. I'll bet she was thinking of herself in black, a widow. My death would have been her salvation. There'd be no clacking tongues to drive her from the Steam Packet, no scandal, no dirty linen to be washed in public. No one need know what had happened. There's something comfortably respectable about widow-hood.

"Is that where he's gone?" she asked more happily, indicating the papers spread on the office desk.

Kate nodded again and Minnie stared in awe at the black headlines. I'm sure she'd no idea what was going on. I expect she thought a war was a bit like a noisy Saturday night at the Steam Packet.

"Well!" she said, and she seemed almost indignant. Her moment of dismay had passed and she was the old Minnie again, self-reliant, selfish and independent, her problems half solved, anxious to make an impression.

"Fancy going off like that. Never a word of goodbye to a girl." She turned to Kate, not realising how much she knew. "Never even bothered to kiss me aw revaw," she said.

"I expect not," Kate replied, then she went on hurriedly, anxious to avoid an argument with a stupid woman: "Nobody did. They didn't have time."

"Well, I think it's a bit thick," Minnie said, and she even managed to force a few tears.

With thin hands that showed a sinewy strength Kate grabbed her shoulders suddenly, unexpectedly, and shook her so that her teeth jarred.

"Shut up!" she said, angered by the act Minnie was putting on for her benefit. "Don't you realise he's risking his life to save stupid people like you?"

The unexpected shaking on top of the nervous strain of the past few days while she'd been waiting for me to turn up at the Steam Packet, while she'd struggled to get her story word perfect and debated the best means of soothing me down, of winning me back now that she'd lost Pat, suddenly brought real tears to Minnie's eyes and she began to wail. She stopped short as she felt a stinging blow on her cheek where Kate slapped her face.

"Pull yourself together," Kate said. "There's no time for hysterics."

Minnie glared. "I 'spect you think he's coming back to *you*, don't you?" she stormed, her passionate temper rising. "Well, you're wrong, Katie Fee. You're wrong. You wait. He's my husband and we'll soon see who he comes back to. Just wait till he spots me, that's all. Then we'll see."

She shoved her hat straight on her head and, grabbing her bag, hurried out of the office…

The day dragged on wearily towards dusk and Kate still waited under the harsh glare of the office electric light. The news that came over the wireless was still vague, but there was a more confident note in it now. England was on her own, but far from humiliated in her suffering. There was rising in her a spirit of pride, a grandeur that came from tradition. There was hope despite the disaster.

As she sat, Kate heard a train shriek in the silence and she guessed that another load of soldiers had arrived, needing shelter and food. Suddenly angry with herself for her fears, she rose to her feet. There were other women with anxieties just then, she decided. She wasn't alone in her misery. There was too much to do to sit still, and the women who were slaving in and around the station and the Town Hall would be glad of help.

She rose and, switching off the light, stepped out into the cool night air and closed the office door behind her.

I was leaving the station with Dig as she turned into the street. She saw me immediately and broke into a run, her heels clicking sharply on the pavement.

"Jess! Oh, Jess!" Her voice broke and became an emotional croak as my hands caught her and steadied her. Then she was hugging me fiercely, her eyes shining with tears.

"Oh, Jess!" she was sobbing. "Thank God you're safe!"

I held her silently, my arms round her, suddenly thankful she was there. My knees felt like water at the thought that she wanted me. I'd known she'd wait for me, but now that she was there in my arms it seemed to crowd the words from my tongue and hold my throat in a choking tightness that wouldn't let me speak. And my eyes were full of stinging tears again.

"Kate," I whispered at last. "I'm glad you were here."

I drew her closer to me. My weary body and tired mind seemed to draw strength from her. Dig was standing nearby, his mouth twisted foolishly into a smile. Then Kate suddenly saw I was hiding the shabby naval sword she'd last seen Old Boxer wearing when he stumbled into the boat-yard that last night. She didn't question it, though she must have guessed why Old Boxer wasn't there to carry it himself, and why Yorky hadn't come back with us.

I knew then that I no longer had any fear of losing her. I should never lose her again after this, however far away a ship might carry me. The sea couldn't ever keep us apart again.

I held her tighter at the thought. I never even noticed the grimy figures who hurried past, all of them too tired, too concerned with food and sleep to see us.

Occasionally we were jostled by the crowd, but we clung together silently, speechlessly, breathlessly. To me there was no longer any question about the future. Kate had decided it for me. All the emptiness and hollowness, all the solitariness had drained away.

"It's been a long and lonely voyage, Kate," I said, "but I'm home at last."

JOHN HARRIS

CHINA SEAS

In this action-packed adventure, Willie Sarth becomes a survivor. Forced to fight pirates on the East China Seas, wrestle for his life on the South China Seas and cross the Sea of Japan ravaged by typhus, Sarth is determined to come out alive. Dealing with human tragedy, war and revolution, Harris presents a novel which packs an awesome punch.

A FUNNY PLACE TO HOLD A WAR

Ginger Donnelly is on the trail of Nazi saboteurs in Sierra Leone. Whilst taking a midnight paddle in a canoe cajoled from a local fisherman along with a willing woman, Donnelly sees an enormous seaplane thunder across the sky only to crash in a ball of brilliant flame. It seems like an accident... at least until a second plane explodes in a blistering shower along the same flight path.

John Harris

Live Free or Die!

Charles Walter Scully, cut off from his unit and running on empty, is trapped. It's 1944 and, though the Allied invasion of France has finally begun, for Scully the war isn't going well. That is, until he meets a French boy trying to get home to Paris and so what begins is an incredible hair-raising journey into the heart of the French liberation and one of the most monumental events of the war. Harris portrays wartime France in a vividly overwhelming panorama of scenes intended to enthral and entertain the reader.

The Old Trade of Killing

Set against the backdrop of the Western Desert and scene of the Eighth Army battles, Harris presents an exciting adventure where the men who fought together in the Second World War return twenty years later in search of treasure. But twenty years may change a man. Young ideals have been replaced by greed. Comradeship has vanished along with innocence. And treachery and murder make for a breathtaking read.

JOHN HARRIS

THE SEA SHALL NOT HAVE THEM

This is John Harris' classic war novel of espionage in the most extreme of situations. An essential flight from France leaves the crew of RAF *Hudson* missing, and somewhere in the North Sea four men cling to a dinghy, praying for rescue before exposure kills them or the enemy finds them. One man is critically injured; another (a rocket expert) is carrying a briefcase stuffed with vital secrets. As time begins to run out each man yearns to evade capture. This story charts the daring and courage of these men, and the men who rescued them in a breathtaking mission with the most awesome of consequences.

TAKE OR DESTROY!

Lieutenant-Colonel George Hockold must destroy Rommel's vast fuel reserves stored at the port of Qaba if the Eighth Army is to succeed in the Alamein offensive. Time is desperately running out, resources are scant and the commando unit Hockold must lead is a ragtag band of misfits scraped from the dregs of the British Army. They must attack Qaba. The orders…take or destroy.

'One of the finest war novels of the year'
– *Evening News*

TITLES BY JOHN HARRIS AVAILABLE DIRECT
FROM HOUSE OF STRATUS

Quantity	£	$(US)	$(CAN)	€
ARMY OF SHADOWS	6.99	11.50	15.99	11.50
CHINA SEAS	6.99	11.50	15.99	11.50
THE CLAWS OF MERCY	6.99	11.50	15.99	11.50
CORPORAL COTTON'S LITTLE WAR	6.99	11.50	15.99	11.50
THE CROSS OF LAZZARO	6.99	11.50	15.99	11.50
FLAWED BANNER	6.99	11.50	15.99	11.50
THE FOX FROM HIS LAIR	6.99	11.50	15.99	11.50
A FUNNY PLACE TO HOLD A WAR	6.99	11.50	15.99	11.50
GETAWAY	6.99	11.50	15.99	11.50
HARKAWAY'S SIXTH COLUMN	6.99	11.50	15.99	11.50
A KIND OF COURAGE	6.99	11.50	15.99	11.50
LIVE FREE OR DIE!	6.99	11.50	15.99	11.50
THE MERCENARIES	6.99	11.50	15.99	11.50
NORTH STRIKE	6.99	11.50	15.99	11.50
THE OLD TRADE OF KILLING	6.99	11.50	15.99	11.50

ALL HOUSE OF STRATUS BOOKS ARE AVAILABLE FROM GOOD BOOKSHOPS
OR DIRECT FROM THE PUBLISHER:

Internet: www.houseofstratus.com including author interviews, reviews, features.

Email: sales@houseofstratus.com please quote author, title and credit card details.

TITLES BY JOHN HARRIS AVAILABLE DIRECT
FROM HOUSE OF STRATUS

Quantity		£	$(US)	$(CAN)	€
	PICTURE OF DEFEAT	6.99	11.50	15.99	11.50
	THE QUICK BOAT MEN	6.99	11.50	15.99	11.50
	RIDE OUT THE STORM	6.99	11.50	15.99	11.50
	RIGHT OF REPLY	6.99	11.50	15.99	11.50
	ROAD TO THE COAST	6.99	11.50	15.99	11.50
	THE SEA SHALL NOT HAVE THEM	6.99	11.50	15.99	11.50
	THE SLEEPING MOUNTAIN	6.99	11.50	15.99	11.50
	SMILING WILLIE AND THE TIGER	6.99	11.50	15.99	11.50
	SO FAR FROM GOD	6.99	11.50	15.99	11.50
	THE SPRING OF MALICE	6.99	11.50	15.99	11.50
	SUNSET AT SHEBA	6.99	11.50	15.99	11.50
	SWORDPOINT	6.99	11.50	15.99	11.50
	TAKE OR DESTROY!	6.99	11.50	15.99	11.50
	THE THIRTY DAYS' WAR	6.99	11.50	15.99	11.50
	THE UNFORGIVING WIND	6.99	11.50	15.99	11.50
	UP FOR GRABS	6.99	11.50	15.99	11.50
	VARDY	6.99	11.50	15.99	11.50

ALL HOUSE OF STRATUS BOOKS ARE AVAILABLE FROM GOOD BOOKSHOPS
OR DIRECT FROM THE PUBLISHER:

Hotline: UK ONLY: 0800 169 1780, please quote author, title and credit card
details.
INTERNATIONAL: +44 (0) 20 7494 6400, please quote author, title,
and credit card details.

Send to: House of Stratus Sales Department
24c Old Burlington Street
London
W1X 1RL
UK

Please allow for postage costs charged per order plus an amount per book as set out in the tables below:

	£(Sterling)	$(US)	$(CAN)	€(Euros)
Cost per order				
UK	1.50	2.25	3.50	2.50
Europe	3.00	4.50	6.75	5.00
North America	3.00	4.50	6.75	5.00
Rest of World	3.00	4.50	6.75	5.00
Additional cost per book				
UK	0.50	0.75	1.15	0.85
Europe	1.00	1.50	2.30	1.70
North America	2.00	3.00	4.60	3.40
Rest of World	2.50	3.75	5.75	4.25

PLEASE SEND CHEQUE, POSTAL ORDER (STERLING ONLY), EUROCHEQUE, OR INTERNATIONAL MONEY ORDER (PLEASE CIRCLE METHOD OF PAYMENT YOU WISH TO USE)
MAKE PAYABLE TO: STRATUS HOLDINGS plc

Cost of book(s): —————————— Example: 3 x books at £6.99 each: £20.97

Cost of order: —————————— Example: £2.00 (Delivery to UK address)

Additional cost per book: —————— Example: 3 x £0.50: £1.50

Order total including postage: ——— Example: £24.47

Please tick currency you wish to use and add total amount of order:

☐ £ (Sterling)   ☐ $ (US)   ☐ $ (CAN)   ☐ € (EUROS)

VISA, MASTERCARD, SWITCH, AMEX, SOLO, JCB:

☐☐☐☐☐☐☐☐☐☐☐☐☐☐☐☐☐☐☐☐

Issue number (Switch only):

☐☐☐

Start Date: **Expiry Date:**

☐☐ / ☐☐   ☐☐ / ☐☐

Signature: _____

NAME: _____

ADDRESS: · _____

_____

POSTCODE: _____

Please allow 28 days for delivery.

Prices subject to change without notice.
Please tick box if you do not wish to receive any additional information. ☐

House of Stratus publishes many other titles in this genre; please check our
. website (**www.houseofstratus.com**) for more details.